TRANSPLANT

TRANSPLANT

Frank G. Slaughter

Hutchinson
London   Melbourne   Auckland   Johannesburg

© Frank G. Slaughter 1986

This edition first published in 1987 by Hutchinson Ltd,
an imprint of Century Hutchinson Ltd, Brookmount
House, 62–65 Chandos Place, London, WC2N 4NW

Century Hutchinson Publishing Group (Australia) Pty
Ltd,
PO Box 496, 16–22 Church Street, Hawthorn,
Melbourne, Victoria 3122

Century Hutchinson Group (NZ) Ltd.,
PO Box 40–086, 32–34 View Road, Glenfield, Auckland
10

Century Hutchinson Group (SA) Pty Ltd,
PO Box 337, Berglvei 2012, South Africa

Printed and bound in Great Britain by Anchor Brendon
Ltd, Tiptree, Essex.

ISBN 0 09 167350 X

British Library Cataloguing in Publication Data

Slaughter, Frank G.
  Transplant
  I. Title
  813'.52[F]   PS3537.L38

  ISBN 0–09–167 350–X

CONTENTS

AUTHOR'S NOTE

Except for historical characters and events, easily identifiable as such, the people and events making up this novel are entirely fictional. If the name of any real person or any actual event appears, such appearance is entirely accidental.

BOOK I

SELENA

i

When the taxi-cab bearing Henry Walters and Selena McGuire from the Mid-Town Manhattan Police Headquarters to his apartment on Upper Fifth Avenue stopped for a traffic light, Henry looked up from the brown study he'd been in since they'd left Police Headquarters, saw the glaring headline – and shuddered. A curbside newsstand occupied the corner and placed so as to be easily visible to passing traffic was a stack of the Wall Street final editions of the *New York Post*, with the heavy type black headline spread across the top of the front page.

Henry turned quickly to look at Selena, hoping she hadn't noticed it. She was still sitting in the corner of the cab, rigid with obvious indignation at the events of the last several hours or so. To keep her from seeing the headline, Henry leaned forward, hoping to block her view through the open window of the taxi. The news vendor, however, took this to mean he wanted a copy of the paper and thrust it at him folded to show the glaring headline.

'Read all about it, mister,' he bawled. 'New sex organ transplant operation makes medical history.'

'Give me that!' Selena leaned across and took the paper while Henry was fumbling in his pocket for a quarter, handing it to

1

the news vendor just as their taxi lurched into motion again with the change of the traffic light.

'BART'S PARTS GET NEW START,' Selena read in a voice dripping with scorn. 'Story on page two by Wilhelmina Dillingham.'

Turning to Henry she asked furiously: 'Do you have any idea what that Dillingham woman will do with this story – and all because of you?'

'Hold on!' Henry protested. 'You're as much the cause of all this as I am.'

'How – ' Selena was momentarily at a loss for words, something Henry had rarely seen happen in the three years since she'd become his editor and publishing mentor at the giant Bennett Press.

'If you hadn't flown off to Boulder to teach that short course and ruined my plans for us to spend the Memorial Day weekend in my cottage in the Catskills, I wouldn't have been in New York when all this happened.'

'There you go, blaming me for something I didn't have any control over. You know perfectly well I had to go to Boulder in place of Nick Darby, when he came down with appendicitis.'

As editor-in-chief of Bennett Press, Nick Darby was not only a close friend of them both but their boss – so to speak – Selena being Darby's first assistant and Henry one of the leading authors published by the Bennett firm.

'If you don't mind,' Selena said loftily, 'would you tell me how my going to Boulder caused you to have your gen – you know what I mean.'

'Archie Bunker called them "gentiles" and mine didn't get transplanted,' said Henry. 'The ones I got came from my twin brother who called himself Bart Bartlemy.'

'Hey!' The taxi driver had obviously been listening closely. 'Ain't Bartlemy the actor that made such a sensation by being photographed naked in last month's edition of that sex magazine for women, *Fun Girl?* Geez! I ain't never seen nothing like the you know whats on that guy.'

'Our pictures are at the bottom of the page.' Henry pointed to the three-column photo, hoping to turn Selena's attention away and assuage some of her anger.

'With my mouth open like a dead fish!' she spluttered. 'And

2

don't tell me that blonde on the other side of you – what was her name?'

'She called herself Gloria Manning.'

'Don't tell me she wasn't in on this whole caper. You knew her before, didn't you?'

'I never saw Gloria Manning in my life until my class ring fell off my finger into her dress on the subway and I reached for it. I explained all that to Justice Peebles just now in court – under oath.'

'I still say she was happy with the publicity, at least. You can tell by the smug look on her face.'

'I don't want to be reminded of *anything* that's happened today,' said Henry as the taxi drew to a stop before the marquee in front of his Upper Fifth Avenue apartment. 'What's the fare, driver?'

'Ten dollars might do it; I don't hardly ever get celebrities in my cab. By the way, who are you, ma'am?'

'Nobody special.' Selena was getting out of the taxi on the other side.

Henry answered for her: 'She's my editor and my fiancée.'

'Ex-fiancée,' Selena corrected him as she counted out twelve dollars from her purse and gave it to the cabbie. 'Keep the change.'

'Thanks, lady.'

'Don't you want to keep the cab, darling?' Henry asked. 'I can make it up to my apartment now under my own power.'

'You've got a novel to finish for Bennett Press,' said Selena, 'so I'd better at least see that you get safely into your apartment.'

'Hey!' The driver was looking at the front page of the *Post* again. 'You're both in the picture and that blonde ain't bad neither. Didn't you say Bart Bartlemy was your twin brother, mister?'

'Yes.'

'Looks like you'll be stepping in his shoes then, don't it?'

'I hope not,' said Henry fervently. 'God, I hope not.'

Selena seized Henry by an elbow – one that had had a lot of the skin knocked off it earlier in the fracas on the subway that had started the whole affair. 'I've got to get back to the office as soon as I can be sure you're safe in your apartment where you can't get into any more trouble,' she said and, when he

3

winced added. 'I'm sorry I took the arm that was hurt but I'll get you some extra-strength Tylenol I've got in my handbag.'

'What I need is extra-strength bourbon,' said Henry. 'You can fix us a couple when we get upstairs and I'll tell you the whole story just as it happened'.

Which he did – thus:

ii

Henry had been pretty low coming back from the airport where he had seen Selena off on the plane for Denver, from whence she would go on to Boulder, site of the University of Colorado and one of the most beautiful spots in the whole Rocky Mountain area. As he pulled his Mercedes to a stop in front of his apartment building, he saw Ezra, the doorman, apparently arguing with a man whose back was turned. From fragments of the conversation, Henry gathered that the owner of the Rolls Convertible with the top down parked just in front of his Mercedes, wanted to leave it there for a while, in spite of the strict no parking rule in front of the apartment house marquee.

'You can put mine in the parking garage when you get a chance, Ezra,' Henry said, tossing the keys to the doorman.

'Right, Mr Walters,' said Ezra. 'I'll get to it in a minute.'

When Ezra spoke Henry's name, the man to whom he had been talking whirled to face Henry, who recognized him immediately. For not only the face but also the rest of Bart Bartlemy, Henry's twin brother, was familiar to millions all over the world.

'Henry?' Bartlemy asked.

'Yes,' said Henry. 'You're Bart.'

'Why did you grow the beard?' Bartlemy asked. 'I'd never have recognized you with it, if the doorman here hadn't mentioned your name.

'It was a good way to keep from being mistaken for you,' Henry said with a shrug.

'I guess you would have that trouble, since the last issue of *Fun Girl* appeared,' said Bartlemy. 'Do you know we haven't seen each other for thirty-two years?'

'Not since our aunts took us out of adjacent cradles and

4

adopted us,' said Henry. 'Come on up to my apartment and I'll give you a drink.'

'No time for that. I've got a job for you'

'A job?'

'Since that *Fun Girl* photo came out my lawyer thinks it would be a good idea for me to write an autobiography. I want you to do it.'

'For God's sake, why?'

'It's their idea, don't ask me,' said Bart. 'But if you'll get in the Rolls here I'll take you down to my lawyer's office. It's down close to Wall Street and we can just about get there before it closes.'

'Then you're really serious about this autobiography business?'

'Damned serious, if it'll make me some money. And it ought to make you some, too.'

'I guess you're right there.'

'Got anything to do for the next couple of hours?' Bart demanded.

'No.'

'Then hop in and we'll go down and talk to Greg about it.'

His curiosity aroused to see what this was all about, Henry took a seat in the Rolls.

'The bar is behind the seat,' Bartlemy told him as the engine roared into life and the big car spurted away from the curb.

'No thanks.'

'Then fix me another,' said the actor. 'I haven't had one in a couple of hours.'

'Do you think you ought to be drinking when you're driving?' Henry asked.

'I drive better when I'm drunk than I do when I'm sober,' Bart Bartlemy laughed boisterously. 'Pour me a shot of bourbon while I look for a ramp to the East Side Drive. We'll get downtown faster that way.'

Busy pouring bourbon from a liberal supply in the rack behind the seat, Henry didn't realize just what direction they were taking, until he handed the glass to his brother and looked up to see a sign that plainly said 'DO NOT ENTER'

Coming down the ramp which the sign forbade, was a big behemoth of a truck and Henry only had time to reach for the

5

seat belt. Not being accustomed to a Rolls, he hadn't located it before Bart asked for the drink – and so was not able to buckle it before the crash came and he was, for a few moments, airborne over the windshield and bonnet.

'Decided to come back to earth, Mr Walters?' The feminine face that floated into Henry's field of vision was middle-aged, plump and topped by a starched nurse's cap.

'The pain!' He moaned. 'It's like a knife.'

'I'll get you a hypo.' The nurse disappeared past a bank of bottles and tubing attached to the corner of what was obviously a hospital bed. She came back moments later carrying a hypodermic needle which she jammed into his buttocks. 'There,' she said. 'That will fix you up.'

'Where am I?' Henry asked.

'In the Manhattan Research Hospital,' the nurse informed him. 'You had an accident on the East River Drive two weeks ago.'

'My God! Have I been unconscious all that time?'

'Yes, with a severe concussion of the brain.'

'If I had a concussion, why do I hurt so much in my bottom?'

'I don't know the details, but there were other injuries besides the concussion.'

'You can say that again,' said Henry, his voice already slurred a little from the effects of the injection.

'I'll tell Dr Sang you're back to life,' he heard the nurse's voice receding as he dropped into a black void.

When Henry awakened again, it was dark outside and a plump doctor wearing the white coat of a staff physician was sitting in the chair by his bed looking through the chart.

'Well, Mr Walters,' he said. 'Glad to have you back with the living. You barely made it, you know.'

'I didn't know and I still wonder,' said Henry.

'I'm Dr Sang,' the doctor told him. 'You were in an accident involving Mr Bart Bartlemy's Rolls which was going the wrong way on an up-ramp to East River Drive.'

'I remember that, and a big truck staring at me through the windshield, but nothing afterwards.'

'You were barely alive when you reached the Emergency Room,' Dr Sang told him.

'What about Bart?'

'I'm sorry to have to tell you that your brother was killed in the accident. Were you very close?'

'This was the first time we had seen each other since our parents were killed in an accident and we were adopted by two aunts, one living in California and the other in Connecticut. What happened to Bart?'

'Well, he was drunk at the time of the accident; I read that he'd been drinking heavily ever since he was featured as the centrefold in that magazine for women – '

'*Fun Girl.*'

'That's the one. When the Rolls crashed into the front of the truck, you were projected over the windshield and across the silver hood ornament that was Bartlemy's insignium.'

'The one that represents the scientific symbol for the male?'

'Yes. The arrow at the top sliced through your belt and removed your external genitalia as clean as a scalpel could have done.'

'My God! I'm a eunuch.'

'Fortunately, your eunuched state – if you wish to call it that – lasted only a few hours,' Dr Sang assured him. 'The accident happened only a few blocks from the hospital else you'd prob- ably have died from haemorrhage and shock.'

'I don't remember any of that. How was Bart killed?'

'He wasn't wearing a seat belt and sustained a crushing injury to his skull. As we do in all apparent cases of DOA, we did an immediate electro-encephalogram on Mr Bartlemy and found no brain waves.'

'Establishing brain death?'

'Unquestionably. Fortunately for you, we also found a copy of what is now sometimes coming to be called a living will in Mr Bartlemy's wallet. It gave us permission to use any part of his body we considered suitable for transplant.'

'I remember signing one of those last year during a TV campaign,' said Henry.

'Naturally, the first thing we did when Mr Bartlemy's body arrived at the Emergency Room was to put him on a respirator and a pacemaker in order to keep him breathing and his heart beating, thus providing oxygen to his body tissues, even though his brain and therefore his legal body, you might say, was dead.'

'Are you telling me – ' Henry stopped. 'But that's never been done before, to my knowledge.'

'We've tried to transplant the external genital organs in several cases but without success,' Dr Sang admitted. 'Fortunately though, a new drug called Cyclosporin has changed all that, so we decided to risk one more try at transplant using the drug to help prevent rejection.'

'I think I'm going to be ill,' said Henry, but Dr Sang took a small object from his pocket and crushed it beneath Henry's nose, reviving him quickly with the pungent reek of aromatic ammonia.

'Meanwhile,' the urologist continued, 'we were doing everything in your case to combat shock and haemorrhage while preparing you for surgery. Naturally, too, we initiated a tissue match between your tissues and those of Mr Bartlemy, as we always do when we are preparing for transplant. But since he had signed a living will making any part of his body available, we didn't wait for the results but went ahead immediately with your surgery. Meanwhile, other surgeons were at work removing tissues for transplant, too.'

'Sounds like you surgeons had a regular field day.'

'I personally spent six hours of it on you,' Dr Sang told him. 'That same day one of Bartlemy's kidneys was transplanted into a young medical student and the other was on the way to New York to save a child dying from nephrosis. Bartlemy's heart is now beating in the chest of a young professor at NYU, a genetic scientist with tremendous potentialities for the good of mankind who had a severe case of rheumatic fever as a medical student and was slowly dying of heart failure. Both corneas also went to two blind children who will now see for the first time.'

'It sounds like everybody in the hospital was busy removing Bart's spare parts,' said Henry. 'I can't help comparing this to the operation of an automobile graveyard.'

'There are certain similarities,' Dr Sang conceded with a smile. 'Fortunately, we were able to do a complete transplant of your external generative organs and while we were doing that, we made an interesting discovery.'

'I think I already know what that means.'

'When we got the result of the first tissue match we couldn't believe our eyes so we did a second – with the same result.'

'Naturally, with Henry Walters and Bart Bartlemy being identical twins.'

'Which meant that a transplant from your brother's body to yours was certain to take, provided our technique was skilled enough to connect up the necessary arteries, veins and nerves, which it appears to have been. Fortunately, a young surgeon on our staff was trained in microsurgery by the same surgeon in St Louis who made the first testicle transplant.'

'I read about that one,' said Henry, 'but I never dreamed that – '

'You may be interested to know that the twin who received the testicle in that case has recently become a father.'

'In other words, I now possess – '

'The most famous and best known set of genitalia in modern history.'

'I'll never live it down,' Henry groaned.

'Judging from the reaction of the feminine public to Bart Bartlemy and particularly to that centrefold, Mr Walters, once they learn what happened in your case, I think you're going to be busy living it *up*.'

'And all because of a twin brother I never saw before, except on the screen.'

'I still don't understand how it happened that being identical twins neither you nor Mr Bartlemy knew each other.'

'Our parents were in an accident near the end of our mother's pregnancy,' Henry explained. 'Father died on the scene and Mother was barely alive when she reached the hospital, but fortunately a surgeon was there and performed an emergency Caesarean section in time to save Bart and me.'

'The *Lex Caesarea* was included in the codification of Roman law in seven fifteen BC, requiring the physician who reaches a dying pregnant woman to remove the foetus so it can live,' Dr Sang observed.

'Neither Bart nor I were injured in the crash and two maternal aunts who didn't have children of their own wanted to adopt us, so the court gave one of us to each of them.'

'The *Solomonic* principle.'

'I suppose that was the only way for everybody to be happy,' Henry conceded. 'Aunt Nadia Bartlemy took Bart to California where he grew up in the movie colony and became a chronic hell raiser and later a movie star of sorts. Aunt Helen Walters took me to Boston, where Uncle John was an associate professor of English at Harvard, so I naturally became a history teacher and later a writer.'

'And neither one of you knew he had a twin brother?'

'We knew and I was sometimes curious actually to contact Bart. But he turned out to be a bad apple and was sent to a reform school when he was thirteen for getting a girl pregnant and after that my family stopped acknowledging kinship.'

'A rather natural reaction,' Dr Sang conceded.

'Isn't it strange that after all these years, it was Bart who gave his life to give me back my manhood?' Henry stopped suddenly. 'Or will I be . . . ?'

'As potent as Bart Bartlemy? Yes. I'm sure of it.'

'But not as promiscuous, I hope.'

'That depends on a lot of things. Both testicles were trans-planted successfully and will no doubt continue to produce a plethora of the sex hormone, as they apparently did for your brother. Nevertheless, your upbringing and a lot of other factors will operate to set a pattern of behaviour.' Dr Sang smiled. 'As I remember from some scenes in your books that I have read – '

'That's just sublimation, according to my editor and fiancée,' Henry interposed quickly.

'Sublimation or whatever.' Dr Sang rose to his feet. 'If you ever decide on reality instead of imagination, you're one of the best equipped lovers in history, a man who could leave Casanova in the shade.'

'One thing I don't understand,' said Henry. 'I saw that photo-graph of Bart in *Fun Girl* and he was a lot more, shall we say, well endowed both for the photograph and for the parts he played in films than I ever was. How do you explain that?'

'A simple matter of physiology, Mr Walters,' said the uro-logist. 'If you've ever seen those who, to use the vernacular, "pump iron" you'll know that there is tremendous hypertrophy of their muscles from lifting weights. The same is true, I'm sure, of any organ that is used excessively.'

'I get it,' said Henry.

'To turn a phrase,' Dr Sang said with a smile, 'you've also got it.'

Henry had just finished lunch a few days after his conference with Dr Sang when the voice of the ward secretary at the desk outside crackled through the small grilled loudspeaker on the wall beside the bed.

'You have a visitor, Mr Walters – a Mr Gregory Annunzio.'

'I don't know anybody by that name but send him in anyway.'

Gregory Annunzio was tall, dark-haired, handsome and impeccably dressed.

'How nice to see you doing so well after such a serious accident, Mr Walters,' the visitor said warmly shaking hands.

'At least I'm better off than Bart Bartlemy.'

'Poor Bart. He just couldn't take fame, not even the kind he gained after that last caper.'

'Well, that's one thing I'll never have to worry about,' said Henry.

'You don't have to be modest, Mr Walters; I'm quite familiar with the literary reputation you've gained through your historical novels. May I sit down?'

'Sorry if I seem ungracious but Dr Sang told me a few days ago just how near I came to dying and I haven't gotten over it yet.'

'That information at least should not depress you,' Annunzio assured him. 'I've been reading your books since I was in law school at Yale. They're very, very good – in their genre, of course.'

'That was a long time ago before the paperback sex epics drove the works of honest writers off the book racks.'

'Your kind will come back; a good book will always find a market over a long period when these – what you call sex epics – have long since been tossed into the waste basket. Besides, I think I have a project that will both interest and intrigue you.'

'Are you a publisher?'

'No. I'm an attorney.' Annunzio opened his briefcase. 'I represent several clients who have formed a company to support the arts.'

'Angels, Incorporated?'

Annunzio laughed. 'Not quite. You see, we commission the

writing of books, dramas and screenplays, as well as furnishing financial support to both stage and screen. For example, we placed Bart Bartlemy under exclusive contract the day after that nude centrefold photograph of him appeared in *Fun Girl*.'

'As an actor?' Henry asked incredulously.

'Well, not exactly,' Annunzio conceded with a smile. 'We figured we could use him in projects that were certain to succeed.'

'Soft porn?'

'Something like that. Anyway, both Bart and my group stood to profit from his, shall we say, attributes?'

Henry had a sudden inspiration. 'Maybe you can tell me whether I can sue Bart's estate and his insurance company over this accident to pay my hospital and doctor bills.'

'You'd be wasting your time and money. Bart's been on a bender for the past six weeks. His car insurance had lapsed and he owed everybody in town.' Annunzio took out a computer printout sheet from his briefcase. 'Your hospital bill, too, in case you would like to know it, is over fifty thousand already.'

'Fifty thousand! How the hell will I ever find that much money writing books that sell twenty thousand copies and aren't even picked up for paperback reprint any more.'

'Precisely why I'm here, Mr Walters,' said Annunzio. 'My clients are prepared to make you an offer for a commission – '

'Who do you want murdered?'

'This project will be both pleasant and profitable for you, I am sure. You may not have known it, but when Bart took the wrong ramp, he was bringing you down to my office to discuss an autobiographical novel about him.'

'He did mention it,' said Henry. 'I came along out of curiosity to see just what was going on.'

'For one thing you are – or rather, were – his twin brother.'

'How did you find that out?' Henry demanded suspiciously. 'Hospital records are supposed to be confidential.'

'We have our sources nevertheless, Mr Walters.'

'But how could I write a biographical novel about Bart when I never saw him in person, except maybe in the hospital nursery or on a film or television, until the day he was killed?'

'We know all that, too,' said Annunzio cheerfully. 'After all, you didn't know King Arthur, Lancelot or Queen Guinevere either, yet you made them come alive in *Lancelot's Return*.'

'But that was research; Bart's dead now.'

'Not in your mind, Mr Walters, or in your files. We happen to know you've maintained a series of scrapbooks containing newspaper and magazine clippings about Bart Bartlemy and his career for many years.'

'How in the hell did you discover that?'

'One of our representatives visited your apartment yesterday afternoon.'

'That's breaking and entering!'

'Not quite,' said Annunzio. 'Your landlady was kind enough to let a relative in with her pass key so he could get some things you needed in the hospital. Judging from the size of your scrapbook collection dealing with your twin brother, you were obviously very much interested in him and his career. And by combining your present knowledge with other material already in our possession, you could produce a very sensational and, I might say saleable biography, about a real person who was very well known to the public.'

'On the order of *In Cold Blood?*'

'Somewhat, but from another angle.'

'Bart was certainly well enough known – especially to young females,' Henry said thoughtfully. 'I think I read somewhere that they went to his movies in droves.'

'They did. You see, Bart Bartlemy was actually a nobody, a second-rate actor playing walk on parts until he posed for the centrefold. But that photograph made him overnight a world-wide sex idol.'

'A lot of men have posed nude in that magazine as well as some others.'

'Admitted. The difference, I think, is that, while most models in *Fun Girl* are either photographed in profile or full face, Bart posed in a quarter profile calculated to bring out his best points.'

'A stand-out as I remember it,' Henry commented.

The visitor laughed. 'You do have a way with words, Mr Walters; it's one of the things I like most about your writings. And why, as soon as I learned that you were alive, the idea came to me that you would be an ideal writer for our projects.'

13

'Didn't I read somewhere that Bart had almost finished a picture before the accident?'

'Enough that we could shoot around him and use some cuttings to finish it out, plus a few shots of you without the beard. After all, you were identical twins.'

'But I'm a lousy actor! Couldn't even make Hasty Pudding at Harvard.'

'Your participation as an actor would be minimal,' Annunzio assured him. 'Besides, poor Bart never won any acting awards either.'

'I can agree with that.'

'One other film we had produced starring Bart was released before the centrefold appeared,' Annunzio continued. 'It did rather poorly the first time but it's being reissued now and we expect it to sweep the nation. Still another one is in the can and I think we can piece this last one together to make a third, while we're also transferring all of Bart's films to video cassettes which are a very profitable market these days.'

'Why do you need me then?'

'Frankly, Mr Walters, my clients like to gamble and stand to profit considerably, if Bart Bartlemy can be made into the sort of legend that James Dean became some years ago, after he died in an automobile accident. Nobody is quite as good as you are in taking legends and creating real heroes and heroines out of them, so we're counting on your literary skill to create a James Dean type of legend around Bart. Incidentally, they were both lousy actors and decidedly unpleasant personalities, too, so the precedent is already established.'

Henry's brain was seething with ideas generated about what Annunzio suggested but he retained enough of his senses, even after the concussion, to realize that this was a time to play very cagily the hand being dealt to him.

'If I can do a job such as you have outlined for a novel about my twin – not the Bart you say he really was but the Bart millions of women imagined he was – it would probably be little more than a series of couplings. You're not going to get a big sale with the same fare that's clogging the book racks these days.'

'I wouldn't be too sure of that, considering the stream of pornos by women writers from Hollywood that have been deluging the market lately,' said Annunzio. 'Actually, however, we chose you because you can create seduction literature – if you understand what I mean – of the highest order.'

'It's not much of a tribute to my own self-esteem as a writer,' Henry said a little bitterly, 'but I do understand exactly what you mean. I also understand that, once this project is finished, Bart Bartlemy will be worth far more to your clients dead than he ever was alive, so what could I expect to get out of it?'

'Fame, Mr Walters – and money. Maybe not the solid kind of fame you've already achieved as a historical novelist but certainly a great deal more money than you could ever hope to make in your regular field.'

'Especially if I use one of Bartlemy's nicknames as the title for the biographical novel – *Superstud*.'

'A stroke of genius,' Annunzio agreed. 'Put that title on a novel and publicize the fact that it's based loosely on a few of the late Bart's more lurid interludes, then add some even more startling fictional events cooked up by your fertile writer's imagination, and you'll produce the best seller of the year. In fact, I and my clients are willing to bet on it.'

'How much?'

'First your hospital and medical bills will all be wiped off the books forever. Second, shall we say half the royalties and subsidiary rights, like book clubs, paperbacks – '

'Three fourths,' said Henry quickly. 'Don't forget that you stand to profit tremendously from reissuing Bart's films and the film rights to the new book, to say nothing of video cassettes, while all I'll get out of it will be royalties.'

'You drive a hard bargain, Mr Walters, especially when we'll be letting you use the material we already have.'

'But you just admitted that I have in my scrapbook collection a lot more information about Bart's exploits than you had when you first thought of this deal.'

'You win,' Annunzio conceded. 'In addition to paying your hospital and medical bills, we will receive a fourth of the proceeds from *Superstud* in return for owning motion picture and television rights. When can you get started?'

'As soon as I get out of here. Dr Sang says that shouldn't be more than another week or ten days.'

15

'Excellent. The sooner we can get this book in print, the larger the sale.'

'One thing more,' said Henry. 'I insist that Bennett Press shall have the first option on the book. And if they decide to publish it, Miss Selena McGuire shall be my editor.'

'We'd be happy to see Bennett publish,' Annunzio assured him. 'With their imprint and your name, nobody could say this is just a hack job of writing in a hurry to profit from the late Bart's rather sudden and violent demise. Incidentally, once the Bartlemy legend is established in the public mind, the possibilities are endless; TV dramatizations using clips from his films; a sex manual describing his technique in love-making – which you might even write; the possibilities are endless. Is it a deal?'

'It is with me but I wonder what Harry Westmore will say.'

'No agent would do anything but approve this deal after you've already driven such a hard bargain,' said Annunzio. 'It's quite okay, however, for Westmore to represent you with publishers both here and abroad. Certainly a well-known agent like Harry can place this book with publishers whom we probably wouldn't even be able to reach. Why don't you call Harry now?'

'He's roaming around Europe somewhere. Can't the deal wait until he gets back?'

'One of my clients wants to hire a Hollywood hack writer he knows for the job but I held out for you,' Annunzio told him. 'I'm afraid delaying it any longer will probably jeopardize your getting the job.'

'Go ahead and draw up the agreement then. I'll send Harry a cable describing the deal.'

'I already have the contracts.' Annunzio opened his briefcase and took out a sheaf of documents. 'All that needs to be done is to fill in the percentages and sign.' Using his briefcase as a desk, Annunzio wrote briefly on four copies of a single letter of agreement before handing them to Henry. 'You can okay the change in terms with your initials and sign at the bottom,' he said. 'We'll get a nurse in here to witness the signature.'

The document was terse but Henry could find nothing wrong with it. Calling in his nurse, he had her witness his signature and handed three sheets back to the lawyer, keeping one for himself.

'Be sure and stop in at the business office on your way out and guarantee my medical bills,' he reminded the lawyer. 'Once that load is off my mind, I can start my background thinking.'

'It's as good as done.' Annunzio stuffed the papers in his briefcase and got briskly to his feet. 'I'll send the material we have on Bart over to your apartment by messenger as soon as you get out of the hospital; no use having it lie around here and somebody finding out what your next project will be. One other thing, too; let's have no publicity unless we both agree to it. As long as nobody knows you're writing this, no hack can do a hurry-up job and get publication ahead of us.'

'Okay, but I'd like to tell Miss McGuire when she gets back from Aspen about the time I get out of the hospital.'

'Of course,' Annunzio agreed. 'A man shouldn't have secrets from his editor, his fiancée – or his wife, especially when he hopes some day to make them one. Good day, Mr Walters. I'm sure our business association is going to be pleasant as well as profitable.'

Ten minutes after Annunzio left, the phone in Henry's room rang.

'This is Mr Jackson in Patients' Accounts,' the caller said cheerfully. 'I thought you'd like to know that all of your expenses, past and future, have been guaranteed, Mr Walters – by Gregory Annunzio.'

iv

The phone beside Henry's hospital bed rang about eight o'clock that night. It was Selena and she sounded happy.

'Are you back in New York already?' Henry asked. 'I thought you were going to be in Aspen another week.'

'I'm going to be there two more weeks,' she said.

'Three weeks! What happened?'

'The Chairman of the seminar has asked me to stay on for another two weeks for a special post-graduate session,' she explained. 'It seems that a convention of publishers and managing editors is scheduled to start here the day after the

17

one I'm teaching ends and he wants me to give them a course on day-to-day editing.'

'If publishers don't know that already, they don't have any business being in publishing.'

'Theoretically, yes,' Selena agreed. 'But with the conglomerate companies taking over so many publishing houses, a lot of people are being put in charge of managing who know nothing whatsoever about the publishing industry itself.'

'Maybe that's why there's so little quality in what they're bringing out these days,' Henry observed.

'Nick Darby said the same thing when I called him to ask whether I could stay the extra two weeks,' Selena told him. 'But he said something about your having an accident. Is that why I had to call the hospital to get you?'

'Oh, just a little car accident,' Henry said quickly. 'I'll be out by the time you get back.'

'That's fine,' she said. 'And for being so nice by not objecting to my staying out here the extra time, I'll let you take me up to the Catskills for the Fourth of July weekend.'

'Now you're talking,' said Henry. 'We'll go the very day you get back. By the way, when is that?'

'I'm not too sure, so I'd better call you when I am,' she said. 'Nick Darby wouldn't tell me the details but he sounded as if your accident was serious.'

'Everything's okay now,' he told her. 'I'll tell you about it on the way to the Catskills. Do you know what flight you'll be on?'

'United F–103, I think. It's supposed to get to Kennedy about two o'clock.'

'I'll be waiting; that'll give us time to get to the cottage by dark.'

But there as it happened, Henry was wrong.

V

At the end of the week, Henry took a taxi from the hospital to his apartment on Upper Fifth Avenue. The place was spotless; his cleaning woman, Mrs O'Toole, had seen to that. It was Saturday morning, too, quiet and an ideal time to work.

18

Anxious to get started on the first draft of *Superstud*, he went to his word processor in its customary place before a window overlooking Central Park and sat down. But no matter how hard he concentrated, he couldn't seem to get started.

Henry had never done much cooking at home, it being simpler to have breakfast and lunch in an excellent coffee shop around the corner from his apartment house. Dinners he usually transferred from the freezing compartment of his refrigerator to the microwave oven. And when he entertained, which was usually for some scholarly friends, other writers and Selena, dinner was sent in by a caterer. Otherwise, he ate in hamburger houses and the fast food outlets on nearly every New York street corner.

When a whole week had passed without his being able to get started on *Superstud*, Henry began to be really perturbed. The first week it had rained a lot forcing him to stay in the apartment most of the time. But when he awoke one morning at the end of the second week after leaving the hospital, he found the sun shining and the day bright, so decided to go for a walk before having a late breakfast.

Everybody in Central Park seemed to be happy. Children were playing tag amidst the shrubbery. Old people were drowsing in the warm, spring sunlight. And two young ones on a blanket in the shade of a tree were engaged in a fervent embrace. Feeling a sudden stirring both in his mind and in the tissues lately reconstructed by Dr Sang, Henry turned away, only to receive a smile from a striking brunette who was leading a large Burmese cat on a leash. He didn't remember ever seeing her before so, when she started to leave the park, he followed, encouraged by an occasional glance over her shoulder. By the time he crossed Fifth to the building on the east side of the thoroughfare, however, Henry was beginning to breathe a little more quickly – and not simply from the effort of walking.

A stab of pain in his nether parts warned him that if he followed the brunette into the apartment house toward which she was heading, he might be forcing the issue Dr Sang had warned him against sooner than was wise, so he ducked into a coffee shop where he often ate, shutting the decidedly attractive brunette from sight. Revived by a cup of coffee and a couple of aspirins, Henry emerged from the coffee shop and made his way to his still stubborn word processor, but it proved as resistant as ever to initiating any creative process toward getting the stubborn *Superstud* started.

Henry had heard no further word from Gregory Annunzio since their conference in the hospital and the signing of the agreement to write the book – which suited him fine since the failure to get started writing was rapidly sending him into a depression. Nearly every day when he'd gone to the park he'd seen a wizened little man perched on a bench across the avenue but thought nothing of it. When shortly before eleven one day he took a taxi to Dr Sang's office in the Manhattan Research Hospital for his appointment, it didn't occur to him that he might be followed and so missed seeing the little man hail a cab and follow his own. When he paid his own cabbie at the entrance to the hospital, the little man did the same a few hundred feet down the street but, again, Henry had no reason to make note of the occurrence.

Dr Sang's examination was thorough but brief and at the end of it he was beaming. 'Everything looks fine, Mr Walters,' he said. 'I don't think you need to limit your activities now in any way.'

'*Any* way?'

'Barring a rejection of the transplant by your tissues, which I would judge very unlikely, since it came from a body the same as your own, your course should be completely uneventful from now on.'

'That's encouraging,' Henry admitted.

'By the way,' Dr Sang asked, 'did you read the *Times* this morning?'

'Not yet. Don't tell me there's anything about me and Bart in it.'

'Not by name but I gave a brief oral report on your operation at the section meeting on urology of the Academy of Medicine last night. It stirred up quite a lot of interest and the reporter who attends the meeting wrote a short description of the procedure and the results for the morning edition.'

'But still without any names?'

'Of course. I wouldn't do that without your permission.'

'Thank God for that!'

'The *Times* reporter knows a lot about medicine so there's a graphic description of the procedure as I described it last night.

20

You might be interested in reading that section of his report on the meeting.'

'Are you sure you didn't identify Bart or me?' Henry asked.

'No, only the fact that you were twin brothers.'

'I guess no harm was done then,' Henry conceded. 'One thing about this whole thing puzzles me, though. Before the accident I used to get horny occasionally but since the accident I'm that way most of the time.'

'For a young man that's nothing to worry about – rather the reverse I would say,' Dr Sang said with a smile.

'Something's happened to my personality, too. It's almost like I've suddenly become another person.'

'I wouldn't knock it if I were you,' Dr Sang told him. 'With the kind of luck you're sure to have, once the news that you've inherited Bart Bartlemy's most famous attributes gets around, I doubt that you'll ever want to go back to being the old Henry Walters.'

'Maybe,' said Henry, doubtfully, 'but I'm still in a hell of a bind.'

'How so?'

'While I was in the hospital I signed a contract to write a novel based on Bart's life emphasizing largely the most lurid aspects of his career.'

'The book should be a best seller right away.'

'I think so, too, if I could ever get it going. But so far, I haven't even been able to make a start.'

'What's the title?'

'*Superstud.*'

'You'll find the right approach, I assure you.' Dr Sang chuckled. 'After all, who could write better about the *old* Superstud than the *new* Superstud.'

vi

A steady drizzle had begun while Henry was in Dr Sang's office. After trying vainly to hail a cab, he gave up and ducked into the nearest uptown subway entrance. He could hardly help noticing the nubile blonde who rode down the escalator from

21

the subway entrance and also took the uptown express, inching into the crowded car beside him. When he smiled instinctively, the blonde smiled back. And with the car packed largely with women in the middle of the day, Henry found himself pressed tightly against her – a by no means unpleasurable situation.

The blonde was holding an overhead strap steadying herself against the rocking motion of the subway car. But since all straps were taken, Henry spread his feet a little and tried to steady himself, aided considerably by the pressure of feminine bodies all around him. However, when the car hurtled around a curve on the tracks, he was thrown off balance and reached up to catch the strap above the blonde's hands. Unfortunately, this action loosened the already loose Harvard class ring on his finger and, to his horror, as he reached for the strap, he saw it fly off his finger and describe an arc whose terminus was obviously the cleft in the blonde's somewhat opulent bosom.

Instinctively, Henry tried to catch the flying ring but, when the car rocketed back into a straight, he was thrown sideways and found his clutching fingers suddenly surrounded by a softness which could have only one origin, the bosom of the blonde. She looked startled but did not appear offended. Nevertheless, a woman holding on to a strap just beside Henry clouted him indignantly with the purse in her other hand forcing him to his knees as the attacker screamed, 'You molester!'

Those around Henry took up the cry and, felled by a rain of handbags, Henry was knocked to the floor. Every head in the subway car, Henry was sure, – although he couldn't see them from his position amidst a sea of female legs and shoes – was centred upon him. Meanwhile, the accusation – however unjust – had been seized upon by a half dozen women around them so that when the angular woman raised her handbag and clobbered Henry over the head with it once again, a veritable torrent of screeches poured upon him from all sides.

Crawling amidst the layer of dust, dirt and cigarette butts on the floor of the car, Henry tried to protect himself and, more important, the transplant. Meanwhile, a rain of kicking feet ensconsed in every sort of torture instrument imaginable was belabouring him from every side.

Only the slowing of the train for another stop saved Henry from serious injury. As the car came to a halt and the door slid open, he was propelled outward upon the subway station in the centre of a still kicking, screaming tide of indignant female humanity. And no sound he'd ever heard was so welcome to his ears just then as an authoritative Irish brogue ordering: 'Break it up! What's going on here?'

The policeman was immediately surrounded by a small army of jabbering and gesticulating females. Finding himself no longer the centre of attention at the moment, Henry tried to crawl through a forest of female legs of many sizes and shapes towards the men's room, the instinctive haven sought by any male when pursued by angry females. He might have made it, too, had not Hawk-face seen him and shouted a warning to the others. Immediately, the tide of handbags and shoes was turned against Henry once more until the policeman waded into the crowd and dragged him, battered and bruised, from their midst.

'Did this man molest you, miss?' the officer asked the blonde, who had also been shoved to the front of the group by Hawk-face and others. A dozen shrill voices answered the question for her, a cacophony of screeching that hardly allowed the young lady to answer: 'He did – in a way – officer.'

'In the middle of all these people?' The policeman sounded incredulous but a chorus of angry voices confirmed the truth of the charge.

'He's a sex fiend,' Hawk-face insisted. 'Arrest him, officer!'

'If you want this man arrested, you'll have to come to the station house and prefer charges, miss,' the policeman told the blonde and while she hesitated momentarily, Henry tried to put in a word of explanation but was promptly squelched.

'If the lady says you molested her, you done it!' Then the brogue softened and the officer's voice was lowered to a tone of admiration. 'But I'll be damned if I see how you made out in the middle of a subway car full of women.'

Seizing Henry by the arm he elbowed him out of the crowd, many of whom, including the blonde, followed them up the stairway to the street. In the holding room for the Mid-Manhattan District Police Court, where he was taken, Henry insisted upon his right to a single telephone call and then had to borrow a quarter from the policeman who brought him in, when he discovered that during the mêlée someone had managed to remove his wallet.

The only person he could think of to call was Nick Darby, Editor-in-Chief at Bennett Press.

'This is Henry Walters,' he told the Bennett Press switchboard operator. 'I'd like to speak to Mr Darby.'

'He's out to lunch, Mr Walters, but Miss McGuire is here. I'll ring her.'

'What are you doing in New York?' Henry demanded when Selena came on the line. 'You're supposed to be in Aspen.'

'I left a day earlier,' she explained. 'You don't sound like yourself, Henry. Is anything wrong?'

'Everything's wrong,' Henry croaked. 'How soon can you come to the Mid-Manhattan District Police Headquarters and get me out of jail?'

'What in the world are you doing in jail?'

'Hurry up, buddy,' the bailiff who was watching Henry ordered. 'Justice Peebles will be back in court any minute now.'

'I'll explain when you get here,' Henry told Selena. 'Just come as soon as you can.'

'I'm coming but – '

Henry had to hang up when the bailiff took his arm and pulled him toward the door leading to the police court chamber.

vii

Magistrate Calvin Peebles of the Mid-Manhattan District Police Court was mellowly content when he took his place on the bench and looked down upon the crowded courtroom. He had lunched at Luigi's around the corner on ravioli and a small bottle of Chianti, then paused for a moment of browsing, as was his want, at Serutano's, a small bookshop nearby that he often visited during lunch time. There he'd had the fortune today of purchasing a copy of Sir Thomas Malory's *Le Morte D'Arthur*, in an edition that appeared to preserve the flower of the Old English in which it was originally written.

'The Mid-Manhattan District Police Court in the city of New York is now in session,' the bailiff intoned. 'Magistrate Calvin Peebles presiding.'

As the rustle of movement in the courtroom subsided, Justice

24

Peebles's eyes canvassed the familiar rows of battered benches. The quick sweep of faces lifted to him, the new offenders hopefully, the old resignedly, formed a moment that he loved. The judicial gaze paused briefly when it came to the handsome, scholarly, though somewhat battered, countenance of the trimly bearded man on the front bench. He frowned momentarily in thought, trying to place a faintly familiar face.

'Do I know you, sir?' he asked.

'I think not, your honour,' said Henry Walters.

'I rarely forget a face. Are you sure?'

Henry nodded and the judge's gaze moved on but a nagging doubt persisted in his mind. The man was certainly a cut above the usual run of muggers, minor thieves and other malefactors who daily paraded through the courtroom. Obviously, the accused – since those with relatives and lawyers always occupied the front seat – had a good taste in women, too. The young lady sitting stiffly beside the bearded man was startlingly beautiful and, looking at her, the judge sighed as a picture took form in his imagination, blasting the clerk sitting beside him with the pungent aroma of garlic.

Next to the two who were together – though the young lady appeared to shun any close contact with the defendant – was a somewhat statuesque blonde, whose air of righteous indignation was already beginning to waver somewhat in the august presence of the magistrate. Justice Peebles had seen enough of those to know what to expect and sat up a little straighter, leaning forward a little the better to enjoy the two examples of female loveliness flanking the somewhat battered male with the beard.

'First case,' he called.

'Henry Walters,' the clerk read and Henry stood up.

'What's the charge?' Peebles asked.

'Molesting a female – Miss Gloria Manning.'

'Just where did this interesting crime occur, bailiff?' Peebles asked.

'In the subway, your honour.'

Peebles blinked. 'Really?'

'That's what it says here, your honour,' said the clerk. 'On complaint of Miss Gloria Manning, Officer Terrance O'Shea arrested the defendant on the charge of molesting a female.'

Peebles regarded the complainant for a moment. She, too,

had stood up when her name was called and Justice Peebles, who could appreciate a good figure when he saw one, especially from the elevated dais, was properly impressed. However, he turned back to Henry, still convinced that he had met the defendant somewhere before.

'Are you perchance an entertainer, sir?' Peebles asked Henry.

'Not exactly,' said Henry. 'I'm a novelist.'

'Author of *Lancelot's Return?*'

'Yes, your honour.'

At the back of the room where the reporters normally sat, when any of them bothered to cover a police court proceeding, an amazon with a camera rose and started down the centre aisle toward the front. She was wearing denim hip-huggers, a dark T-shirt that fitted almost like her own skin, a fringed jacket and blue canvas sneakers. All of which combined to emphasize a striking, if slightly bizarre figure. Seeing her, Justice Peebles blinked, knowing that if the almost legendary Wilhelmina Dillingham – known to her intimates as Willy the Dilly – was covering this case, something decidedly out of the ordinary must be involved.

As the decorative reporter settled into a chair at the far end of the second row, camera ready for whatever might rise, the magistrate turned back to the accused.

'Mr Walters,' he said, 'I'm curious to know your source for the legend of the escape of Guinevere and her reunion with Lancelot.'

'It was mentioned in an old edition of *Le Morte D'Arthur*, your honour.'

'Like this one perchance?' Peebles held up the small volume he'd just bought.

'That looks like the same edition.' Henry was still too dispirited and hurting in too many places for it to seem important that the Justice, who would decide his fate – at least in the lower court – was also a student of the Arthurian legends and, presumably, inclined to be friendly.

Recognizing the knock of opportunity, though, Selena gave Henry a push from behind that made him stumble nearer to the bench, placing him beside Gloria Manning and adding to the misery he was already experiencing – a misery that was considerably increased by the flash of a bulb above the camera in the hands of Wilhelmina Dillingham.

'If you would let me see the book,' he suggested dispiritedly to the magistrate, 'I might be able to verify the edition.'

'Please do, Mr Walters.'

Henry had some trouble studying the small somewhat beaten volume Justice Peebles handed down to him, largely because one of his eyes was almost closed by a truly gargantuan mouse. But after a brief perusal of the small volume, he handed the book back up to the magistrate.

'It's the same edition, sir,' he said. 'You'll find the reference to Guinevere and Lancelot being joined later in a bibliography at the back of the book.'

'A most fortuitous meeting, Mr Walters.' Justice Peebles beamed at this proof of his good fortune by an expert. 'Didn't I read somewhere that *Lancelot's Return* is to be made into a film?'

'Twentieth Century Fox will be casting soon, I believe,' Henry admitted.

'Do you have any idea who will play the leads?'

'I don't think they've selected the cast yet, your honour, and in any event authors are never consulted about such things.'

'I shall look forward to seeing the film and hope it will be as good as the book,' Justice Peebles said as he turned again to the clerk. 'What was that charge against Mr Walters, again?'

'Molesting a female, sir. The complaint is signed by Miss Gloria Manning.'

'Well, Miss Manning?' The magistrate's tone as he turned to face Gloria Manning was decidedly forbidding.

As for her, she glanced quickly toward the back of the court-room, as if to consult someone there, but Henry was too despondent to notice. Whoever or whatever she saw seemed to give her courage for she turned back and spoke firmly in answer to the justice's question: 'He made advances to me, your honour – in the subway.'

'You were alone in the car together?'

'Well – no, sir.'

'The car was packed with women, your honour,' Officer O'Shea volunteered. 'There's a sale on at Macy's today.'

'These advances, Miss Manning,' Justice Peebles asked.

27

'Wouldn't you say that making them in a crowded subway is a rather remarkable feat under the circumstances? Though' – he added gallantly – 'I must say a very natural male reaction.'

'That's all it was, your honour,' said Henry. 'A reaction.'

'I saw him do it, your honour,' said the hawk-faced woman who had slugged Henry first when he sought to reclaim his seal ring. 'He reached right into her dress – between the boobs – '

'What a target,' the bailiff observed *sotto voce*, and a wave of laughter passed through the room, until Justice Peebles banged it into silence with his gavel.

'In view of what's been happening to young women in New York lately, particularly in the subway, Mr Walters,' said Peebles, 'this could be a very serious charge. May I ask whether the young lady with you is your counsel?'

'My name is Selena McGuire, your honour.' Selena joined Henry before the Bench. 'I'm Mr Walter's editor at Bennett Press.'

'How fortunate for such a distinguished author to have so lovely an editor,' said Justice Peebles gallantly.

'Thank you, sir.' Selena spoke briskly. 'May Mr Walters go now?'

'I'm afraid not,' said the magistrate with obvious reluctance. 'There's still the matter of the complaint – unless Miss Manning wishes to drop the charges.'

Once again, Gloria Manning glanced toward the back of the courtroom but Henry still didn't even try to see why. Standing despondently beside her with Selena on the other side, stiffly disapproving as she'd been since she'd arrived at the courtroom a few minutes after Henry was arraigned, he was wishing it was all over and he was once again comfortably in jail – or wherever Justice Peebles was going to send him.

'There were witnesses to the attack, your honour.' The hawk-faced woman spoke loudly from the front row and an indignant hum came from a dozen or so of her cohorts.

'Do you still insist that Mr Walters laid hands on you, Miss Manning?' the magistrate asked.

'Yes, your honour. He put one of them inside my dress.' She reddened in embarrassment. 'From above, of course.'

'Naturally – since you were in the subway,' said Justice

Peebles. 'But tell me this, had you encouraged Mr Walters in any way before the incident occurred?'

'Oh, no, your honour,' Gloria Manning protested. 'We were pressed pretty close together there in the subway. In fact, it was hard to even breathe – '

'Did Mr Walters give you any warning that he might be planning to, I believe you said, molest you?'

'Oh, no, your honour. It was, you might say, the reverse.'

The magistrate blinked. 'If I understand your meaning – and I believe I do – wouldn't you say that what Mr Walters did was a very natural reaction, perhaps one you've experienced before?'

'I didn't think much about it then, your honour.' Miss Manning looked somewhat embarrassed again. 'When you're pressed close to a man in the subway, you know what usually happens.'

'Let's say I still remember,' said the magistrate, on a note of sorrow. 'Please proceed.'

'Well, the subway went around a curve and we were all sort of thrown around. Before I realized what he was doing, he was reaching down – you know. Then that lady there' – she pointed toward Hawk-face – 'recognized what he was doing and started beating him over the head with her handbag.'

'What happened then?' Justice Peebles inquired.

'Nothing, your honour. Mr Wal – , the defendant, was crawling around on the floor when the train stopped and the doors opened. We were all carried out onto the platform where Officer O'Shea arrested him.'

'Thank you.' Justice Peebles turned to Henry. 'What's your story, Mr Walters?' he asked courteously. 'Are you guilty of molesting Miss Manning?'

'Well, not exactly the way the accusation is phrased,' said Henry. 'You see, I've recently had an operation and lost some weight and the class ring I wear is loose. When the car hit a curve and I was thrown to one side, I instinctively reached up to grab the strap Miss Manning was holding above her hand. As I did so, my ring flew off and landed – do I need to describe exactly where?'

'I think not, Mr Walters,' said Justice Peebles, 'since the evidence would be relatively conclusive.'

'I do remember reaching to try to catch the ring,' Henry confessed, 'and I suppose, inevitably, Miss Manning could have considered that I was molesting her – '

'Granted,' said Justice Peebles. 'Please continue.'

'Well, you see, these women were pressing close to me and, having recently had an important operation, I was afraid something might be injured, so I naturally protected myself in the only way I know how.'

'He was squattin' on the floor, holding his hands over his – you know what,' Hawk-face volunteered.

'You're not a witness, madam,' Justice Peebles said sternly. 'If you are called, you will be allowed then to give details of what you saw.' Turning to Henry, he added, 'Just because you happened to be in a crowded subway and have recently had an operation doesn't exactly justify your, shall we say, becoming familiar with a lady when your ring happens to drop into her bosom, Mr Walters. I'll admit that your fictional heroes would certainly do a better job than that.'

'All I was trying to do at first was to get the ring. But when that lady' – he nodded toward Hawk-face – 'clobbered me with her handbag, my first impulse was to protect myself and the transplant.'

When he saw the amazon reporter on the second row shoot up like a jack-in-the-box, Henry realized he'd said the wrong thing, but it was a matter of record so he couldn't change it.

'Have you had a transplant operation, Mr Walters?' Justice Peebles asked.

'Yes, your honour.'

'How long ago, may I ask?'

'About a month.'

'It was just a month ago that a well-known figure in the film world named Bart Bartlemy had a fatal accident; I remember now that you were involved, according to police records, although you were guilty of no crime.' The magistrate leaned forward, his eyes alive with interest. 'According to a report by Dr Sang to the Academy of Medicine last night – as mentioned in the *Times* this morning – a number of transplants were made, using organs from Bartlemy's body. Did you perhaps receive one of those?'

'Yes, your honour,' Henry admitted, not able to see any way of denying it when he was under oath.

'Most interesting.' The jurist leaned back in his seat. 'I happen to know, Mr Walters, that Dr Sang is one of the best-known urologists in the country. Was this transplant you received perhaps in his area of expertise?'

'Yes, your honour, but I'd rather not elaborate on it. Bart Bartlemy was my twin brother, although we were separated shortly after birth. And, besides, I have contracted to write a novel about Bart's life.'

'Mr Bartlemy's anatomy had become quite well known, Mr Walters, through his appearance in certain magazines.' Justice Peebles asked the sixty-four thousand dollar question Henry had been dreading. 'Did you perhaps receive the most famous parts?'

'Yes, your honour,' Henry said miserably.

Wilhelmina Dillingham triggered another flash bulb and the room literally exploded as reporters raced for the doors and the telephones outside. Had Henry been looking, he would have seen the tall form of Gregory Annunzio leaving at the same time but he was too concerned with his own discomfort to care.

'However, reluctantly, I'm going to have to sentence you to ten days in jail or fine you one hundred dollars, Mr Walters,' said Justice Peebles. 'After all, you did admit to molesting Miss Manning.'

'Thank you, your honour.' Henry reached for his wallet, then suddenly remembered that someone had lifted it while he was rolling on the floor of the subway car.

'Is anything wrong?' the magistrate asked.

'I'm afraid my wallet's been stolen with all my credit cards. I don't even have a chequebook with me.'

'In that event–' the magistrate started to say but Selena broke in before he could finish. 'I can pay the fine, your honour, if you'll just give me time to go back to my office for the money.'

'That's all right, Miss McGuire,' said the magistrate gallantly. 'We'll let Mr Walters sit here in the courtroom until you come back with the fine.'

viii

'I guess you're hardly to blame for everything that's happened,' Selena conceded when Henry finished the story of his recent painful misadventure. They were in his apartment and Henry was in bed holding an empty bourbon glass whose contents he had just swallowed. 'Just a minute,' she added, 'and I'll get another drink. After what happened to you this morning and this afternoon as well, you certainly deserve one.'

'Did I really hear you tell Justice Peebles that you're writing a novel about the life of Bart Bartlemy?' she asked when she came back and handed Henry his drink.

'Yes.'

'How did that come about?'

Henry gave her a brief summary of the visit from Gregory Annunzio while he was in the hospital and what had developed.

'Do you have a copy of the agreement?' she asked when he finished.

'It's in the top drawer of my desk. I was saving it to show to Harry Westmore.'

'I should think you would.' She went into the living room where he customarily worked before a window overlooking the park, and came back with a single sheet in her hand and a frown on her face. 'This is unbelievable, Henry,' she said.

'Annunzio wanted half of the take but I held out for seventy-five per cent and won,' Henry said proudly.

'Do you have any idea who Gregory Annunzio really is?'

'The lawyer for a group that gives financial support to the arts, is what he told me. I suppose you could call it some kind of a syndicate.'

'The syndicate part is right, at least. Annunzio is a legal laundryman for Big John Fortuna and his group.'

'Laundryman?'

'The Syndicate invests in many legitimate business activities to clean up the money they skim from the rackets and the Las Vegas gambling tables. Annunzio's law firm handles the job of placing a lot of cash for one of the biggest groups of racketeers in the country.'

'How do you know so much about it?'

32

'The same group wanted to take over Bennett Press last year; it would have been ideal for them, with foreign sales and all. Of course. Annunzio did the talking for them. He even tried to date me but I would have no part of him.'

'Let's hope not,' said Henry fervently. 'You did say the deals he negotiates are legitimate, though, didn't you?'

'Yes – if you don't mind handling that kind of money.'

'The only money I've gotten is payment of my medical bill; the rest will have to be earned by the book I'm going to write. Incidentally, Bennett Press is also going to make a lot of money publishing *Superstud*.'

She gave him a startled look. 'Is that what you're calling it?'

'What else? It was Bart's nickname all over Hollywood. If you saw that *Fun Girl* centrefold – '

'Don't insult my taste in literature – '

'I'm not talking about literature, I'm talking about photos. Did you or didn't you see the centrefold?'

'Well, I did glance at it.' Selena blushed, making her Irish peach complexion even lovelier. 'But only because everybody was making such a fuss over it. Incidentally, even though you've contracted to write a book about Bart Bartlemy, Bennett Press hasn't contracted to publish it yet.'

'What about the options in my contracts?'

'Options are to keep authors from leaving publishers. A publisher can let an author go whenever he wants to.'

'What do you think of the possibilities of *Superstud?*'

Selena winced. 'Written with all the stops out, it's a natural, of course. But are you the one to write it?'

'Annunzio thinks so and his clients agree. Can you give me one good reason why I can't do it?'

'This has got to be a super-lusty book, Henry. I don't want to hurt your feelings but, frankly, I'm not at all sure you're lusty enough to write it.'

'You should know something about that, after those weekends we spent at my cabin in the Catskills.'

'I'm talking about something else, Henry; something like tenderness and gallantry – and love. I don't think those emotions characterized very many of Bartlemy's liaisons, but they come naturally to you. Besides, you'd have to do a lot of research.'

'I've got a whole file of clippings and other information about

Bart. Annunzio has sent down several hundred other pieces, too, so everything I need to start writing is here in this apartment. The only trouble is – '

'What?' she asked when he didn't finish the sentence.

'I'm having trouble getting started.'

'That's just what I've been telling you. You might be able to write convincingly about Bart Bartlemy but the difference between just another hack novel about a Hollywood womanizer and a real study of a complex character isn't going to be enough to make it really successful. You need to feel what you're writing and you're too much of a gentleman ever to be able to ape your brother in that respect.'

Henry's patience was being tried very hard. 'What you're saying is that, in order to acquire the emotional capacity to think like Bart and put it down on paper, I've got to shack up with some broads. Or maybe even come by the office with obscene pictures to prove I've turned into a lecher.'

'Lecher!' Selena exclaimed. 'That could be it.'

'What the hell are you talking about?'

'You're about the most un-lecherous man I know, Henry. But for this book to be a runaway smash in sales, you need at least to write it as if you appeared to be the sort of person your twin brother was.'

'That's absurd,' said Henry firmly. 'I've still got a writer's imagination and Annunzio doesn't mind if I take some liberties with facts.'

'Maybe you could recreate Bartlemy in your imagination,' Selena considered. 'Certainly you were successful in the love scenes between Guinevere and Lancelot.'

'Then what are you worried about?'

'Something about the whole affair smells,' said Selena. 'Are you absolutely certain that blonde followed you into the subway?'

'I told you that an hour ago.'

'Then her being next to you on the train could very well have been more than just a coincidence.'

'Now you're being absurd.'

'Maybe not. Twice during the hearing, when Justice Peebles asked her whether she still wanted to press charges against you, Gloria Manning, or whatever her real name is, looked at

34

somebody in the back of the room as if for advice. And each time whoever was back there apparently signalled her to go ahead.'

Henry stared at Selena in astonishment. 'Are you trying to tell me I was framed so the whole story of the transplant would come out in Justice Peebles's courtroom where it would receive the maximum of publicity?'

'That certainly fits what happened. Can you think of any set of circumstances where the announcement would get more publicity?'

'No. But why?'

'I've just finished telling you I don't think you're the kind of writer who can turn out the sort of stuff this novel has to be, if it's to become the best selling blockbuster Annunzio and his crowd obviously want.'

'So what should I do next?'

'As soon as you feel like it, write something like a movie treatment of the story – you know, a long synopsis. Send it over to me and I'll present it to the Bennett Press Fiction Group and we'll see how they feel about it.'

'There's one other thing,' said Henry. 'Ever since I left the hospital, I've been feeling a lot more like Bart Bartlemy than I have like Henry Walters.'

Selena gave him a startled look. 'What do you mean?'

'Well, some of Bart Bartlemy's lusty instincts – your own word, remember – may have come to me with the transplant.'

'Heaven forbid!'

'Don't knock it until you've tried it,' said Henry. 'We could still make that trip to the Catskills you promised me from Aspen.'

'I'll have to take the offer under advisement,' said Selena. 'Are you sure nothing else happened while I was away?'

'Nothing I haven't told you,' Henry lied manfully. 'If I didn't hurt all over from where those women kicked and beat me in the subway, I'd be out of this bed chasing you around the apartment.'

'You've made your point,' she conceded. 'If you're convinced that part of Bart Bartlemy's sex appeal was transferred to you, even though that couldn't possibly have really happened, maybe

35

you also have the imagination needed to write *Superstud* after all.'

'Now you're talking my language,' said Henry with fervour.

'Do you have any plan for the story?'

'I've got a perfect one; found it in one of the publicity releases about Bart. You see, the first girl he ever had was named Leonora. According to this article, Bart and Leonora had a brief love affair, then she ran away and got married. Since then, he's gone from love affair to love affair, always seeking what he found so briefly in Leonora but never finding it.'

'What you're building is a framework for recurrent seductions.'

'Isn't that what most modern fiction is about anyway?'

'No doubt about that.'

'Then you approve?'

'So far, but what about the end. Does Bart find Leonora and, if so, how are you going to handle the accident?'

'Maybe Bart finds his Leonora and is rushing to marry her when the accident occurs,' said Henry. 'It's the sort of riding off into the sunset motif that will have every woman reader who's bored with her husband crying into her beer.'

Selena got to her feet in a studiedly casual movement that carried her well away from the bed.

'What's the matter?' Henry asked maliciously. 'Is whatever portion of the old Bartlemy sex mystique that came over to me with the transplant giving you the hots already.'

'Of course not,' she said, but the sudden rush of colour to her cheeks belied the statement. 'When are you going to start writing?'

'I've been trying for a week and can't even get the story off the ground. I guess I've got a case of writer's block and what happened this afternoon is going to make it worse.'

'I think I can take care of that.' Selena picked up the telephone from his desk.

'What are you doing?'

'Making an appointment for you – with a psychiatrist I know.'

'Why would I need a shrink?'

'Obviously the block you say you've had for a week is a revulsion on the part of Henry Walters, the highly respected

36

author of fine novels, to writing the kind of junk *Superstud* will have to be in order to be a smash.'

'Call the shrink!'

'Dr Schwartz helped me once,' said Selena as she was dialling.

'You'd be the last person I'd ever expect to lose your marbles.'

'I didn't lose anything – except some of my self confidence. Dr Schwartz sent me to some people who put me back in touch with things.'

'What I need is someone to help me *stop* touching things.'

'You *do* seem to be in an acute stage,' Selena conceded with a chuckle. 'Did you recognize the tall woman in denim with the camera?'

'I didn't recognize anything, except that I was hurting like hell where I got kicked in the – '

'That was Wilhelmina Dillingham.'

Henry gawked. 'Willy the Dilly?'

'I'm glad to see your brain wasn't damaged. She claims to get her best stories in hospital emergency rooms or police courts. This afternoon she hit the jackpot.'

Henry didn't need to be told more about the famous Wilhelmina Dillingham. The reputation of Willy the Dilly – a title by which she was known to intimates and public alike – as a crack newspaper woman and poison-pen demolisher of human foibles in her column, 'Dallying with Dilly', was as formidable as was the list of her amours.

'She's bound to be the one who thought of that Bart's Parts headline,' said Henry. 'I'll never live that down.'

'This is Miss McGuire,' Selena said into the phone. 'Could Dr Schwartz possibly see an emergency case for me – Mr Henry Walters, one of our authors?'

There was a pause, then Selena spoke again. 'You have a cancellation for tomorrow at eleven? Fine. Put Mr Walters down for it, please. The trouble? Writer's block.'

'Dr Isadore Schwartz, Ninety-fifth and Park,' said Selena as she picked up her handbag and prepared to leave. 'Eleven tomorrow morning.'

'I'm wounded,' Henry protested plaintively. 'You can't leave me here alone.'

'Nonsense. You're only bruised a little.'

'I need encouragement, too; the kind of encouragement an

editor is supposed to give to an author. Why don't you have dinner with me?'

'I've got to teach a course in editing at NYU tonight, but I'll have your dinner sent in from the delicatessen you like so much around the corner. Don't forget Dr Schwartz, tomorrow at eleven.'

'Marry me and I'll never have writer's block.'

At the door, Selena turned and he saw something in her eyes he'd never remembered seeing there before – an elfin gleam, as if she'd been touched momentarily by the Little People.

'After what's happened, you might turn out to have a split personality, Henry,' she said. 'And I don't really think I could stand having both you and Bart Bartlemy for husbands.'

BOOK II

GLORIA

i

Dr Isadore Schwartz was a tall man with a strong resemblance to Abraham Lincoln. Just looking at the doctor's smiling face made Henry feel better.

'I've been an admirer of your writings for some time, Mr Walters.' Schwartz waved Henry to a chair; there wasn't a couch in the room. 'Miss McGuire told my secretary you were having some difficulty but I didn't realize exactly what the trouble might be, until I saw the papers last night. I didn't hear Dr Sang's presentation at the Academy but, from what the newspapers said, I judge that the transplant has been outstandingly successful anatomically.'

'Anatomically, yes,' said Henry. 'Functionally remains to be seen. Maybe I'd better tell you the whole story.'

'I think that would be a good idea.' Dr Schwartz switched on the tape recorder on his desk.

'I guess that's all there is,' Henry said when he had finished the account. 'I've tried for a week to get started with the first draft of *Superstud* but nothing's happened.'

'Have you ever had a block like this before?'

'Occasionally. All writers do.'

'What makes you think this one won't pass like the others did?'

39

'I guess what really bothers me is what Wilhelmina Dillingham said in her article,' Henry admitted. 'Bart had quite a reputation with women and before I write a novel about him, I've got to do a lot of things he did.'

Dr Schwartz looked surprised. 'I should think you would look forward to this, er – research – with pleasure, even anticipation. All you need now is to indulge in a number of romantic episodes in the name of research – if that will ease your conscience – and write them down in the form of a fictional narrative. And since you write far better than most authors already making fortunes in sex fiction, you should achieve even greater returns.'

'But it's Selena – Miss McGuire – I want, not a lot of other women.'

'Oddly enough, close analogies exist between economics and marriage, Mr Walters. The man other women want usually gets the one *he* wants. Or, to put it simply, when he's in short supply because of increased demand, the ardour of the one he really desires usually increases.'

'Are you saying I should run after other women?'

'Isn't that the dream of every red-blooded American male?'

'Well – yes.'

'In your case, I believe you have an excellent chance to win the young lady of your choice, while still having a ball – and at the same time write a very saleable novel.'

'Provided you can fix me up so I'm confident of my ability, without getting clobbered like I was yesterday in the subway.'

'I think I can do that, Mr Walters, and I'm confident that we can remove your writer's block. After all, you now have all the equipment necessary for a great lover.'

Henry brightened. 'And Selena can't blame me because it was her idea for me to do research and also to come to you. Doctor, I think you've got something. When do we start?'

'Right now, Mr Walters.'

Dr Schwartz flipped a switch beside his chair and the room was darkened as motor-driven shades covered the windows. Seconds later, in answer to another switch, a vibrating ball of light appeared on the wall behind the psychiatrist's left shoulder.

'Please concentrate upon the light,' Dr Schwartz directed. 'Keep your eyes on it and try to remove from your mind everything except what I shall tell you.'

ii

It was past noon when Henry came out of Dr Schwartz's office and the streets were crowded, mainly with women of all ages, sizes and shapes. None of that troubled him at all, however; in fact, he no longer found himself observing them with apprehension but instead with pleasure and a certain anticipation.

As to just what had transpired after the doctor turned on the vibrating light, Henry had no real memory. Not knowing didn't trouble him, though, nor did the cheque for fifty dollars he'd given the secretary outside. The important thing was that he felt like a new man in every way, even to a marked lessening of the aches and pains from yesterday's subway encounter. On an impulse, he stepped into a drugstore and, dropping a coin into the slot of a telephone in a booth at the back, dialled the Bennett Press editorial office, and asked to be put through to Selena.

'How about having lunch with me?' he asked.

'I'm sorry, Henry, we're having a luncheon conference of the non-fiction publishing group here at the office in ten minutes.'

'How about dinner?'

'I'm teaching a class in publishing at NYU tonight.'

'How about tomorrow then?'

'I'll have to call you tomorrow. I'm presenting the plan of your novel you summarized for me to the Fiction Group in the morning. Did you see Dr Schwartz?'

'Just came from his office.'

'Does he think he can help you with the block?'

'He already has.'

There was a moment of silence, then she asked, 'How?'

'I'm not sure exactly what he did but whatever it was, I'm a new man. In fact, I feel like Bart must have felt in his prime.'

'Isn't that rather risky considering your medical history?'

'Dr Sang says I'm okay and so does Dr Schwartz. Incidentally, how about going with me to my shack in the Catskills for the weekend?'

She laughed. 'You really are fired up. I'll let you know tomorrow, when I give you the opinion of the fiction group.'

'They're bound to be happy with a super best-seller coming up. We can celebrate at dinner tomorrow evening.'

41

'I'll let you know in the morning whether I'm free,' she promised.

iii

After a highly productive afternoon with his computer/word processor, Henry was crossing the living room of his apartment to the kitchen, planning to pour his five o'clock bourbon, when the door buzzer rang. Going to the door he opened it to find Miss Gloria Manning standing outside smiling warmly. His first impulse was to shut the door in the visitor's face, but Miss Manning thoughtfully stuck her foot inside the frame and he was forced to give up the idea.

'Please, Mr Walters,' she said beseechingly, 'I came to apologize for yesterday, and give you this.'

When she held out his signet college class ring that had started all the trouble yesterday, he could hardly refuse. Looking at her under more pleasant circumstances, too, than he'd been able to do yesterday, and particularly with a new feeling of confidence generated by Dr Schwartz's vibrating light, Henry could see a rather marked resemblance between Gloria Manning and the heroine of many of today's best-selling novels as depicted on the jackets.

'Where did you find the ring?' he asked as he let her in.

'It was in my bra,' she confided.

'I was about to have a drink,' Henry told her as he accepted the ring and put it on his finger. 'Would you join me?'

'I'd love to,' said the visitor. 'It's very nice of you to ask – considering.'

'Think nothing of it,' said Henry grandly.

The kitchen bar had a countertop that gave an excellent view of the living room, so he could hardly escape the sight of Miss Manning dropping her jacket on the back of the chair to reveal that she wore a rather tight sleeveless angora sweater. Taking a seat upon the sofa, she crossed really superb legs and made herself comfortable.

Fixing the drinks – doubles – Henry felt his interest in the blonde visitor rising steadily, as evidenced by a similar reaction

42

in the transplant. Bringing the glasses into the living room, he handed Miss Manning hers and took the lounge chair across from her.

'This is delicious,' she said after downing half of the drink in one swallow. 'It's hot outside and I was very thirsty.'

Henry felt the potent bourbon hit his empty stomach and be rapidly absorbed.

'I really do owe you an apology, Mr Walters,' said Miss Manning. 'But under circumstances like yesterday's, I'm sure you realize that a girl can never be quite certain of a gentleman's intentions.'

'I understand fully.'

'Under different circumstances . . .' She left the sentence hanging but he understood her meaning fully and felt the excitement of pending conquest build.

'I'm glad you're so understanding, Miss–'

'Please call me Gloria.'

'Of course, Gloria. It all must have been embarrassing for you, too.'

'A little. But you were really paying me a compliment.'

'A well deserved one,' Henry heard himself say and realized that the devilish genie of Bart Bartlemy's spirit, which Dr Schwartz had somehow managed to free with his vibrating light, had now seized command of the situation. More important, the genie was doing a darn sight better job than the old Henry Walters would have ever dared to try.

Emptying her glass, Gloria rose and went to examine the bookshelves on the wall, which were largely devoted to foreign editions of Henry's own writings.

'Are your books really published in all those countries?' she asked.

'Those and a few others. Won't you have another drink?'

'That would be nice.'

Henry couldn't see that the double bourbon Gloria had downed was affecting her at all, although he was beginning to feel as if cushions of air were under the balls of his feet. While he was making the second drink – hers a double and his a single – she came to the door of the kitchen.

'Didn't Judge Peebles say something about one of your novels being made into a picture?' she asked.

43

'*Lancelot's Return* has been bought by Twentieth Century Fox.'

'I read that book.' She took the glass he handed her. 'It was beautiful.'

'Thank you. I felt the world should know that Guinevere was every inch a woman, besides being a queen.'

'I'm in show business,' Gloria confessed. 'Just some modelling and a few walk-ons on TV so far, but I have hopes.'

'You could certainly play the heroine in *Naked Lust*.' The new Henry Walters – courtesy of Bart Bartlemy – could recognize opportunity when it knocked, by using the title of the latest sex epic as a come-on.

'Do you really think so?' Her warm smile of pleasure enveloped him.

'I'm sure of it.'

'*Your* book hasn't been cast yet, has it?'

'Not to my knowledge.'

'I brought some photos – in colour. Do you suppose you could possibly get someone at Twentieth Century Fox to look at them – just in case they might be able to use me.'

At another time, Henry would undoubtedly have told her the truth – that he hadn't heard from Fox, nor expected to, since he'd signed the contracts and cashed the first of five annual cheques for film rights to his most recent novel, *Lancelot's Return*. But not the genie Dr Schwartz had somehow managed to release.

'I'll be happy to,' he assured the lovely visitor. 'But naturally I can't promise anything.'

'I understand.' From her large handbag, Gloria took an envelope and handed it to him.

'They're a bit realistic,' she warned as he was removing the photos from the envelope.

Prepared by her warning, Henry managed not to gape at what he saw – six poses of her in full colour, all completely nude.

'Beautiful!' Henry's grip almost crushed his glass. 'Absolutely beautiful.'

'A compliment means so much coming from a man of the world like you with such an understanding of a woman's emotions and her needs, Mr Walters,' Gloria breathed.

'Call me Henry, please.' It was then that the lightning stroke of inspiration struck and, taking a deep breath, Henry launched his ploy: 'I'm engaged in research right now for the new novel.'

'Research?' The blank look in Gloria Manning's eyes told him the meaning of the word had escaped her in that context. Which didn't surprise him for he'd never used it in exactly the same circumstances.

'It's about Bart Bartlemy,' he confided.

'I saw that centrefold in *Fun Girl*. He was quite a man.'

Henry decided to play his ace. 'Did you know that many authors use models for their heroines? Just like artists do?'

'I didn't know that. How interesting.'

'Like I said, my novel about Bart will be very realistic.'

'It would have to be to do justice to his memory. Do you have a title yet?'

'It will be called *Superstud*.'

Gloria's eyes widened suddenly and he saw that she fully realized the implications. 'You'll make a million! A cool million!'

'You said just now that you'd done some modelling so you can imagine what the publicity will do for the model I use for the heroine.' Henry followed up his initial ploy, exactly as he surmised Brother Bart would have done. 'Her picture might even be on the jacket.'

'Oh yes!' Gloria breathed. 'After seeing my photos, do you think I might pose for some of the scenes – maybe even the jacket?'

'The photos are helpful, of course, but for the realistic descriptive passages, I need living flesh – you know, for skin tones and all that.'

'I understand.' She put down her empty glass and got to her feet. 'Is that a bedroom at the back?'

'Yes.'

'I remember just the scene from *Naked Lust;* I was reading it last night. It's where Esme – her name's really Esmeralda but he calls her Esme – comes out of the bedroom.' She gave him a warm smile. 'Don't go away, I'll be right back.'

'I wouldn't think of it.'

Henry was pacing the room like a stallion at bay. When Gloria finally posed in the bedroom doorway, it was worth all the waiting and all the lies.

'Will this do?' she asked, turning slightly so he could get the full impact of her profile.

'Perfectly,' he said hoarsely.

'When are you going to start your research?' she said, and this time Henry knew the exact answer.

'Right now!' he said. 'The first chapter will be a bedroom scene so we might work better in there.'

iv

Henry Walters awakened to the sound of birds singing outside his window and the mellow sunshine of a summer morning caressing his face through the open window. He lay in bed for a while, luxuriating in the undiluted pleasure of remembering the sequence of events – some quite active – which had followed the appearance of Gloria Manning at his door the evening before.

They had dined somewhere around nine o'clock he recalled, on scrambled eggs, bacon and toast. Gloria had departed around midnight, fervently promising to return whenever he might need her for other modelling activities and, moreover, obviously pleased with the hundred he had insisted on pressing upon her as a fee for professional services.

Remembering his tentative dinner date with Selena, Henry shaved and showered before breakfasting at a drugstore around the corner from the apartment house. After breakfast, he took a brief walk into Central Park, enjoying the warm sunshine and pausing now and then to admire the chic young matrons walking their poodles and Weimarieners there. So pleased was he by the events of the last twenty-four hours – and in truth somewhat depleted hormonally – that only once did he feel his interest begin to stir, when the striking brunette whom he had seen walking her Burmese cat on a leash there almost every morning smiled at him.

'Good morning,' Henry said warmly. 'We seem to be regulars.'

'Rashid demands it,' said the young woman. 'I'm Elena

46

Hartsfield; we're neighbours since I have a condominium in the same block.'

'I should spend more time talking to my neighbours,' said Henry gallantly. 'But I must admit that I have seen you here on a number of occasions.' He glanced at her left hand and seeing the ring there, felt his ardour subside somewhat.

'I still keep the name Hartsfield, although Carling and I have been divorced for about six months.' Elena answered his question for him. 'You've been in the news quite a lot lately.'

'Not by choice, I assure you,' said Henry, 'but these things happen.'

'And often for the best,' Elena smiled warmly. 'In fact, I may be able to help you with your new book.'

'So? May I ask how?'

'Before I came to my senses and married money – in the person of Carling Hartsfield – I was a contract starlet for almost a year in Hollywood,' she told him. 'I knew your twin brother, Bart, well. Very well, in fact, since we had a brief affair.'

'Then you should be able to give me a lot of information about Bart that I will need very badly for my book,' Henry said promptly. 'You see, we were separated by two aunts shortly after birth and they had different philosophies, you might say, about the quality of life.'

'I know,' said Elena Hartsfield. 'The Hollywood milieu is certainly quite different from that in Cambridge, where I read in the paper this morning that you grew up.'

'This morning?' Henry said, surprised. 'I didn't know I had become so famous so quickly.'

'Wilhelmina Dillingham has written quite a piece about you in the *Post*,' said Elena Hartsfield, 'and you even made the *Times* this morning.'

'*Sic transit gloria mundi*,' said Henry. 'I went for years as a moderately successful writer and suddenly found myself famous for no reason of my own at all.'

'That should make a very fascinating part of your book about Bart Bartlemy, Mr Walters – '

'Henry.'

'Certainly. I'm Elena. If you can spare the time, I would like to tell you a great deal about Hollywood and what happened to Bart there.'

'I've already had breakfast,' said Henry, 'but we could make it for lunch.'

'Let's make that the day after tomorrow at dinner, Henry,' she said. 'I managed to earn my way through Vassar as a waitress in a short order restaurant but I can still do a considerably better job than hamburgers and french fries.'

'I can't wait,' Henry told her. 'Shall we say eight o'clock?'

'That will be fine. I'll be looking for you.'

About half past eleven that morning, as Henry was writing the first chapter of *Superstud*, a messenger arrived with a cablegram from his agent, Harry Westmore. It was from Paris and exuberant:

PARIS MATCH carried story your transplant and arrest. Valery-Gestalt ecstatic over bio novel re Bart Bartlemy. Also Bannister. Expect to hear from Davidof before nightfall. Salutations to the new Henry. Home Thursday. Happy hunting.
Harry

Valery-Gestalt was Henry's French publisher, from whom came almost a fourth of his annual royalties. Bannister was the English publisher with about half as much and Davidoff handled the Scandinavian countries. Obviously, the new novel was already a hit – in the opinion of very knowledgeable people in the publishing world – with only a few pages yet written.

Selena called just before lunch. 'The Fiction Editorial Group meeting has been moved up to three o'clock this afternoon,' she said. 'Mr Bennett saw the mention of your new novel on Nick Darby's morning schedule and had the meeting postponed until after his afternoon nap. He loves your books.'

'Even at his age, Abner is bound to appreciate *Superstud*,' Henry assured her. 'This could be a very good break.'

'I hope so.' Selena didn't sound as encouraged as Henry was. 'I'll tell you the result at dinner. The meeting will probably run late; where should I meet you?'

'How about the Peacock Alley? It usually isn't crowded for early dinner. Shall we make it at, say, six o'clock?'

'I'll meet you there. Goodbye.'

'Cheer up,' Henry admonished her. 'We've got the world by the tail and so has Bennett Press.'

At ten of six, Henry took a stance in the lobby of the Waldorf Astoria near the delightful and expensive nook called the Peacock Alley. Watching Selena cross the lobby from the Park Avenue entrance, he felt a considerable surge of pride – plus another emotion. No young woman in the lobby of the famous hotel that afternoon could hold a candle to her and even the familiar reaction of yesterday beginning to arise with him once more did not trouble him now.

After his session with Dr Schwartz, Henry was confident of being able to act in the true Bartlemy manner, holding himself in check through a period of preliminary courtship of the reluctant seducee or, riding roughshod over tremulous objections, like Lancelot in full armour galloping to free Guinevere.

'You look lovely,' Henry greeted Selena as, taking her elbow, he guided her gently in the direction of the maitre d'hôtel who was waiting deferentially.

'Hello, Henry.' She sounded dispirited.

'What's wrong?' he asked when they were seated at the table in the corner he had reserved.

'Everything. I need a drink.'

'Of course. What would you like?'

'Whatever you're going to have. You know I don't drink much.'

'A stinger is delicious but mild,' he lied nobly, giving the order to a hovering waiter.

'I didn't know this was one of your haunts,' Selena observed, looking around her while they waited for the drinks.

'I come here every now and then – for a change.'

'That's what I need – a change.'

'What's the trouble?'

'Just something at the office. I'll tell you about it after dinner.'

'May I say again that you're looking particularly lovely today.'

'You'd better not look at me like that, Henry. I mean in your condition.'

'Your friend, Dr Schwartz, took care of everything,' he assured her.

'With just one consultation? I can hardly believe it.'

'It's almost unbelievable but I'm practically a new man.'

'You've certainly changed,' she told him. 'There's an air of assurance – almost a certainty of success – about you that wasn't there before.'

'Which do you like best?'

'Right now, you're acting like Bart Bartlemy and I rather think I prefer the old Henry.'

'You're responsible for the new one,' he reminded her. 'Plus Dr Schwartz, of course.'

'I guess that's what troubles me. I read somewhere that in the Far East, if a man saves another's life, he becomes responsible ever after for the one he saved.'

'An excellent idea! You can start being responsible for me right now.'

'I already am as your editor.'

'I don't mean just as my editor. Marry me and let me take you away from all this.'

Selena's eyebrows rose. 'For what you call *this*, most girls would give their eye teeth.'

'That isn't what I want from you,' he said as a waiter placed their drinks before them.

'What you want is quite apparent from the look in your eyes,' Selena assured him as she lifted her glass. 'Cheers!'

'Cheers!' said Henry, and was surprised when she drank the potent drink almost as rapidly as Gloria had downed the bourbon the night before.

'I believe the research you're doing into the life of Bart Bartlemy is having an effect on you already,' she said as she put down her empty glass.

'Marry me and it won't have to go any farther – as research, I mean.'

'Just how far has it gone already?'

'Oh, you know.' Henry sensed this was not the time to tell Selena about Gloria Manning – if ever. 'I've been checking up on Bart's sex life, his first love affairs, things like that.'

'Who was first?'

'A high school classmate; you wouldn't want the sordid details.' Henry was beginning to perspire although the temperature in the Peacock Alley could no more vary by more than half a degree whatever the season, than the sun could stand still. Then he had an inspiration.

'Of course, the kind of language and writing that will make

50

Superstud succeed means practically learning a new tongue for a former Professor of English Literature,' he said.

'I suppose so.' To Henry's surprise, Selena agreed to a second round before they ordered.

'I was going to put off telling you as long as I could but I might as well get it over with,' she said when they were well into the second stinger. 'I'm sorry, Henry, but you won't have to do any more research.'

'Why?'

'Mr Bennett was at the Fiction Group meeting this afternoon.' The second round had added a faint tint of pink to the alabaster perfection of Selena's skin and Henry signalled the waiter surreptitiously for another round. 'I might as well tell you now. He doesn't like the idea of *Superstud.*'

'The hell you say! Didn't Nick Darby like the project as you outlined it.'

'Nick flipped when I briefed him on it before the conference.' She looked suspiciously at the third stinger which had just been placed before her. 'What are you trying to do anyway, Henry? Get me tight and entice me to your lair?'

'That's the best idea I've heard today, but remember I've also offered to make it legal.'

'I was so shaken up by Abner Bennett's reaction to your story that I lost my cool and spoke very sharply to him.'

'Better your virtue than your cool.'

'Who said that?'

'It's going to be a line from *Superstud.*'

'Don't tell me you've already started writing?'

'Only the opening lines. Want to hear them?'

Before she could answer, Henry started declaiming the words in a voice – courtesy of the alcohol in his bloodstream – somewhat louder than his normal tone:

'*She stood in the doorway, drowsily unaware it seemed, that she was naked.*

'*"Who are you?" she asked.*

'*"My name's Bart and I'm hungry."*

'*"You were hungry last night, too. Or aren't those your teeth marks on my –"*

She moved closer as she spoke. "See?"

'*"They're not mine," said Bart. "I prefer little bites."*

51

'"Well, whoever you are, mister, you're just in time for breakfast."'

'Henry! Stop it!' said Selena.

'Sorry, darling, the writer in me got carried away.'

'From the look on your face, somebody else was about to be carried away and for a minute I was afraid it was going to be me.'

'Now there's an idea,' said Henry enthusiastically. 'Finish your drink and we'll go home where I can fix one of those omelettes you like so well.'

'I'm not very hungry and with three of these in me, I might pass out right here and disgrace you, so maybe that's a good idea,' she said. 'Are you sure all this research you've been talking about is being done at home?'

'Every bit of it, except of course the charge I get out of merely looking at you.'

'But I've let you down,' she wailed. 'I thought I was doing the right thing for you but now – '

He reached across the table to take her hand. 'You couldn't do me wrong, darling – not ever.'

'I'm trying to tell you Bennett Press isn't going to publish *Superstud!*'

'What?'

'I guess it really isn't *they*,' she admitted. 'It's *Him*.'

In the Bennett Publishing empire, only one man was always *Him* – behind his back, of course. To his face it was always, 'Yes, Mr Bennett. No, Mr Bennett. By all means, Mr Bennett.'

'What did *Him* – I mean *He* do?' Henry asked.

'Well, first I made the presentation of *Superstud* to the Fiction Group.'

'It's too bad you couldn't have quoted the opening lines I just gave you – but I hadn't thought of them then.'

'Even they wouldn't have stirred Abner Bennett,' she assured him. 'He said he reads your historical novels and likes them because they put him to sleep – no offence of course.'

'At Abner's age, Little Bo Peep would put him into a coma – without the sheep,' said Henry with some bitterness. 'Did you tell him what a bonanza this book could be for Bennett Press?'

'I gave the conference the whole promotion and Nick Darby backed me up. An interview on the Today Show at publication date. Books shipped early so word can get around that we've got a hot one – '

'As hot as the place where Bart probably is now, I suspect.'

'Please, Henry. This is no joking matter.'

'I know, darling. Go on.'

'You played fair with me by telling Gregory Annunzio I had to handle the book. I even assured the committee that you really can deliver it.'

'And that we were bound to have a sure winner with that story written by a real writer with an established reputation who also was the twin brother of the main character?'

'Mr Bennett still wouldn't hear of it,' she told him. 'He held up *Lancelot's Return* as a perfect example of the historical novel. Like so many old people, I suppose he lives mostly in the past, when virtue was triumphant and right living always paid off.'

'I guess I was like him until *you* put me wise,' Henry confessed. 'I didn't even suspect Lancelot of fooling around with Guinevere, until I saw Tyrone Power and Ava Gardner in the film and got the idea for writing *Lancelot's Return*.'

'Neither did King Arthur, I suspect.'

The bill came and Henry signed the American Express voucher. Selena was leaning rather heavily on his arm as they left the lobby of the Waldorf and Henry wasn't too steady on his feet either. Outside, they had to wait a few minutes before the doorman was able to get them a taxi at that time of day.

'Bennett Press had its chance and muffed it,' Henry said while they were waiting. 'Harry Westmore will be back from Europe in a day or two and we'll go to another publisher.'

'I'd hate to see you do that,' she told him. 'Have you talked to Harry about this already?'

'No, but I had a cable from him this morning. The story in the newspapers about the subway incident was picked up in Europe. Valery-Gestalt and the other publishers over there are ecstatic. When Bennett turned *Superstud* down, that put it in the public domain as far as publishing is concerned. We can go to anyone else we wish, regardless of Bennett Press's options. I'll make a success of it with some other publisher and give you a check for the advance as a wedding present.'

'How do you know anyone else will take it? After all, this is a field where you haven't proved yourself.'

'You heard the opening lines I quoted just now. Do they sound like a failure?'

'No, but – '

'Is your doubt now because you think no other publisher has an editor on his staff who can bring out the tiger in Henry Walters? Tell you what, why don't *you* be my model?' Henry said as he handed the doorman five dollars and helped her into the taxi which had finally braked to a stop before the marquee of the Waldorf.

'Be serious,' she said as she settled back against the worn seat covers.

'What's more serious than asking the girl you love to marry you?'

'I've already told you I'm going to marry you some day,' said Selena. 'But I'm making a success at Bennett Press and I don't want to go into marriage until I've reached a better editorial level than now.'

'You can go to another publisher, too, if I insist,' said Henry. 'I told Gregory Annunzio in the beginning that I wouldn't write the novel unless you were my editor and that holds true no matter who publishes it.'

'You still can't be sure another publisher will accept *Superstud*,' she said. 'After all, who's going to contract for a sex novel by a writer who pleases Abner Bennett?'

'That was a low blow, Selena.'

'I'm sorry, darling, I'll make it up to you.'

And she did.

V

The shaft of sunlight peeking through the window as dawn broke over New York in all its polluted glory, woke Henry. He had long since discovered that he worked best in the early hours of the morning and had formed the habit of waking when the rays of the rising sun struck his face through the window. He moved gingerly so as not to disturb Selena – still asleep with the rich masses of her hair, unbound since about seven o'clock yesterday, spread out on the pillow. She was beautiful all over, lying there in his bed, her face flushed with sleep, her lips full and ripe from the kisses they'd shared during the long passion-filled hours before midnight, when they'd finally fallen asleep, exhausted.

Moving to the computer/word processor, Henry switched it on and, turning the chair so he could see Selena through the open bedroom door, began to write. No need to use his imagination now, the wonder of what had happened since yesterday was all the stimulus he needed for words to begin flowing beneath his flying fingers. He'd been writing for an hour when a slight creak of the bed called his attention to the real, as opposed to the fiction, world.

'What time is it, darling?' Selena asked, yawning.

'Seven a.m.'

'Goodness.' She sat up in bed. 'You mean I slept here all night?'

'Part of it.'

She stretched luxuriously and created a diversion that took his mind off anything except the reality of her loveliness. When he came into the bedroom and leaned down to kiss her, she put her arms around his neck and held him tight for a long moment.

'You're quite a lover, Henry Walters,' she said when the kiss ended finally. 'I guess I'm going to have to marry you to keep one of Brother Bart's old flames from grabbing you off while you're doing what you call research.'

'That's the best news I've heard today, even though I've used up all the arguments I know in favour of marriage over the last six months, but you wouldn't listen – '

'Until you deliberately got me stoned yesterday afternoon,' she accused him. 'I came home with you because I was so worried about Abner Bennett nixing *Superstud*, that I couldn't even think what I was doing. I'm cold sober now, though, and I love you even more that I did yesterday.'

'The City Hall Marriage Licence Bureau doesn't open until ten,' said Henry. 'Unless you'd rather go to Connecticut.'

'After last night, we couldn't be much more married than we already are, so I guess we can afford a few days of a meaningful relationship between the sexes.' She gasped suddenly and reached down to disengage his roving hands. 'Do that again and I'll be totally unable to resist you. If you need something

55

to do, fix us coffee and toast while I get a shower and take some precautions against bearing your child embarrassingly close to our wedding day.'

The coffee was perking and Henry was busy scrambling eggs and making toast, when he heard a scream from the living room. Rushing in from the kitchen, he found himself part of a tableau like something out of *Oh, Calcutta!*

A naked Selena, fresh and glowing from the shower, was standing in the doorway of the bedroom, covering herself with her hands about as effectively as did September Morn. In the open door from the hall outside stood Gloria Manning, fully clothed and looking very much embarrassed. She was holding Henry's keys, which he suddenly remembered he'd left in the lock yesterday afternoon, when he'd carried Selena across the threshold and kicked the door shut behind them.

'I'm on my way to work, Henry,' said Gloria, as he took the keys and dropped them on his desk. 'Just stopped by to see whether I possibly left my earrings in the bedroom when I was modelling for you the other night.'

'Oh!' A snort of indignation came from Selena, since any female knows very well that, model or not, only one thing makes a woman take off her earrings in the bedroom of a man's apartment. Before Henry could answer – and after all what could he say? – Selena disappeared into the bedroom, slamming the door behind her with a finality that left no doubt of her feelings about the situation.

'I hope I haven't given the wrong impression,' said Gloria concernedly.

'The young lady is my fiancée,' Henry croaked.

'Congratulations! I'm so happy for you and for her.' Gloria glanced toward the bedroom door. 'Under the circumstances, I guess she already knows what a fortunate girl she is.'

'Thank you, Gloria,' said Henry. 'I'm sorry but I haven't seen your earrings.'

'That's all right. I thought they might have gotten knocked off the bedside table when – well, you know.'

Henry prayed that Selena wasn't listening behind the bedroom door but was pretty sure she was.

'If I find them, I'll give you a ring,' he told Gloria.

'I hope your fiancée doesn't misinterpret our relationship.

56

Sometimes it's hard for wives to understand just what models do.'

'I'm sure she'll misunderstand,' said Henry sadly. 'Goodbye!'

Gloria winked. 'You look real cute in that apron.'

Remembering that his sole garment was a small and frilly kitchen apron Selena had given him last Christmas as a joke, Henry started toward the bedroom. Just then, however, the unmistakable smell of burning toast sent him rushing to the kitchen where the percolator was boiling over on the stove and the toast switch, of all mornings, had stuck and the toaster was filling the kitchen with a cloud of black smoke.

He was struggling to open the kitchen window when he heard a loud 'Humph' from the door and, embarrassingly conscious of how he must look from the rear, wheeled to face Selena. She was fully clothed, except that her hair was still down upon her shoulders and her eyes were shooting sparks.

'You! You!' Words failed her, something he'd never seen happen before.

'Louse?' he suggested, but she shook her head.

'You're lower down than a louse, Henry Walters. Now I know what you meant yesterday by research and getting a model. How did *she* look standing nude in the bedroom doorway?'

'Not as good as you did,' he volunteered, but that only lit another fuse.

'Gloria Manning! I'll bet that's not her real name?'

'She's a professional – '

'Anybody can see that.'

' – model.'

Before he could say more, Selena began to quote in a falsetto tone:

' *"Boy, were you hungry last night – Aren't these your teeth marks on my – "* She moved closer as she spoke, *"See." ' ' "They're not mine,"* said Bart. *"I prefer little bites – " ' '*

'You lecher,' Selena resumed in her own voice. 'I hope I never see you again.'

She started across the living room, a picture of indignant loveliness that filled his heart to overflowing with love and also with fear of losing her.

57

'You forgot *your* earrings,' he reminded her.

Like a drill sergeant on parade, Selena marched into the bedroom and out again, carrying the earrings as if they were tainted by a skunk.

'Selena, please!' he called but she kept on through the door and out in the hall.

Stopping only to unplug the toaster and the percolator, Henry raced through the doorway into the corridor – just in time to see her enter the elevator, do an 'about face' and push the 'down' button.

As the elevator started to descend, he heard a door slam behind him and knew at once what had happened. The breeze from the open kitchen window had just blown his apartment door shut, leaving him stranded in the hall with only a somewhat libidinous, and very tiny apron for a garment – and no key.

vi

After borrowing a pass key from the elevator starter and cleaning up a kitchen that looked like the aftermath of a small holocaust, Henry decided to go out for breakfast. On the way, he picked up Selena's reading glasses from the bedside table where she'd dropped them after letting her hair down last night. Briefly he considered stopping by the Bennett Press offices on Madison Avenue after breakfast and leaving the glasses. But realizing his action might be interpreted by other Bennett employees to mean exactly what it did mean, he decided to send them to her office by messenger instead.

Returning to his apartment after breakfast, Henry sat down before the word processor from force of habit and switched on the printer. As the words he'd written that morning, while waiting for Selena to wake up, chattered to paper from a floppy disk, he read them. And when they came to a halt, the memory of Selena in the big bed was still so vivid that he allowed his authorial imagination to conjure up a picture of what might have happened had Gloria Manning not interrupted. He continued to write on and on, stopping only for a glass of milk and a sandwich about two o'clock.

By six thirty, his normal quitting time, he had written thirty pages and felt utterly depleted, as he always did when he had written vividly. While the printer transferred what he'd written to paper, he put a TV dinner in the oven and had his usual bourbon as he watched the national news. After eating a solitary dinner and watching TV briefly, he crawled into his bed, strangely empty now after two nights of feminine companionship.

Henry was busy writing the next morning, when the door buzzer sounded shortly before ten. He opened it and found Harry Westmore waiting outside. A broad-shouldered man in his fifties, Westmore was one of the smartest literary agents in the business, besides being a close friend.

'When did you get back?' Henry asked.

'An hour and a half ago. Came straight here from Kennedy.'

'Then you can use some coffee, I was about to make some. Been busy the last several days getting my research down on paper.'

'Research? According to the newspaper accounts you're not writing an historical novel.'

'I need to sort of get inside Bart for the biographical novel about him,' Henry explained. 'And the best way seemed to be by doing some of the things Bart did.'

'Didn't lose any time, did you?'

'Less than you'd think.' Henry spread the photographs of Gloria out on the kitchen table. 'Here's the jacket photo.'

'Wow!' said Westmore. 'Maybe you'd better start at the beginning; all I know is what I read in the European papers about the transplant.' He looked down at the photos again, then back to Henry. 'I presume that Bart's parts are working.'

'Like clockwork.'

'I don't think that's quite the right comparison but go ahead. I still can't believe all this happened to you, of all people.'

'What do you mean by that?' Henry asked in a tone of some indignation.

'Until all this started, you were one of the quietest and mildest guys I know. You did your research – '

'That's all I've been doing – research.'

'With her?' Harry Westmore held up one of the photos.

'Yes.'

59

'Tell me more. I'm beginning to wonder whether they transplanted part of Bart in – '

'On.'

' – On you, or *you* on the most important part of *him*. Before you get started on the sordid details, though, it's only fair to tell you that I called Nick Darby from the phone downstairs in the lobby to see how all this was going to affect your relationship with Bennett Press,' Westmore continued. 'Nick told me Selena McGuire came to work and threw you out of her stable of authors.'

'I know.'

'You don't get editors like Selena very often – or chicks either. Maybe you'd better tell me what all this is about.'

'It's kind of personal.'

'I knew you were carrying a torch for her, Henry. What happened?'

'Everything was coming up roses until old Abner nixed Selena's plan for Bennett to publish *Superstud*.'

Westmore blinked. 'How did a horse get into this?'

'*Superstud* is the title of the novel I'm writing about Bart – '

'The one you've been researching by bedding beautiful broads?'

'You could say that.'

'I don't know of a more appropriate title – or research, considering Bart's well know proclivities. But where does Selena come in?'

'She was pretty mad at Abner Bennett for nixing *Superstud*. After the Fiction Group meeting yesterday, we met at Peacock Alley and got stoned together.'

'Bedding two gorgeous chicks in two days! I can see why Willy Dillingham labelled you a sex fiend. Maybe you'd better go back to where all of this started, with the accident when Bart's Rolls met that truck head on while going up the off ramp.'

vii

'That's the damnedest story I ever heard,' said Westmore when Henry finished the account. 'If you could write it down – '

'That's what I'm doing. Nobody would expect a biography of a Hollywood sex symbol to have much truth in it anyway, so I sort of let myself go.'

The agent frowned. 'Have you been writing without a contract?'

'This is preliminary research. What's more, it's deductible.'

Harry placed his right hand over his heart. 'Henry, my boy, let me salute genius – pure genius.'

'My writing isn't that good.'

'I'm not talking about writing. Ever since the income tax amendment was passed, people have been trying to make sex deductible and you've succeeded where everybody failed before. If I weren't your agent, I'd say take the rest of your life to research and write this book.'

'Did Nick Darby say anything else when you talked to him this morning?'

'He's worried about what your next book for them will be. Since Selena threw you out of her stable, Nick's going to be responsible for you at Bennett Press.'

'That's kind of him, considering that they don't want to publish what *I* want to write,' Henry said on a caustic note.

'They'll publish what you *write*, as long as it's what Abner Bennett likes to *read*. Nick says the Old Man made it abundantly clear that you're to be given the red carpet treatment for your historical novels.'

'Can even the Bennett sales force sell books that put Abner Bennett to sleep?'

'That's what's got us all worried. The question now is what to do with *Superstud*.'

'We can always go to another publisher.'

'Bennett Press has an option on your next book according to the contract.'

'Selena gave them a chance to pick up the option at the Fiction Group conference, when she presented a synopsis of the book. Old Abner wouldn't have it, so that lets us out.'

'Legally, yes,' Westmore conceded. 'But Bennett Press has been good to you, Henry, so a question of loyalty is involved, too.'

'Is Abner Bennett loyal to me when he wants me to starve,

just so he can read about knights jousting for the favours of fair ladies?'

'If the knights got the same favours you've been getting lately, you just might have your cake, and eat it, too.'

'Suppose I did write one of those operas-in-armour – with the sort of stuff thrown in that sells books nowadays in the mass paperback market – and Abner lowers the boom again. I'm left with a dud. Besides, it will be hard to sustain a sex scene while a guy's getting out of armour – unless the lady's willing to help with the can opener.'

'You've made your point.'

'There's something else I haven't told you.'

'Let's hear it,' said Westmore. 'Nothing could be more exciting than what I've been hearing and my sclerotic old heart has taken that okay.'

'I never would have gotten into this in the first place if a fellow named Gregory Annunzio hadn't come to see me in the hospital.'

'He's the Syndicate lawyer,' Westmore exclaimed while Henry rummaged in his desk and came up with his copy of the agreement with Annunzio.

'Let me see that?' Westmore read the single sheet, then looked up reproachfully. 'You could have waited 'till I got back from Europe to sign this.'

'Annunzio said they were dickering with another writer. It had to be signed that day or I would have lost the chance.'

'That could be; Annunzio's a smart lawyer and he'd have no reason to con you. But why *you?*'

'He'd read some of my books and he said a novel about Bart Bartlemy written by his twin brother, who can also really write, will have wider sales than a hack job would.'

'He's right there. What's more, with his clients owning Bart and you the closest relative, you're free to write anything you want about him, without fear of being sued.'

'Everything that's happening to me has been going down on the paper as happening to Bart,' said Henry.

'What about the title?'

'That's mine. Thought of it myself.'

'Well, you signed the agreement so you're committed,' said Westmore. 'Can I have what you've written so far? I'll have it xeroxed for my files and send the original back to you by messenger later on today.'

'Sure, but where do we go from here?'

'I want to talk to Barney Weiss first. Maybe we three can have a drink somewhere around six – unless you've got another seduction scheduled for then.'

Barnard Ellington Weiss had become an almost legendary figure in publishing annals in a few years, through being the first to see the possibilities in exploiting a series of sex operas in tune with the new permissiveness – before it became permissive. It was Barney Weiss who had recognized the potential of Suzanne L'Anglais, the French novelist whose latest, *Satyr's Quest*, was at the top of the best-seller list. Weiss had also created her now famous décolletage, too, and the emeralds she wore in her navel at its lowest point was the sort of bizarre touch that was now almost traditional with a Weiss author or authoress.

'Take some of these, too, while you're at it.' Henry gave Westmore a couple of views of Gloria Manning. 'There's the jacket ready made.'

viii

The Louis Fourteenth Restaurant in Rockefeller Centre is an ideal place for discreet conferences, especially around six o'clock, when the bar is only moderately crowded and the dining area not yet heavily frequented. When Henry came into the restaurant a few minutes before six, he recognized immediately the tall man sitting at the bar with a drink before him.

'Mr Walters, I'm Barney Weiss,' the publisher greeted him. 'Harry called to say he'd be about ten minutes late, so why don't we have a drink here at the bar while we're waiting for him?'

'I'll take a Bloody Mary,' said Henry taking a seat beside Weiss.

The publisher gave the order and turned back to Henry. 'It may surprise you to know that I was at Harvard, too, though some years before you, class of nineteen fifty.'

'College – Sixty. Grad School sixty-five.'

'After I got my AB, I took a Masters in English Literature at Columbia,' Weiss told him. 'I even taught Chaucerian Literature there for a couple of years.'

'Chaucerian?' Henry asked, startled.

Barney Weiss laughed. 'The old English unexpurgated version. But when I discovered that my students were far more interested in what was then called dirty words in Chaucer than they were in either literature, characterization or the beauty of poetry, I decided the publishing world had much more to offer.'

'You've certainly had a successful career.'

'All due to a flair for publicity and promotion, I assure you – along with a lack of scruples. What we really sell has had a rather good market since the Garden of Eden and Lilith. Packaging made the difference, once we got back to the same costume that existed in the Garden.'

'I've never heard the mass market sex novel craze explained just that way before,' Henry admitted.

'Publishing in general – I don't mean outright pornography, of course – only came to adopt my point of view, as far as fiction is concerned, after I proved how successful it could be. Until then, most publishers – and authors, too, if I may say so – were a bit like the Emperor's new clothes in the children's tale. Everybody protested that literature must reveal some new outlook upon life, in spite of the fact that practically everything really important any novel has ever said can be summed up in a few of the old Testament stories, particularly those about one man – King David.'

'I've never written any biblical fiction.'

'Take my advice and don't start; right now anything in that field is a drug on the market – which is a shame. David winning over Goliath is a classic account of man's struggle against insuperable odds. His lusting after another man's wife and placing Uriah, the Hittite, in the front of the battle so he would be killed, is the basis for the eternal triangle, too. Can you imagine a more poignant tragedy than David's grief over the death of his son Absalom, even though the boy tried to kill his father and gain control of the kingdom.'

Harry Westmore appeared just then and the three moved to a table *en banquette* against the wall. Henry was still a little

64

stunned by Barney Weiss, who was much different from what he had expected of the most sensational sex novel publisher in history.

'What were you two discussing so earnestly, when I came in?' the agent asked.

'Nothing concerning Mr Walters' writings, I assure you, Harry; I never make the mistake of discussing business with an author when he has an agent, especially a sharp guy like you,' said Weiss. 'I've long been an admirer of Henry's skill in making history live; it's too bad the troubles of the present no longer give us time to think about the beauty of the past.'

'Mr Weiss – ' said Henry.

'Call me Barney, please. Everybody does – except my enemies.'

'Barney has been giving me a lesson in not being impressed by my own importance as a writer, Harry,' said Henry.

'Don't listen to the shyster,' Westmore advised. 'He's only trying to make us take a lower guarantee.'

'For what?'

'*Superstud* – what else? He's going to publish it.'

'Did you make that decision on just thirty or forty pages?' Henry asked Weiss.

'That and the way Harry says you plan to construct the story,' said the publisher.

Henry shook his head slowly. 'At Bennett, I always had to do at least half the book before contracts were signed.'

'I can recognize genius when I see it, Henry,' the publisher assured him. 'You're going to get rich from this book – and so am I.'

'What do you figure I'll get out of this altogether?' Henry asked the agent, still a little dazed by the rapidity of events.

'Somewhere between a half million and a million,' said Harry Westmore. 'That's before taxes, of course, but you're in the driver's seat there, too. We'll lump everything except the hundred thousand guarantee into one year. Then, with income averaging, you can spread it back over at least four previous years – plus the provision against the tax bite of more than fifty per cent of earned income. You may lose a third to the Internal Revenue Service – besides the twenty-five per cent to Greg Annunzio's clients – but you'll still wind up a rich man.'

65

'What about my historical novels?'

'Bennett Press can keep them,' said Weiss. 'I wouldn't want Abner to have insomnia.'

'Is it a deal, Henry?' Harry Westmore asked.

'All this sort of overwhelms me,' Henry admitted. 'I need a little time to think.'

'Suppose I hold the offer open for forty-eight hours as an option on the package at those terms,' Weiss suggested.

'What's the hitch, Henry?' the agent asked. 'Aren't the terms satisfactory?'

'The terms are fine but if I accept them, it means embarking on a whole new way of life. I can't make a decision like that without some thought.'

He couldn't tell them what was the real drawback, something that had to be settled before he took the final step into the earthly paradise the agent and the publisher were offering. Once he signed the contract with Barney Weiss, he sensed, there could be no return to the simple pleasant ways of the past and he couldn't take that step without making one more try at persuading Selena to marry him.

'I've got to run,' said Weiss as he scribbled his name at the bottom of the bill. 'I hope we'll be doing business together, Henry, but if we don't, I'll understand. After all, if it hadn't been for the dirty words in Chaucer, I'd still be a college teacher.'

ix

The Bennett Press offices were closed by the time Henry entered a telephone booth in the underground city that lies between Fifth Avenue and the Avenue of the Americas on either side of Fiftieth Street, but Selena answered her home number on the second ring.

'Don't hang up,' he said quickly. 'I've got to talk to you.'

'What do you want?' Her tone made Henry shiver.

'I've got to make an important decision within forty-eight hours and you're the only one who can help me.'

'I told you I never want to see you again.'

66

'I know – but this is business, Selena. It involves Bennett Press, too.'

'Nick Darby's your editor now.'

'I don't have anything against Nick, but I'm not going back there except with you as my editor. Can't we meet somewhere?'

'I just washed my hair and was getting ready to make a sandwich.'

'I can be there with a pizza and a cold six-pack in twenty minutes.'

'Leave off the six-pack, you only want me to get stoned again.'

'Two people couldn't possibly get stoned on a six-pack.'

'You'll have to talk fast, too,' she warned. 'I've got a manuscript to read tonight.'

'A half hour is all I need. Then you'll either marry me or I'll walk out of your life forever.'

'The latter alternative is one I couldn't possibly resist. Make the pizza Italian sausage with anchovies.'

Selen's apartment was in Gramercy Park, some twenty minutes by cab from where Henry was, so he flagged down a taxi going past.

'Know of a first-class pizzeria near Gramercy Park?' he asked the driver.

'Sure, Antonelli's.'

'Take me there and wait while I get one.'

At Antonelli's, Henry selected the biggest pizza available with sausage and anchovies. It was almost a yard across and he waited impatiently while the beaming proprietor slipped it into a box and took his money.'

'I hope you brought your toothbrush,' said the taxi driver when Henry came out staggering under the size of the box in a brisk breeze. 'Nobody in his right mind would spend that much on his wife.'

'Take it into the kitchen,' said Selena as she opened the door to the apartment. There was no welcome in her voice but he could see her lips begin to moisten as the delicious aroma seeped around the edges of the box and started to fill the apartment.

Neither of them spoke while Henry placed the pizza on the kitchen table. He was amazed to see two bottles of Blue Ribbon already there but made no comment. Selena had done a quick job of drying her hair, too, he noticed and it now lay in dark red masses upon her shoulders. She'd also taken the trouble to put on make-up – including eye shadow.

'You've already used ten minutes of your half hour,' she warned. 'What's the ploy this time?'

He gave her a quick rundown on his conversation with Harry Westmore and Barney Weiss.

'Do you want to know whether it's a good deal?' she asked.

'That isn't what I came for.'

'You'd be a fool not to accept it. Even if Abner Bennett had given me the okay for *Superstud*, Bennett Press wouldn't give you nearly as good terms.'

'I came to ask about something else.'

She glanced at the kitchen clock. 'You've got five minutes left to make your play.'

'Will you marry me, Selena?'

'You know the answer to that. No.'

'What if I don't take the Barney Weiss offer just to prove how much I love you?'

'You mean you haven't – '

'It's on a forty-eight hour option. If you'll marry me and go back to the way things were before – '

'Before what?'

'Anything.'

'Gloria Manning?'

'I'll even go back to the day I met you – I've been nuts about you ever since.'

'What about this research you've been doing?'

'You'll be my only subject from now on,' he promised. 'After last night – '

'Don't nauseate me with the sordid details of how you plied me with strong drink under false pretences – '

'There wasn't anything false – '

'About labelling a stinger mild? You knew they were dynamite all along.'

'Well, anyway, nothing about the rest of it was sordid. It was all very beautiful and so were – are – you.'

'What I don't understand is how you could ever have seen anything in that blonde.'

'It was all an accident,' he explained. 'While we were in court, Gloria heard me say *Lancelot's Return* was to be filmed. She came to the apartment to bring my ring and asked me to help her get a part in the picture. When I told her about *Superstud*, she wanted to pose for the jacket – '

'You made her pay the price, I suppose.'

'How could I promise to put her on the jacket when I've barely started the book. Besides, you already told me the costume epics I've been writing have lost out in sales to sex fiction and advised me to read things like *Naked Lust*.'

'Don't try to blame me for this career of debauchery you've embarked upon.'

'I'm not blaming anybody. I love you and I'm willing to give up half a million dollars – before taxes – to prove it. What else do you want?'

'What happens if I agree?'

'I'll throw what I've written – it's only forty pages or so – into the trash can and you can take over as my editor again. I'll even write something for Abner Bennett to go to sleep by and we'll live happily ever after – penuriously, of course, but happily.'

'I insist on keeping my job.'

'Keep anything, only keep me,' Henry said earnestly, detecting a possible change of feeling in her voice.

'I guess a girl couldn't want greater proof of a man's devotion than giving up half a million, but you really don't have to give that up either.'

'Come again?'

'There may be a way to have your cake and eat it, too. Does this contract you signed with Gregory Annunzio name a delivery date for the manuscript of the Bart Bartlemy story?'

'No.'

'Then you could write what you call a costume epic first for Bennett Press and do *Superstud* for Barney Weiss immediately afterward.'

'I'm not sure that would work,' said Henry doubtfully. 'It would take me six months to do another Round Table type of story and – '

'You made a big point of the research you've been doing,' Selena had the grace to blush. 'In six months of marriage I can promise you there will be a lot more to write about in *Superstud*.'

The prospect she held out was so dazzling, he could only

gulp, lost for words at the moment. Then all he could say was, 'Gosh!' But Selena understood.

'I've always had my heart set on being married in a church but it will take maybe a week to get my wedding dress and invite a few friends,' she said. 'The contract for your next historical novel at Bennett can be arranged right away, though, and you can start working on it to keep yourself out of the kind of trouble that seems to be getting a habit with you lately. I'll send the contracts to Harry Westmore's office tomorrow or the next day.'

She stood up and came around the table where the remains of the pizza lay. Henry pushed his chair away, too, and, since the kitchen was small, they were face to face for a moment, their bodies almost touching. Unnerved by her proximity and her loveliness, he reached for her but the softness he loved rested only momentarily against his palms before she slapped his hands away.

'No more handling the merchandise until it's yours,' she said. 'Not this – or any other. Understand?'

'Yes, darling,' said Henry, happily full of pizza, beer and love. 'We can meet at the Licence Bureau tomorrow and get things started; I think it takes three days.'

X

Henry had just returned home from his visit to Selena when the telephone rang. It was Gloria.

'I've been trying to get you for several hours, Henry,' she said.

'I was out.'

'How have you been?'

'Fine.'

'Is everything all right between you and the young lady with the red hair?'

'We're going to be married in a few days.'

'Congratulations! She's very beautiful.'

'Thanks, Gloria.'

'I was worried about running in on you like that so early the other morning but the key *was* hanging in the door outside.'

'It's all right.' Henry couldn't be mad at anybody tonight.

'You sure I didn't cause you any trouble?'

'It's all straightened out now and I'm very happy.'

'Then I'm happy, too, Henry. Like I told you before I left you the other night, you're the greatest – '

'Oh, I wouldn't say that.'

'I would – and my opinion is worth something.'

'May I say that you were wonderful, too,' Henry said gallantly.

'I don't usually have any complaints. Did the scene in your new book I posed for go all right?'

'It was perfect.' Henry was beginning to sweat as the reason for Gloria's call began to penetrate his brain. 'No scene I've ever written went more smoothly.'

'I'm so glad,' she said. 'Then my picture – one of those I gave you – will be on the jacket of the book?'

The moment of truth had come and Henry faced up to it manfully. 'I'm afraid not, Gloria.'

'Why?'

'Mr Abner Bennett owns the publishing house that handles my books and I have contracts with them. He doesn't like that sort of book.'

'Wouldn't someone else publish it?'

'There are options in my contract. I'm sorry, Gloria, real sorry.' Henry felt relieved at having gotten out of it so easily. 'You would have looked fine on that jacket.'

'I was particularly anxious to have my picture on a book by you because you're so nice, Henry,' she told him. 'Are you sure you're not going to write it?'

'Maybe later – after I do another historical novel.'

'How long would that be?'

'Six months, at least. And there's no guarantee I would do *Superstud* even then. I'm sorry, Gloria.'

'So am I, but I hope everything turns out all right for you, Henry. You're the nicest man I've ever known.'

'Thanks. Miss McGuire and I are going to be married in about a week. I'd invite you to the wedding, Gloria, but under the circumstances . . .'

71

'I understand, Henry. Goodbye.'
'Goodbye, Gloria.'

xi

Henry called Harry Westmore at home early the next morning
and told him of his decision to postpone writing *Superstud* while
he turned out a costume epic for Abner Bennett. Westmore's
answer was a gulp, followed by a period of silence.

'You still there, Harry?' Henry asked.

'I'm here but if you ask me, you're out of your mind.'

'I know what I'm doing.'

'Anybody who'd throw away a half million certain and maybe
more, even for a gorgeous chick like Selena, has to be nuts.'

'She's all that's important to me, Harry,' Henry explained. 'I
have to do a book for Bennett first to prove how much I love
Selena, but that doesn't mean I can't do *Superstud* afterward for
Barney.'

'My boy, opportunities like the one you've been given don't
wait. You have to strike while the iron is hot and this one is
red. Have you talked to Gregory Annunzio?'

'No.'

'He and the people he represents are not going to like this.'

'There's nothing in the agreement I made with them about
a delivery date for the manuscript.'

'But you'd already started writing and in a book like this,
timing could be everything.'

'I promised Selena,' was all the answer Henry could give.

There was another period of silence on the phone, he guessed
while Harry Westmore gained control of his anger at a client
who was – by any except purely romantic standards – the
greatest fool in history.

'When's the wedding to be?' the agent asked.

'In about a week. We're applying for the licence at noon.
Selena said to tell you that the contracts for the new historical
novel will be ready by tomorrow.'

'What?'

'There shouldn't be anything complicated about the

contracts. The terms will be the same as before and Selena says as soon as I do the historical for Bennett – maybe in six months – I can go back to work on *Superstud*.'

'What about your research?'

'From now on I'll be doing that at home.'

'With Selena as the model?'

'Who else?'

'I can think of a lot of others but it looks like you're hog-tied, Henry.'

'All right. I'll try to talk Barney Weiss into waiting for *Superstud*. But if some hack comes up with the same idea before then, you've lost the most saleable sex novel since *Fanny Hill*. By the way, congratulate Selena on the ideal way to promote herself to Senior Editor because Abner Bennett has insomnia and goes to sleep by reading your books.'

'I'm not that bad, Harry.'

'You're good in your field, Henry. Very good. So is Seneca.'

xii

Henry had just arrived back from the Licence Bureau late that afternoon where he and Selena had made the necessary applications, when the telephone rang. It was Elena Hartsfield.

'You haven't forgotten our dinner date this evening, Henry?' Elena asked. 'I tried to call you several times today but you were away.'

'I had some things to attend to.' Henry decided it was just as well not to tell her exactly what.

'I've got so many things to tell you that happened while I was living with Bart. We'll have a casserole with a bottle of a special wine that Carling used to have imported from France.'

'That – ' Henry hesitated only momentarily, 'That sounds fine.'

'I'll look for you at about eight o'clock, then,' she said.

'Informal dress, I imagine,' said Henry and Elena's laugh sent a tingle of anticipation through him.

'To start with anyway,' she added.

A tray of martinis was already prepared by the time Henry

arrived. Elena was wearing something filmy and clingy, both filmier and clingier than Henry had expected and revealing several reasons why she had been at least a starlet in Hollywood for a brief period.

'I hope you like martinis,' she said, handing him one from the group on a large silver tray.

'Love them,' said Henry, accepting the glass she handed him. 'I also brought a small tape recorder to record some of the facts about Bart and Hollywood, if you don't mind.'

'I don't mind in the least,' said Elena. 'After all, the newspapers are saying that this book of yours is going to be very realistic and name real people.'

'That's the plan,' Henry heard himself saying and wondered momentarily why he didn't tell her the truth, but, following her to the den which, he could see through an open door, led to a very feminine bedroom took away any desire to tell her the truth about his plans for the future. As for the present, the genie had already taken things pretty well in hand.

The martinis were potent, the food delicious, the company more and more stimulating as time passed and they talked about Hollywood and Bart Bartlemy and how Henry would write *Superstud*.

It was eleven o'clock when he looked at his watch and realized how quickly the evening had passed. When he got up to go, Elena came close, and when he instinctively reached for her, she came into his arms. The kiss she gave him was warm and eager and before it was finished, Henry had forgotten all about Selena, Abner Bennett and everything except the reality of the present.

'You don't really have to go unless you want to, Henry,' she said against his lips.

And he didn't.

The clock in Elena's intimately decorated bath said eight when Henry finished a quick shower. He was tiptoeing across the room trying to keep from awakening her, when she spoke from the queen-sized bed.

'I forgot to tell you last night, Henry,' she said, 'but "Bart's Parts" as Willy Dillingham labelled them, look a lot better on you than they did on Bart. He'd been doing a beer commercial for about three months and was getting quite a pot belly from it, but you're in much better shape than he was.'

'Thanks,' said Henry. 'I try to run five or six miles several times a week.'

'I know,' she said. 'I've seen you running in the park. You're a much superior lover than Bart was, too. He belonged to what is called "wham, bam, Thank you, Ma'am" school of love-making but you're gentle and warm and obviously understand a woman's role in making love.'

'I do remember that we broke the tape several times together last night,' Henry admitted as he finished dressing. 'And it was wonderful.'

'I know a lot more about Bart that I haven't told you,' she said. 'We'll have to do this again some time.'

'Absolutely,' said a throaty voice that Henry recognized vaguely as his own, 'but I'd better be going now or people will start talking. Goodbye – and thanks for everything.'

'I should thank you,' she said, 'and I do.'

'By the way,' he asked from the door of the bedroom, 'where is Rashid?'

'He's shut up in Carling's room,' Elena laughed. 'When I take him for his walk this morning in the park, I know he's going to be mad as hell, so don't make the mistake of getting in range of his claws.'

'You can be sure of that,' said Henry. 'Goodbye.'

On the way back to his apartment, Henry stopped at the coffee shop at the end of the block in which his apartment house stood. Sybil, his usual waitress, served him and when she brought him the bill, she asked, as she had dozens of times before: 'Anything else, Mr Walters?'

'Well, I might use a little of that.' As he had often done playfully in the past, Henry gave her a pat on the rear where the rounded prominence threatened to burst through the green nylon.

'I think that can be arranged,' he was startled to hear her say. 'I have a coffee break in about thirty minutes. You still have the same apartment, don't you?'

'Yes,' Henry heard the same voice answer that he'd heard in Elena Hartsfield's apartment earlier that morning. 'I'm going up there now.'

'I won't be far behind you,' Sybil told him. 'That is, if you're ready.'

She wasn't and he was.

xiii

'I really didn't have any space in my schedule,' said Dr Schwartz when he ushered Henry, shaking like a leaf in the summer's breeze, into his office shortly after ten o'clock. 'But you sounded very disturbed over the telephone.'

'I'm possessed, Doctor! By the spirit of Bart Bartlemy – or rather his demon.'

Dr Schwartz went to a cabinet in the corner and, pouring two green capsules in his hand from the bottle there, brought them back with a cup of water. 'Take these,' he commanded.

'What are they?'

'Only a mild tranquillizer. In your disturbed state – '

'You'd be disturbed, too, if you were possessed by Bart's demon. When Dr Sang did the operation he turned me into a split personality.'

'We often treat split personalities in psychiatry, Mr Walters, but we haven't believed in demons for hundreds of years.'

'That's because you've never been seized by one. You released Bart's spirit from the transplant the first time you treated me with the vibrating ball of light and now it's trying to control my life.'

'Come now, Mr Walters,' said the psychiatrist. 'All I did was induce hypnosis and allay your fears that you weren't capable of living up to the possibilities afforded by the transplant.'

'I've lived up to them,' said Henry. 'Now it's trying to take control of my life.'

'Could you be more specific?'

'Night before last, Selena McGuire agreed to marry me but made me swear I'd never look at another woman.'

'Young wives often do that but it rarely ever works.'

'I *want* it to work this time, Doctor – at least the part of me that's not controlled by Bart Bartlemy's spirit does. I really intended to be true to Selena but forgot that I had a dinner

76

date last night with a very beautiful young divorcee who lived in Hollywood with Bart Bartlemy for a while. We dined in her apartment and talked about their relationship for several hours – '

'But when the time came for you to go, you didn't?'

'Not only that but when I was eating breakfast in the coffee shop around the corner from my apartment building this morning, after spending the night with another woman, I gave Sybil, the waitress, a little pat on the rear when she gave me the bill, something I often do. Before I realized what was happening, though, Sybil was upstairs in my apartment shedding her uniform. Would you believe that she was back downstairs bedded – as I say in my historical novels – and dressed in twenty-nine minutes?'

'Why the rush?'

'Sybil only had thirty minutes for a coffee break,' Henry explained. 'But how can I be true to Selena if I never know something like that isn't going to happen whenever I get close to a well-stacked female?'

'What is it you want me to do, Mr Walters?'

'That first treatment helped wonderfully. I felt loose, where women were concerned, for the first time in my life.'

'If I could get that result with every patient,' said the psychiatrist a little wistfully, 'I'd be a millionaire.'

'All I want to do is get rid of this demon.'

'Exorcism is out of my line, Mr Walters, but I can assure you what's happened is merely that the real you has been released by Dr Sang's operation. Some of your normal tendencies may have been intensified, too, by knowing that you've got the finest sexual apparatus to appear in modern times, perhaps in history.'

'Can't you bring the instinct under control a little without disturbing the apparatus?'

'What a waste of superb equipment that would be, Mr Walters,' said Dr Schwartz. 'It would almost be like besmirching the memory of Bart Bartlemy.'

'I don't give a damn about Bart! He's wrecking my marriage before I'm even married, even though he's dead.'

'There's another difficulty, Mr Walters. A major psychiatric operation – even if I were able to perform it, which I can't guarantee – might destroy the functioning of the transplant.'

'You mean . . . ?'

'Tampering with something that's functioning so spectacularly now could possibly make you incapable of sex for life. You might marry Miss McGuire, only to discover that you were a husband in name only. Are you prepared to take that risk?'

'My God! No!'

'Then why tamper with a normal physiological process that is functioning, I might say, with striking success?'

'I've just finished telling you that I'm not normal any more,' Henry objected.

'If you're not – and I don't accept that either, Mr Walters – millions of men would give a lot to possess your particular kind of abnormality. My advice is to fortify yourself against temptation with tranquillizers until your marriage is consummated. From what you've told me today, I believe the situation will probably take care of itself after that.'

Outside Dr Schwartz's office the day was warm and the streets were crowded with lunchtime migrants, mainly female. Eyes downcast, lest he be tempted by the profusion of stimuli offered to his senses, Henry scurried for the nearest taxi stand and dived into the battered interior. At the apartment, he paid the cabbie and got out, moving around a slender man with a thin almost expressionless face and a long scar on his cheek, who was standing near the curb talking to Angus, the doorman.

'Mr Walters,' an unfamiliar voice called, when he was half way to the door.

Henry turned to see that, besides the doorman – who for some reason looked scared – and the man with the scar whom he'd had to walk around, a long black limousine was also parked against the curb a little distance away from the apartment house marquee. Another young man was under the wheel while a third and particularly elegant looking gentleman was sitting in the back.

It was Gregory Annunzio.

'Someone wants to see you,' said Scar-face, beckoning to Henry.

When the thin man's coat tightened across his chest with the motion, Henry could have sworn he saw the outline of a weapon in a shoulder holster briefly revealed beneath the fabric.

Opening the door of the limousine, the man with the scar took Henry's arm and muscled him into it as easily as he would have handled a child.

'Don't be alarmed, Mr Walters,' said Annunzio. 'I merely want to have a talk with you and this is such a pleasant day for a drive through the park.'

'I have an appointment – '

'I promise not to keep you long. May I congratulate you on the success of the transplant? I have it upon good authority that you're as much of a man as Bart Bartlemy was any day.'

'Gloria!' Light suddenly broke through Henry's brain. 'She works for you?'

'Not me, Mr Walters. Miss Manning – as she likes to call herself professionally – is the sister-in-law of a client, one of the patrons of the arts we discussed when I last saw you at the hospital.'

'Then the subway brawl was planned?'

'Not exactly the way it happened; we weren't clever enough for that. Gloria was only supposed to follow you and be invited into your apartment, where certain events could be counted upon to occur. Then she would give an interview to a reporter for the *Post* – '

'Willy the Dilly!'

'Miss Dillingham came to the courtroom at my suggestion, after Gloria telephoned me before the hearing,' Annunzio admitted. 'Fortunately for us, Justice Peebles's curiosity gave us the newsbreak we were waiting for and the secret of the transplant was revealed dramatically, plus the fact that you're writing a biographical novel about Bart Bartlemy.'

'Your original plan would have been a lot easier for me.'

'But not nearly so effective as the real drama turned out to be; even your facile imagination could hardly have conjured up that rapid sequence of events. I don't mind telling you my clients and I were quite happy about the way the whole plan was working out – until this morning.'

Henry felt a sudden shiver of dread. 'Until . . . this . . . morning?' he stammered.

'When I learned quite accidently, that you planned to write another Round Table novel before finishing *Superstud*.'

'You don't understand, Mr Annunzio,' Henry pleaded. 'Miss

McGuire will marry me but she insisted I do the historical novel before I do *Superstud*. Abner Bennett wants it that way.'

'To put it bluntly, Mr Walters, my clients and I want it the original way.'

'Writing historical novels is my career; I can't afford to cut myself off from Bennett Press,' Henry protested.

'Once *Superstud* is finished, you can write whatever you like,' Annunzio assured him.

'And lose Selena – '

'Miss McGuire is much too intelligent a young lady not to see where your best interests lie, once she realizes how much éclat being your editor with Barney Weiss will give her in the publishing world.'

'But I'm not going to write *Superstud* now.'

With much the same fascination as a cobra emerging from a basket not three feet away would have exerted upon him, Henry observed the fingers of the young hood with the scarred face move idly across the front of his jacket and unbutton it.

'I heard a rumour to that effect this morning, but I could hardly believe it.' Gregory Annunzio's voice had cooled perceptibly.

'This must all be a dream,' said Henry dazedly. 'Or a nightmare.'

'I can assure you that making at least a half million dollars, and probably more, for six months' work, perhaps even less, is no dream, Mr Walters. I would personally much prefer that it not become a nightmare either, but life is real.' The naked threat was in the words and Henry recognized it for what it was.

'If I write your book, I lose my fiancée,' he protested.

'If you write the book according to the way you've been living since the day you bumped into Miss Manning on the subway, you'd be a fool to marry anybody,' said Annunzio bluntly. 'Play your cards right and you'll be well on your way to becoming a bigger sex symbol than Bart Bartlemy ever was.'

'I can't do it,' said Henry, 'and there's no point in telling me you'll have me rubbed out – '

'Please!' Mr Annunzio looked pained.

' – because if you do, you'll lose the chance that I might decide to do the novel later.' Henry had played his trump and hoped it was high enough to take the trick, but the lawyer didn't appear to be intimidated.

'Quick thinking, Mr Walters, and worthy of one of your best plots, but not very much in accordance with real life, I'm afraid.'

'What does that mean?'

'You're not indispensable, nobody is. Shall I tell my clients that you're definitely not going to write *Superstud* first?'

'Definitely.' Henry wished his voice wouldn't squeak.

'In that case, nothing is to be gained by our wasting each other's time. Back to Mr Walters's apartment house, Jerry.'

'I'm sorry you refuse to co-operate,' said Annunzio as the car drew up before the apartment house and Angus opened the door. 'No hard feelings?'

'Of course not.' Henry was willing to concede almost anything now that he was home safe. 'Please give Miss Manning my regards.'

'I shall,' said Annunzio. 'She has nothing but the highest praise for you.'

As Henry stood watching, the limousine slipped smoothly from the curb and into the flow of traffic northward.

'Are you all right, Mr Walters?' the doorman asked.

'Certainly. Why?'

'You look sort of pale. By the way, I recognized Annunzio. See him and his boss at the track together sometimes.'

Henry hesitated, then asked the question that was foremost in his mind: 'Who is his boss, Angus?'

'Big John Fortuna. He's the head of the Family here in New York.'

xiv

Even a busy but highly pleasurable half hour with Sybil at three didn't restore Henry's composure either. No matter how often he assured himself that he had handled Annunzio with all the skill and firmness of the knightly heroes in *Lancelot's Return*, he somehow couldn't rid himself of the feeling that everything was not as it should be. When the telephone rang shrilly just before six, he jumped to answer it.

81

'Mr Walters?' The voice was flat like none he remembered, yet somehow sinister.

'Who is this?'

'My name doesn't matter. Just say I'm a good Samaritan who rescued your fiancée, Miss Selena McGuire, from certain death beneath the rails of a subway train a few moments ago.'

'Wha – ?'

'She's in the Emergency Room of the New York Hospital.'

'Is she badly injured?'

'Miss McGuire was shaken up a little and has a few minor cuts and bruises – plus a mild concussion. The next time she may not be so fortunate.'

'The next time?' Henry knew how the men riding in the tumbrels of Paris had felt when they saw Madame Defarge at her knitting in the looming shadow of the guillotine.

'You ought to take better care of Miss McGuire, Mr Walters,' the sinister voice continued, but before Henry could speak – or rather squeak – the receiver clicked in his ear.

Henry wasted no time staring at the telephone but raced to a closet, grabbed a jacket and left the apartment, pushing the elevator button twice to let the doorman downstairs know he wanted a taxi. It pulled to the curb just as he ran from the building and he collapsed, panting, on the seat.

'Emergency Room, New York Hospital,' he told the driver.

'You sick, mister?' the driver asked as he swung the cab expertly away from the curb.

'No. A friend was in an accident in the subway.'

'Dangerous place, the subway. I stay scared to death the minute I get off work till I get home.' The driver was threading his way through the maze of late afternoon traffic as he spoke, grazing a fender here, standing Henry on his head there, slamming on the brakes just in time to keep from crunching the front end of the taxi against a massive delivery truck.

When the taxi, miraculously still intact, pulled into the circular drive of the Emergency Room at the towering New York Hospital, part of the Cornell Medical School teaching unit, Henry handed the driver ten dollars – twice what was on the meter, and ran through the door. He had no trouble finding Selena; she was arguing heatedly with a tall doctor in white.

82

More important, she appeared to be all right, except for a few patches of surgical dressing here and there.

'I've got a perfectly good apartment in Gramercy Park, Dr Crawford,' she said. 'You're not going to shut me up in a hospital ward with a lot of riff-raff where I could catch who knows what.'

'But, madam – '

'*Miss* McGuire, Selena McGuire.'

'We only want to observe you overnight, Miss McGuire. After all, you *were* unconscious.'

'Only for a minute.'

'I'll be glad to look after my fiancée, doctor,' Henry told the Emergency Service Resident.

Selena wheeled upon him. 'I didn't send for you, Henry Walters.'

'I know – '

'I'm perfectly able to look after myself.'

'If Mr Walters will be responsible, you may go, Miss McGuire.' Dr Crawford obviously welcomed the chance to shift responsibility.

'I know what to look for, doctor,' said Henry. 'I was a medic in the Army.'

'Just sign the release, please.' Dr Crawford held out a paper attached to the chart clipboard he had picked up from the desk beside which Selena had been sitting. 'Miss McGuire has had a mild concussion and in case you have any difficulty in arousing her, bring her to the Emergency Room right away.'

'I understand, doctor.'

'She's been given a mild sedative, too, and should sleep, but not so soundly that you cannot arouse her easily.'

'Humph,' said Selena, apparently determined not to let even the sedative have any effect upon her.

'Where do I pay the bill?' Henry asked.

'At the cashier's window over there.' The doctor gave him a charge slip and moved away to attend another in the constant stream of battered and sick humanity flowing through the room.

'Are you all right, darling?' Henry asked solicitously, taking Selena's arm and guiding her toward the cashier's window.

'I can walk under my own power.' She took two steps but staggered and caught on to him for support. 'Must be the drug he gave me. I didn't want to get on the stretcher in the subway, but a brawny cop practically manhandled me, with everybody looking and my skirt over my head.'

Henry slid the charge slip under the grilled window with two twenty dollar bills and a rubber stamp crashed down marking it 'Paid'.

'Forty dollars for that?' Selena exclaimed indignantly as Henry was guiding her towards the exit. Outside he helped her into a taxi and got in beside her.

'Gramercy Park,' he told the driver, and added the street number.

When he put his arm about Selena, she collapsed against him like a sleepy child who no longer felt it necessary to flaunt her bristling Irish independence in the face of authority.

'How did it happen?' he asked.

'It was all so quick I can hardly remember.' The words were already slurred a little from the sedative she'd been given in the hospital. 'I was waiting for a subway train, when this man brushed against me and knocked me off the platform.'

'You could have been electrocuted!' he exclaimed, horrified.

'It was on the side toward the platform, not the third rail that carries the current.'

'Did you get a good look at the man who pushed you?'

'Who can tell anybody from anybody else in the subway during the rush hour? But it was a man – I saw that much. And the train was coming; I could feel the vibration on the rail during the moment I lay against it.'

'It's a wonder you were ever able to climb out.'

'I didn't. Another man reached down and pulled me back up on the platform, just as the train came around the curve toward the station. When I realized how near I'd been to being killed, I – I guess I did pass out for a moment or two. The next thing I knew they were putting me on that stretcher – '

'Could you tell anything more about the man who pulled you out?'

'Not much. He had sort of pale skin and a keen face with practically no expression at all, except a long scar. It's a funny thing, Henry, but I could swear that, just before I passed out, he said: "*You ought to make Mr Walters take better care of you, Miss McGuire.*" '

84

Henry felt the cold sweat that had been building up just beneath the surface during her recital, suddenly pop out of his skin.

'*You ought to take better care of Miss McGuire, Mr Walters,*' the caller who'd told him of Selena's accident had said and Henry knew now exactly what those words had meant.

'Why would he say that, Henry?' Selena asked sleepily. 'I'd be willing to swear I'd never seen him before.'

'It was probably somebody who'd seen you at the Bennett Press offices. You're pretty decorative, you know.'

'But he knew your name, too.'

'Our names were linked in the newspaper account when I – when that business happened in the subway the other day.'

'That doesn't make much sense,' Selena murmured, 'but I'm too sleepy to worry about it.'

'Don't worry about anything, darling. I'm going to take care of you from now on.'

'Good old Sir Lancelot to the rescue.' A soft snore punctuated the speech.

What Selena had just told him about the accident crystallized a decision, one that might remove Henry's chance to use the marriage licence he was carrying in his wallet, but that didn't matter now. The important thing was that she was safe and he had it within his power to keep her that way, at least as far as the people who had ordered the demonstration of just what could happen to her were concerned.

Selena leaned heavily on Henry when they got out of the taxi and went into the building. At her floor, they shuffled down the hall to her apartment and he opened her door with her key, being careful to remove it from the lock before shutting it again and locking it from the inside before guiding her to the door to the bedroom.

'Think you can get into pyjamas alone?' he asked.

Selena giggled, the effect, Henry was sure, of the drug she'd been given. 'I bet you hope I say no.'

'Of course I do.'

'Then I'll do it myself.'

When he didn't hear from her in ten minutes, Henry pushed the door of the bedroom open and found her lying across the bed, fast asleep and still in her clothes. Undressing her, he took pyjamas from the closet and put them on her, trying – but not quite succeeding – to keep his eyes from feasting upon the loveliness which, until today at noon, he'd expected soon to belong only to him. She roused once while he was buttoning the pyjamas and drowsily put her arms around his neck.

'Kiss me good night, darling,' she said and he obeyed with alacrity but felt her lips go slack beneath his own as the drowsiness from the sedative claimed her fully.

With Selena stretched out on the bed beneath the sheet, Henry counted her pulse and found it to be eighty. Her respirations were a relaxed sixteen and, when he lifted the eyelids, both pupils contracted from the effect of light – all fairly good indicators, he knew, that she had sustained no real brain injury. Pulling down the shades to darken the room against the remaining evening sunlight, he went out into the kitchen to look for something to eat.

A slice of the pizza he'd bought from Antonelli's was carefully packaged in Saran wrap in the freezer compartment of the refrigerator. Taking it out, he put it into the microwave oven to heat and, when it was ready, opened a can of beer. While he ate the pizza, he reviewed the events of the past twenty-four hours, a climactic series of happenings beginning with Gloria Manning's telephone call and leading to Selena's carefully arranged near-brush with death.

No matter how he approached it, the answer came up the same: he had no choice now but to write the book Harry Westmore and Barney Weiss – but most importantly of all, Big John Fortuna, Gloria Manning and Gregory Annunzio – wanted him to write. Moreover, it had to be a best-seller which meant going back to his research in the graphic description of intimate scenes which were now *de rigueur* for such opuses.

After putting the dishes he'd used into the dishwasher, Henry went into the bedroom and checked Selena once more but found no cause for alarm. She was sleeping peacefully from the sedative Dr Crawford had given her, he was sure, and not from the mild concussion that had been her only potentially serious injury from the accident. It was the next accident he had to prevent at all costs, however, and there was only one way of doing it. Picking up the telephone beside Selena's bed, he rang Harry Westmore's number.

'This is Henry,' he said when the agent answered. 'I apologize for calling you after office hours.'

'When would a Judas be expected to demand his thirty pieces of silver?'

'How about a million pieces?'

'Where are you?' the agent's voice was suddenly excited. 'And how many drinks have you had?'

'The answer to the first question is Selena's apartment. To the second, none.'

'What's Selena doing?'

'Sleeping. She had an accident in the subway during the rush hour this afternoon and the doctor in the Emergency Room at New York Hospital gave her a pretty strong sedative.'

'I seem to remember seeing something about that on the seven p.m. news but no name,' said Westmore. 'It sounded very close.'

'It looked close because it was staged that way.'

'Come again?'

'I'm going to tell you something, Harry, if you'll promise never to divulge it.'

'Christ, Henry! Who can you trust if not your agent?'

Henry gave Westmore a quick résumé of the call from Gloria, the visit of Annunzio and Selena's accident.

'There's no question about its being staged to make you do what they want,' Harry agreed when he finished the account. 'I don't like it, Henry.'

'Neither do I. But do you doubt that the threat to Selena exists?'

'Not for a minute. What are you going to do?'

'Write *Superstud* first, of course. It's the only way I can save Selena.'

'I guess you're right.'

'I've already got part of it written; you've seen that. For the rest, I'll just tell the story as it's happening right now.'

'Do you think that's safe?'

'Jung once said: "*Everything that's secret degenerates; nothing is safe that does not show it can bear discussion and publicity.*" If nothing is safe unless it can be discussed and publicized, ergo whatever is given full discussion and publicity becomes safe – for Selena and for me. I intend to write this book so everybody will know who the people in it are in real life.'

'Like *In Cold Blood*. This just might be the success of the century, but you're taking an awful chance, Henry.'

'I don't think so. As long as nothing can be proved against these people, they love being in the limelight, so what've they got to lose? They get the book and Bart's old films, to say nothing of *Superstud*, become gold mines. Will you call Barney tonight and tell him I'm going ahead with the book?'

'As soon as you hang up. We can have the contracts ready in less than a week.'

'First thing in the morning have your secretary report Selena to the Bennett Press office as being sick. If I do it, there's liable to be talk.'

'By the way, what does she think of all this?'

'She's still asleep but my guess is she'll be mad as hell when she wakes up and I tell her I'm going to do *Superstud* first.'

'And that you're doing it to protect her?'

'No. She'd only go storming into Annunzio's office – or Fortuna's – and queer the deal.'

'Good luck, Henry. I've got an idea we'll need it before this is over.'

The only telephone number listed in the directory for Gregory Annunzio was obviously an office, which meant that the lawyer had an unlisted phone at his home. When Henry rang the number, a feminine voice answered after the first several rings.

'Mr Annunzio's answering service. Can I help you?'

'Can you get a message to Mr Annunzio for me?'

'Certainly, sir. He usually calls in several times during the evening.'

'Just tell him Mr Walters called.'

'Would you spell the name, please?'

Henry spelled the name.

'And the message, sir?'

'Tell Mr Annunzio I got the message.'

'Just that, sir, "I got the message"?'

'Yes, he'll know what I mean.'

'Thank you, Mr Walters. Mr Annunzio will get the message.'

BOOK III

Patty

i

Henry awakened on the sofa to the sound of humming in the kitchen and the smell of bacon frying and coffee perking. He lay there for a while savouring the pleasure of the moment, unwilling to destroy it by starting the inevitable quarrel that would certainly begin when he told Selena of his decision last night.

'Are you going to sleep all day.' Henry turned over to see Selena standing in the doorway to the bedroom. She was fully dressed, wore a frilly apron, and showed no ill effects from her close shave the night before, except a few patches of adhesive tape.

'*I* have to go to the office, even if *you* don't,' she added.

'They're not expecting you,' Henry told her. 'I asked Harry Westmore to have his secretary call and tell them you'd had an accident.'

'You don't think I'd let a few bruises keep me from going to work, do you?'

'You had more than a few bruises.'

'Didn't miss a trick either, did you?' she said but without rancour. 'Did you *have* to strip me and put on pyjamas?'

'You had a spot of blood on your slip so I had to find out why. Incidentally, you ought to have that strawberry birthmark on your tush removed. It apparently was scraped when the man

89

in the subway pulled you up to the platform because it was bleeding a little bit when I took off your pantyhose.'

'That birthmark is a family characteristic; it's inherited. How do you like your eggs?'

'Over light.'

'They'll be ready in five minutes, just time enough for you to wash up.'

When Henry came out of the bathroom, Selena was sliding the eggs out of the pan onto his plate which already contained toast and bacon. 'Did you find a wedding dress yesterday afternoon?' Henry asked while she poured the coffee.

'No. I remembered that I had to get the contracts for your new historical novel ready for Harry, so I went back to the office. That's why I was in the subway.'

Henry was having his second cup of coffee when the question he'd been dreading came.

'You said you asked Harry Westmore last night to have his secretary call the office this morning and say I wouldn't be in. What reason did you have for calling your agent at that time of night?'

Henry didn't even consider lying; a Lancelot might put horns on his king, but no *bel knight sans reproche* could ever tell an untruth.

'I called to tell Harry I'm going to do that book for Barney Weiss first.'

Selena stood up suddenly, looking – from his worm's-eye view – about seven feet tall. Her cheeks were flushed with anger, her eyes snapped and he thought he'd never seen her more beautiful – except once.

'After promising me – ' She was too angry to go on.

'Selena, you don't understand – '

'Letting me cook breakfast for you when you'd already stabbed me in the back while I was unconscious.'

'It's not what you think – '

'How do you know what I think?'

'Well – '

'That blonde is involved in all this, isn't she? Don't deny it.'

Henry didn't try, since he couldn't reveal the truth without causing Selena to do something that might well lead to a fatal accident, instead of only the near-one she'd had yesterday afternoon.

'Get out of here,' she said ominously. 'Get out of here and don't come back.'

'Selena – '

'If you're going to write that novel for Barney Weiss, you'd better get going with your *research*. I'm sure Gloria' – she choked on the word – 'Manning will be glad to co-operate.'

ii

The two eggs Henry had eaten at Selena's were still a fist-size lump in his stomach when he returned to his own quarters and let himself in. Mrs O'Toole, who took care of the apartment for him, was cleaning and he told her to go on with her work while he took a shower.

'You look sort of down in the mouth, Mr Walters,' said Mrs O'Toole when he came out of the bathroom. 'Anything wrong?'

'Everything,' said Henry.

'A spat?'

'Worse than that – *kaput!*'

'Lovers' quarrels always look like that the first few hours, but they blow over,' Mrs O'Toole assured him.

'Not this one.'

'The Irish girl, eh?'

'Yes.' Right now he didn't want to talk about it but Mrs O'Toole was inclined to be philosophical – and good cleaning women were hard to find.

'That's always the way with the Irish. We never do anything by half but we never really mean half of what we say.'

Momentarily, Henry considered allowing himself to be cheered by Mrs O'Toole's words but remembering Selena's face, decided it wasn't worth the trouble.

'How are you coming with your new book, Mr Walters?' Mrs O'Toole asked.

'I don't know. There are difficulties – '

'Like that Annunzio fellow?'

'How did you know about him?'

91

'Angus told me. Him and me are right concerned about you, sir.'

'Not half as much as I am concerned about myself,' Henry said and could have added with even more force 'and about Selena', but didn't.

'Whatever it is Big John Fortuna wants you to do, you'd better do it, Mr Walters,' the cleaning woman advised. 'The people who work for him are pretty tough characters, especially the one called Al with the scar on his face. He's a killer –'

'Don't use that word!' Henry shuddered. 'I'm allergic to blood – especially mine.'

'They're not going to kill a goose that can lay golden eggs as long as you keep on laying,' Mrs O'Toole assured him. 'Just play the hand you've been dealt close to your chest, Mr Walters, and you'll come out ahead.'

Which, Henry told himself as he sat down to the word processor, wasn't really much of an insurance policy – but it was all he had to go on. Listlessly, he picked up the last several pages he'd written and looked them over. They were good, there was no denying that, for they'd been written when he was in the full heat – so to speak – of creative inspiration. He felt no stir of inspiration now, however, only the depressing fact that he'd had to break his promise to the girl he loved in order to save her life. Since she would never know why, she'd never forgive him either, unless he could let her know exactly what had happened. Then in a sudden burst of inspiration, he realized where the answer lay; by describing the subway accident and the ominous telephone call to his apartment just as it happened in the book, Selena would at least know the truth when the book was published.

The door buzzer rang while Henry was thinking and he went to open it. Gloria Manning stood outside.

'Gregory Annunzio's office called me this morning,' she told him. 'He said you need a secretary.'

Henry could recognize the voice of authority when he heard it, even second hand, and opened the door.

'Don't tell me you can type, too,' he said.

'I once went to business school. Graduated, too, at the head of the class.'

'Congratulations.'

92

'Of course, that was before I discovered I could make a lot more money modelling. I see that you use a word processor. I can work on one of those, too.'

'That's a great help. It will save me typing.'

'Well,' she said brightly. 'Where do you want me to start?'

Henry looked at the blank monitor of the computer where he'd been trying to write – and getting nowhere – then back to the somewhat lush figure of Gloria Manning. With the rest of his world shattered about him, maybe she did represent a rock to which he could cling while he gained a foothold and a new start toward emancipating himself from the chains Gregory Annunzio and Big John Fortuna had forged about him.

'You can take off your clothes in the bedroom,' he said.

iii

Somewhat to Henry's surprise, Gloria had considerable skill with the keyboard of the computer/word processor. After the first day he stopped writing by hand and began to dictate the rapidly moving story as it unfolded itself in his mind, while she tapped it into words, sentences and paragraphs on the monitor where corrections could be made before the letters were transferred by the printer to manuscript pages. From a normal pace of some two thousand words a day – eight double-spaced typewritten manuscript pages – he soon moved to three thousand as the narrative flowed on.

Gloria was a comfort to have around, too. Besides being a skilled cook, she could always suggest interesting – and very pleasant – diversions whenever the creative muse lagged. Most of those shortly afterward found their way into the typewritten pages chronicling the tempestuous and largely fictional career of Bart Bartlemy, as he searched for his Leonora in the most pleasant of possible ways.

In something over two weeks, Henry wrote roughly thirty-five thousand words, a good third of the novel. As it was finished, each week's batch of manuscripts were sent by messenger to Harry Westmore's office. He hadn't heard from Harry yet but didn't worry because he could feel the vividness of the novel as it appeared on the monitor and sensed its dramatic impact.

Late one afternoon toward the end of the third week, just before he usually knocked off writing around five o'clock and joined Gloria in a drink before she left, the doorbell rang and Henry went to answer it. Outside was Barney Weiss, accompanied by a tiny but remarkably symmetrical woman whose silvered hair effectively camouflaged her age.

'We were up this way, Henry,' said Barney, 'and I thought we'd stop by so you could meet Patty O'Flynn.'

Henry didn't need to be told who the diminutive visitor was. An acknowledged genius in the highly specialized branch of the public relations profession having to do with book promotions, she boasted of never having lost an author, no matter how outrageous the stunts she devised to publicize potential bestsellers.

'How do you do, Miss O'Flynn,' said Henry. 'By all means come in.'

Gloria was at the word machine wearing her favourite working costume, a string bikini.

'This is Miss Manning,' Henry added. 'Miss O'Flynn and Mr Weiss.'

'Hello,' said Gloria, smiling. 'I'll be through in a sec and be going home.'

'After all I've heard about you lately, Mr Walters, don't tell me you let something like Gloria go home at night.' Patty O'Flynn's eyebrows shot up like twin punctuation marks.

'Gloria is my secretary,' Henry explained. 'And a very good one, too.'

'Besides being a character in *Superstud* and the model for the jacket photo,' said Barney Weiss.

'Be sure you don't forget the last part,' said Gloria as she pressed the switch for the printer to put the last page of the day's work into manuscript and placed the sheet on top of the rapidly accumulating pile beside her on the desk.

'I won't, Miss Manning,' Barney Weiss promised. 'In fact, I'll be sending the jacket material to the printer soon.'

'In colour?'

'Of course. Nothing else would do justice to your, er, qualifications. Don't you agree, Patty?'

94

Patty O'Flynn was looking Henry up and down appraisingly, giving him the absurd feeling that, as far as the press agent was concerned, he was even less clothed at the moment than Gloria.

'We might even use Mr Walters,' the publicist started to say but Henry cut her off with a firm 'No!'

'It *could* get your book banned in Boston,' she protested.

'To say nothing of boycotted in the Keokuk Public Library,' Barney Weiss added.

'I'm sure Gloria is quite decorative enough for the jacket,' Henry said firmly.

'If you're leaving now, Miss Manning, I'll be glad to drop you somewhere,' Barney offered as Gloria started to the bedroom. 'Henry and Miss O'Flynn need to go over the plans for the initial promotion.'

'That's very nice of you, Mr Weiss.' Gloria's smile was warm. 'I'll be only a sec. Don't go away.'

'I wouldn't dream of it,' said Barney.

Gloria came out of the bedroom a few minutes later, dressed for the street. 'See you in the morning, Henry,' she said and took the arm Barney Weiss extended to her.

When Henry came back from closing the door behind them, he found Patty O'Flynn standing by the card table on which Gloria had stacked the manuscript, reading the topmost sheet.

'I guess you know you're going to make a fortune out of this book, Henry,' she said.

'I certainly hope so.'

'Why don't we go somewhere and have a few drinks and maybe dinner, while we discuss the whole subject of the promotion.'

'That sounds fine to me.'

'Barney's picking up the tab, so we might as well go to a nice quiet place – like the Four Seasons.'

Henry had rarely been inside New York's most expensive restaurant, but if his future income was going to be anything like what Harry Westmore and Barney Weiss seemed confident it would be, he decided that he might as well accustom himself to higher living.

'Give me a minute to change,' he said. 'Would you care for a drink in the meantime?'

'Let's start even at the Seasons. Take your time, I'll be looking over this last batch of manuscript while you're changing.'

'This is hot stuff, Henry,' the publicist said as they walked to the door. 'You certainly have a way with words – and women. Is it all really true like Barney claims?'

'Every word.'

'You've packed a lot of living into the past week or so.'

'Things just sort of happened.'

'Letting nature take its course is always the best way – with a little help at the right moment, of course.'

'That's the way I think the book should be launched,' Patty O'Flynn said over coffee and brandy several hours later in a dimly lit banquette at the Four Seasons. 'We'll start with a kick-off press conference when you sign the publication contracts. Barney has had what you've written so far xeroxed, along with a brief summary of the book. He sent it to the various paperback people and bids should be in soon.'

'Do you think they'll buy the book without even seeing the finished version?'

'Harold Robbins sells the whole package with only a line or two telling what the book's about. Those opening sequences of yours should convince anybody that it's going to take off like a rocket.'

'Sort of takes your breath away.'

'Unless I miss my guess, this will be one of the most valuable fiction packages ever sold in one unit. Harry Westmore has been talking to Gregory Annunzio and they'll be ready to announce the plans for filming *Superstud* by the time we stage the press conference. We can make that announcement at the same time and from then on, the public will be panting until the book gets off the press.'

'When do you plan to stage the launch, as you call it?'

'In another few weeks, when the paperback and movie bids are in.' Patty put her hand over his on the table and squeezed it. 'I hope all this isn't going to change you, Henry.'

'I – I – don't know what you mean.'

'Obviously you're a pretty swell guy, but if this book turns out the way we're all pretty sure it will, your whole life is going to change.'

'It's changed already.'

'Nothing to what it's going to be,' she assured him. 'Female sex symbols are a dime a dozen these days; the movies can create one with a good blonde rinse, some Edith Head gowns, and enough padding in the bra. A male sex symbol like Bart Bartlemy has to be authentic, though, and fortunately for you, he made sure of that. I wouldn't be surprised if you didn't out-Bart Bart!'

'Is that bad?' Henry asked.

'With all the money you'll make, you're going to get so accustomed to this' – her wave took in the discreetly expensive scene around them – 'that pretty soon it will become a way of life. You'll find yourself spending more money than you ever thought existed and saving less all the time. Did you know one publisher had to create a separate imprint, just to bail out one of America's best-selling novelists from his tax liens?'

'I'm afraid I'm not very hep – '

'Barney would kill me if he knew I'd said this to you, but it's still not too late for you to back out.'

'I'm afraid it is.'

'Nothing's been paid – '

'There are other factors, things I can't talk about.'

'I thought so – from rumours I've heard. But it will all turn out okay if you keep your cool.'

iv

When no contracts had been signed, although Henry was now more than half way through the book, he called Harry Westmore to see what was holding things up. The terms Harry and Barney Weiss had dangled before him that evening in the Louis the Fourteenth Restaurant still seemed too good to be true and he was afraid he might wake up and find this was all a dream.

'What's the trouble?' Harry sounded happy, as any agent would be with an author of Henry's financial potentialities for a client.

'I was wondering if there's any hitch in the contract?'

'Everything's fine, my boy – especially your love-life, judging

97

from what I've been reading and hearing lately. That's quite a harem you're accumulating.'

'They seem to fall into my lap – '

'Vice versa would appear to be more the case.'

'Please, Harry – '

'All right, Henry. I know you're sad about losing Selena, but that should work out, too.'

'I carry the marriage licence in my wallet, in case she changes her mind, but that's not likely unless I can catch her when she's been drugged,' Henry said sadly.

'Take heart, Henry, you're still easily the catch of the year and Selena's a smart girl.'

'What about the contracts, Harry?'

'They've already been drawn but Patty and Barney want to make a big splash over the signing – '

'She told me that much.'

'They want to stage something like a preview of the novel and the film to build up sales interest.'

'Aren't you afraid the interest will sag between now and publication date if you reveal what it's all about?'

'Barney thinks he's got that licked, too. He's going to start setting your copy next week. By the time you write the last page, we'll have proofs of at least the first half for you to read and correct. That way, we should have the book in the stores sixty days after you put down the last word.'

'I still haven't figured how to bring Bart and Leonora together at the end – or myself and Selena,' Henry admitted.

'If you solve one, you solve the other, don't you?'

'Probably. But I haven't solved either.'

'You can always leave Bart shacked up with his most recent conquest. That's the way sex novels usually end.'

'But I love Selena and still want to marry her.'

'*This book* and *your* love-life don't necessarily have to go the same way, you know. Bennett Press will get one of the first sets of proofs of *Superstud* and you can bet your life Selena will see them. She's smart enough to recognize the handwriting on the wall.'

'She's pretty mad at me now,' Henry said doubtfully.

'Which means the fire must still be burning,' Westmore assured him. 'September tenth is publication date but long before that you can be working on Abner Bennett's next sleeping pill and Selena will be back in your bed.'

'If Abner doesn't fire her before then.'

'I talked to Nick about that. Bennett Press published all your historical novels and, when *Superstud* becomes the success it's certain to be, their sales are going to boom in paperback reprints so they have everything to gain by keeping you happy.'

'I'm not going to do any more books for them unless Selena is my editor – '

'Nick understands that, too, so the sooner you solve the problem of bringing Leonora and Bart – I mean you and Selena – together and finish the book, the better it will be for everybody.'

'What about the film?'

'Gregory Annunzio and I are working on that. He thinks he's got Aldo Palmieri set to produce it for release by Columbia Pictures.'

'I guess I couldn't hope for more.' Henry didn't have to be told that Aldo Palmieri was the hottest producer in Hollywood at the moment with a string of sex/nude films that had barely escaped an X-rating and therefore made millions.

iv

The press conference announcing the signing of contracts for *Superstud* in both book and film was staged at the Hotel Plaza late one afternoon and Patty O'Flynn came by to take Henry to it. Gloria had asked for the day off and, since he was too perturbed about whether any members of the press would actually show up, Henry had seen no need for her services that day. He still wasn't sure just what the tiny publicist and Barney had in mind and Patty didn't help much as they rode to the Plaza in a taxi. Besides, it was raining which seemed to add an ill omen to the entire proceedings.

'Why would reporters come to a contract signing anyway?' Henry asked as they were entering the hotel.

'This is news, darling.'

'Sex novels come out every day.'

'Not by the recipient of the first sex organ transplant in history. Besides, we are going to exhibit a big mock-up of the jacket.'

'A picture of a naked girl is a picture of a naked girl, even if you blow it up to ten feet. You can see a dozen or more in any issue of *Playboy*.'

'The artist Barney has had working on this jacket has done a beautiful job – you can depend on that. When you add the publicity campaign, the buyers will be panting to get into the bookstores.'

'I've been wanting to speak to you about that,' said Henry. 'You're making me into a sort of super sex symbol and I'm not really – '

'You'll do until one comes along. Besides, you're part Bart.'

'It's supposed to be the other way around, anatomically, at least, but I sometimes wonder. If you ask me, the spirit of Bart has practically taken over my life.'

'You're much nicer than Bart ever was,' Patty assured him. 'I did the promotion for one of his pictures and, believe me, after the doctors took from him what you got in the transplant deal, there wasn't anything left except a very dull guy.'

'Are you sure anybody's going to be here for the press conference?' Henry asked for about the tenth time as they crossed the hotel lobby.

'Only reporters and gossip columnists, plus book page editors from all the papers and news magazines in town. To say nothing of the wire services, television cameramen – and whoever else can wrangle an assignment where the drinks are free.'

'I still don't see – '

'You've never been to a Patty O'Flynn promotion, Henry. Just leave everything to me, dear, but be sure and be nice to the lady reporters, particularly Willy Dillingham. She eats authors alive.'

'I'm already beginning to feel like a fool.'

'Just hold that innocent look. It never hurts an author to look inexperienced.'

'Even when he's written this sort of thing?'

'That's even better. Well, here we are.'

They had reached the door of the parlour where the conference was to be held and Henry stopped in the doorway, unable to believe the evidence of his eyes. The room was jammed with people, mostly crowded around two bars set up at the back behind the rows of chairs. Television cameras were elevated on a platform above seat level and the profusion of photographic equipment on chairs, while the owners queued up at the bar, left no doubt about the coverage the occasion would receive.

The set on the stage at the end of the room had been built to resemble a book standing upright and partially open, with the end, front, and part of the back cover showing. Beside the mock-up a desk had been arranged for Henry. Complete with a computer/word processor with a page from *Superstud* on the monitor, it was a replica of Henry's own working nook.

What he could see of the back cover was devoted to a photograph of the author but the front cover was hidden by draperies. These, he supposed, would be drawn back at the climactic moment to reveal the mock-up of the jacket Patty O'Flynn had mentioned, along almost certainly with a blown-up photograph of Gloria Manning.

Barney Weiss came forward to greet them with Harry Westmore and a tall man in a turtleneck sweater and a sports jacket. An expensive raincoat was draped across the latter's shoulder and his deep tan and sparkling white teeth seemed more appropriate for an actor than a reporter.

'This is Aldo Palmieri, Henry,' said Harry Westmore.

'Charmed, I'm sure, Mr Walters,' said Palmieri. 'This will be the most successful motion picture in history.'

'I hope you're right,' said Henry doubtfully.

An older man, distinguished and scholarly looking, appeared at Harry's elbow. 'This is Paul Biddleman of the Publisher's Guild,' said the agent.

'Henry and I met at a Bennett Press cocktail party some time ago,' said Mr Biddleman. 'We're very proud to have bought the Book Club rights to your novel, Henry.'

'I still can't believe it's happening.'

Paul Biddleman laughed. 'From what I hear, some of the things that have been happening in your life should happen to me – but no such luck.'

'Gentlemen and ladies!' Barney Weiss had ascended to the platform where the set for the announcements was located and was waiting now for the drinkers to take their places. 'The bar will be open again *after* the press conference.'

There was a round of applause before he continued: 'The purpose of the conference is to announce the signing of contracts between the distinguished author, Mr Henry Walters, who will shortly be introduced to you, and various communications media, including my own small empire. In order to set the stage for what is to follow, Miss Patty O'Flynn, whom you all know, will read to you the taped transcript of a police hearing that took place about two months ago and led to the writing of the novel we're about to unveil to you.'

Patty proved to be quite an actress. As she read the account of what had happened in Justice Peebles's court, her voice changed inflection with the words of each person who spoke, giving the story a dramatic quality Henry had not realized it possessed at the time. When the reading was finished, he noticed several women reporters in the front row of the chairs sit up straighter and take a decidedly more intense interest in the proceedings – among them the amazon he remembered from Justice Peebles's court. Seen under somewhat more favourable circumstances, Wilhelmina Dillingham was a much more handsome representative of her sex than he remembered from that occasion, perhaps because she no longer wore a camera suspended from a strap around her neck.

'This series of events stirred my interest, as I think it will stir yours,' said Barney, when the scene from the courtroom was finished. 'I am privileged at this time to present to this audience a distinguished writing talent, Mr Henry Walters.'

Amidst scattered applause, Henry moved to the platform and faced what was probably as sophisticated and hard-boiled a group of book commentators as could be found anywhere in the world. The sudden glare of TV floodlights almost blinded him, too. 'If I had realized I could stir up so much activity by nothing more than an accident and a little literary research, I would probably have started earlier,' he admitted.

The crowd applauded and Henry took a seat behind the desk at his side of the stage.

'First in the order of business will be the signing of the standard publisher's contracts between Mr Walters and Barney Weiss, Incorporated.' Barney spread out the contracts on the small desk while flash bulbs popped and the red eyes beneath the lenses of the television cameras glowed. Henry scrawled his name upon the contracts along with Barney.

'I might say for the benefit of the press,' Barney added as he folded up the signed contracts, 'that our first printing on *Superstud* will be one hundred thousand copies.'

'Next,' he continued, 'it is my pleasure to announce that the book will be a selection of the Publisher's Guild, with the largest first printing in Guild history already planned. Also, contracts have been signed with Paperback Press for publication rights to the book for the guarantee of one million dollars.'

'How does it feel to be a millionaire and a sex symbol at the same time, Mr Walters?' The speaker was Wilhelmina Dillingham.

'You'll have to ask the Internal Revenue Service that question, Miss Dillingham,' he said. 'We're sort of partners on this job, with them in the majority.'

'Although I have no share in the proceeds,' said Barney Weiss, 'it does give me a great deal of pleasure to announce that Aldo Palmieri will produce the film version of *Superstud*. Will you join me at the podium, Aldo?'

Palmieri ascended the platform and transferred the raincoat from his shoulders to the back of Henry's chair. There was a stir from the audience and more popping of flash bulbs as the producer took a folded document from the breast pocket of his jacket and spread it out with a flourish upon the desk before which Henry was sitting.

'I have the pleasure to show Mr Walters a contract for filming his book when finished,' Palmieri announced. 'The film will be produced by my own company in conjunction with other investors and will be distributed by Columbia Pictures. It will also co-star the divine Tatiana.'

Henry wondered how a Finnish sexpot, whose main contribution to motion pictures so far seemed to be the ability to remove her clothing, no matter what the weather, could play Leonora, Bart's childhood sweetheart.

'And now the event you've all been waiting for,' Barney Weiss announced. 'The preview of what I feel sure you will all name the most arresting and artistic jacket ever designed for a book.'

The lights in the room were dimmed, except for a pair of

powerful spots centred on the closed draperies hiding the other side of the elaborate set. They remained closed for a pregnant moment, then swept apart to reveal Gloria posing in the spotlight just as she had posed for the photographer who had taken the pictures she had given Henry the day after the affair in the subway.

There was a moment of awed silence, then pandemonium broke loose as photographers stood on chairs and bumped into each other, trying to get different angles for their frantically clicking cameras. On the elevated dais at the back of the room, TV cameras were grinding away, too, while Gloria smilingly made publicity history.

Then suddenly, above the voices in the room, rose a strident call familiar to everyone – a man with a bullhorn voice shouting from the back of the room the traditional warning:

'Cheezit! The cops!'

Henry saw them instantly, a phalanx of stern blue-uniformed figures striding down the aisle. He saw Gloria's sudden look of fright, too, and recognized that, like him, she hadn't dreamed this would happen. Moreover, as the original cause of whatever happened to her next, he realized that he was responsible. And with that knowledge, a surge of chivalrous determination filled his breast, urging him into action like Lancelot riding to splinter a lance upon the helmet of a foe.

Seizing Palmieri's raincoat, which was still draped across the back of his chair, Henry stepped quickly around a portion of the scenery marking the end of the book into the front cover, planning to wrap Gloria in the folds of the coat. She was already in flight, however, and so the television cameras on the raised platform, as well as any still photographer alert enough to have kept his lens trained on the stage, caught for posterity the picture of a naked Gloria Manning running like a fleeing doe toward the back of the stage. Behind her was Henry, the raincoat thrust under his arm, seemingly in hot pursuit like nothing so much as the old man in *Satyrs's Quest* – a top seller on the *New York Times'* best-seller list for twenty weeks – chasing the nymphet-heroine – except that nobody could possibly have mistaken Gloria for a nymphet. Only when she was stopped by a beefy policeman at a backstage door, was Henry able to wrap the

104

raincoat around her. Shaking with fear, she huddled against him.

'I'm sorry, Henry,' she whispered as he stood with his arm about her forthrightly defending her from the Law. 'When I saw those policemen coming down the aisle, I remembered one time I was posing in a photo club and the place was raided. I – I can't stand being shut up in jail.'

'You won't be,' Henry assured her with a confidence he was far from feeling at the moment. 'At least not for long.'

'I was cursing my luck in being assigned to the back door but things turned out all right,' said the cop who barred their escape. 'Come along, you two.'

'Where are we going, officer?' Henry asked.

'To jail. Where else?'

'On what charge?'

'Indecent exposure and staging a strip show without a permit for openers; we'll think up a few more on the way. A half dozen females are parading up and down in front of the hotel carrying signs calling you every bad name they can think of, mister, so we shouldn't have too much trouble making the charges stick. What do you do anyway except chase naked women?'

'He's a writer,' said Gloria proudly, 'and he's just signed contracts for several million dollars.'

'Anybody making that much money is bound to be a crook,' said the officer. 'Where do you come in, sister?'

'I'm his secretary and his model.'

'Some people have all the luck. Come on, the paddy wagon's waiting outside.'

vi

Henry used his one allowed telephone call trying to reach Gregory Annunzio but had no luck. Nevertheless, two hours later, while Gloria and Henry were still behind bars, the lawyer appeared at the jail. He was impeccably dressed as always and appeared to find the aroma of the jail oppressive to his sense of smell, something Henry had already noticed, too.

'Who sent for you?' Henry demanded.

105

'Miss Manning called one of my Assoc – '

'Big John Fortuna?'

Annunzio shrugged. 'Names aren't necessary.'

'I felt like calling you a few since Miss McGuire was almost killed in the subway,' Henry told him with some heat.

'Believe me, Henry, I don't approve of such measures,' said Annunzio. 'That was somebody else's idea.'

'You did nothing to prevent it.'

'She was in no danger, I assure you. The, er, participants are experts in such matters.'

'You still should be ashamed of yourself for being mixed up in such things.'

'We all have to make a living, some one way and some another,' said the lawyer. 'Do you approve of everything Barney Weiss is doing to sell your book?'

'Well, no.'

'But you go along with it because the dollars will soon be rolling in. Incidentally, what happened this afternoon was one of the slickest publicity jobs I've ever seen. It could easily be worth a hundred thousand in sales to you, less our twenty-five per cent, of course.'

'Are you implying this whole affair was staged?' Henry asked.

'What else? The fine Machiavellian touch of Patty O'Flynn is plastered all over it.'

'Not Gloria's part?'

'Miss Manning – as she prefers to be called – has no greater ambition than to become the new sexpot queen of TV and film and this affair may very well make her just that. Don't forget what a nude calendar photo did for a girl named Norma Jean a long time ago.'

'What are you going to do about these charges?' Henry asked.

'Get you both off, of course.'

'And have everybody know I'm connected with the Syn – '

'Please!'

'With Big John Fortuna then, if you're going to split hairs. I don't want that and, since you go to some lengths to hide your own connection with Fortuna, you must know how I feel.'

'You're no doubt right,' Annunzio conceded. 'Has Barney Weiss got you a lawyer yet?'

106

'Not that I know of,' said Henry grimly. 'That's another thing I –'

'Don't feel hard toward Barney, Mr Walters; nothing helps sell a book like yours than for the author to be involved in a *cause célèbre*. It's actually to Barney's advantage for this case to be prolonged as much as possible.'

'You mean he'd let us rot in jail?'

'So would I – for a while – if it were left up to me. And so, I suspect, would Patty O'Flynn.'

'Well, I don't intend to let that happen,' said Henry firmly. 'Do you know who will preside at the hearing?'

'Justice Peebles, I'm told. This is his court.'

'I know him; we're fellow students of the age of chivalry.' For the first time Henry saw a ray of hope. 'He collects books on King Arthur and the Round Table and I verified one of the early editions for him, when I was arrested before.'

'What can I do behind the scenes?'

'Could you get a few of those colour prints of Gloria like the one we're using on the jacket of the book?'

'That should be easy. I'm going to see her when I leave you and she can tell me where to look for them in her apartment.'

'Just get them to me before we go into Justice Peebles's court,' said Henry. 'I'll take it from there.'

vii

Henry and Gloria – the latter still wearing only Aldo Palmieri's raincoat – were sitting on the front bench of Justice Peebles's court, waiting for the magistrate to come in. As he had been hustled from the cell to the courtroom, someone – Henry never saw who it was – thrust a large manila envelope into his hand. It was stamped 'PHOTOS – DON'T BEND' and a quick glance inside told him Gregory Annunzio had done his work well.

'I don't like jails, Henry.' Gloria looked subdued and kept close to him for comfort. 'They bug me.'

'You won't be in this one that long,' he assured her.

Gloria managed a weak smile.

'Just do as I tell you and I'm sure everything is going to be

107

all right,' Henry instructed her. 'When it's over, you may even get that Hollywood offer you've been wanting – '

'Oh, Henry! If you manage that, I'll love you forever.'

Justice Peebles entered the jammed courtroom just then and Gloria clutched the raincoat around her as she stood up along with the rest of those in the room. The coat was rather short and, even though Gloria was not quite as tall as Aldo Palmieri, it still allowed a provocative glimpse of thigh.

'First case,' said Peebles.

'Gloria Manning and Henry Walters,' the bailiff intoned.

'We're both present, your honour,' said Henry, hoping he was using the right litany.

'So I see,' said the magistrate. 'When you were here on a former occasion, Mr Walters, I believe Miss Manning brought charges against you.'

'That was all a mistake, your honour,' said Gloria.

'Miss Manning is now in my employ – as secretary and model for many scenes in the book I'm writing,' Henry hurried to explain.

'A very successful book already, judging from the papers – even though it's not even finished.'

'It soon will be, your honour.'

'What is the charge this time, clerk?' the magistrate asked.

'Indecent exposure, your honour. And staging a lewd entertainment.'

'So?' Peebles looked surprised. 'This is a far cry from knights in armour, Mr Walters.'

'A different era, your honour – but the same principle nevertheless.'

'Would you care to elucidate?'

'As one who appreciates literature, I'm sure you will agree that a book jacket is a work of art.'

'An interesting cultural point, perhaps even a legal one,' Justice Peebles conceded. 'Please go on.'

'My publishers and I thought it would be appropriate to reveal such a work of art in its entirety, so we arranged for a gathering of the press at the Hotel Plaza this afternoon in connection with the signing of a number of contracts.'

'*Large* contracts, if the radio and the afternoon editions are to be believed.'

'Yes, your honour. The climax was the unveiling of a large-scale model of the book jacket, for which Miss Manning was kind enough to pose.'

'Sort of a living tableau, would you say?'

'Yes sir – like the ones we used to watch in the circus a long time ago.'

'With a difference, I'm sure.'

'Times change, your honour. So do cultural standards.'

'I will accept your point as valid, at least for the moment, Mr Walters. This is only an informal hearing to determine whether you and Miss Manning should be charged with the allegations made in connection with your arrest and bound over to a higher court.'

'It is my contention that, until the arrival of the police this afternoon, what was being presented was indeed an artistic exhibition,' said Henry. 'You might say, a living example of the way the final book jacket will look.'

'An interesting point. Do you have any proof of what you say?'

'Miss Manning was in the same pose as this photograph that will appear on the jacket of the book.' Henry drew a single photo from the envelope and pushed it across the desk to the magistrate.

'An exact duplicate of this pose, did you say?' Peebles asked without taking his eyes from the photo.

'With no motion whatsoever, which I believe has a legal bearing – '

'It did a long time ago, Mr Walters, about the same time as those circus tableaux you mentioned. But not much any more.'

'I'm also willing to offer proof that Miss Manning's pose was an exact duplicate of the jacket photograph, your honour.'

'Proof, Mr Walters?' The magistrate looked up from the photo, his eyes gleaming with renewed interest.

'If you will ask the clerk and the bailiff to move to the back of the courtroom, we will proceed with a demonstration for your eyes alone. I believe it will make clear the truth of my statement.'

At a nod from the justice, the two men moved away, albeit with considerable reluctance.

'Miss Manning will now assume the pose in which she was photographed this afternoon.' Henry helped Gloria remove her

109

arms from the sleeves of the coat while still hiding as much of her body as could be expected of a rather short garment.

'Please examine the photograph again, your honour,' Henry requested when Gloria had arranged herself in a position before the dais upon which Justice Peebles sat. 'Then examine the pose Miss Manning has assumed.'

Waiting until the justice's eyes lifted from the photo, Henry quickly spread the raincoat wide open, hiding Gloria from the courtroom, but decidedly not from Justice Peebles's eyes. The jurist swallowed once, then glanced down at the photo again as if to reassure himself and back at Gloria.

'Charges dismissed,' he said a little hoarsely and whacked his gavel upon the desk. 'Next case.'

viii

Gloria came to work the next morning bubbling over with happiness. 'You made me a celebrity, Henry,' she told him. 'On the bus this morning, three people recognized me. My pictures are in all the papers.'

'You're on your way to fame and I hope to happiness,' Henry told her. 'I wish I could say as much.'

Gloria was instantly concerned. 'Miss McGuire?'

'After yesterday she'll never speak to me again. Mind if I ask you a question or two, Gloria?'

'Not at all. Shoot.'

'Do you remember when you called me that night about being on the cover of my book and I told you I wasn't going to write it?'

'Certainly. I was real disappointed.'

'Did you tell anybody else about it?'

'Nobody but my sister, Maria.'

'The one that's married to Big John Fortuna?'

Gloria's blue eyes opened wide. 'Why, yes. How did you know that?'

'Never mind. Did you ask your sister to get her husband to see if he couldn't persuade me to write *Superstud* first?'

'Oh, no, Henry. I just told her how disappointed I was.' She stopped. 'You don't mean–?'

'I was persuaded to write the book, yes.'

'But how? They couldn't make you.'

'Miss McGuire had a near-fatal accident in the subway the next afternoon. Somebody pushed her off the platform and a man pulled her up again, just before a train arrived.'

'Oh, Henry! You didn't think that I. . .? But you did, didn't you?' Gloria sat down suddenly. 'I remember now that you acted sort of funny, when I came in that morning and told you Greg Annunzio said you needed a secretary.'

'I did think you were in on it at first,' Henry admitted. 'But after you turned out to be such a fine secretary – '

'Maria must have spoken to John and he had two of the boys fake the accident.'

'I think that's exactly what happened. Incidentally, Annunzio came to the jail yesterday offering to help us get off but I wouldn't let him.'

'Because of the subway incident?'

'Partly, but mainly because I didn't think it would do either of us any good to have Annunzio defending us, when he's known to be associated with your brother-in-law – no offence, of course.'

'That Maria is always making a mess! I've told her more than once to stay out of my business!' Gloria said angrily. 'I only called her that night because I was so disappointed and wanted her to know I could associate with a real nice man like you, Henry – a best-selling author and all that.'

'Thank you, Gloria.'

'Are you sure you don't hold any of this against me?'

'Of course not.'

'And not what happened yesterday afternoon either?'

'That was staged by Patty O'Flynn.'

'She sure knows how to do it – except the raid, of course.'

'I'm pretty sure she knew how to handle that, too. I'll find out when I see her again.'

Henry got Patty O'Flynn on the phone a little before five o'clock. 'I've got a bone to pick with you,' he told her.

'Let's pick it over a drink at Louis Fourteenth – a half hour from now in the bar. You know where it is, don't you?'

111

'I certainly should. I bartered my soul to Barney Weiss there and I've been in trouble ever since.'

'The kind of trouble you've been having shouldn't be wasted on young men. See you at Louis's.'

Henry was sitting at a table eating peanuts when Patty O'Flynn arrived – as usual like a small hurricane.

'How's Gloria?' she asked.

'Fine.'

'I hope she didn't catch cold from all that exposure the other afternoon.'

'Gloria's got the constitution of an ox – no, a cow would be better, I suppose.'

'You ought to know, Henry. What's bugging you?'

'That raid yesterday – it was staged, wasn't it?'

'Are you implying that I can manipulate the New York Police Department?'

'If you set your mind to it you could put a lock on the Pearly Gates and organize a heavenly demonstration outside for a Department of Soul Music.'

'Why, Henry! You say the sweetest things.'

'Never mind the blarney. You did arrange it, didn't you?'

'Well, I do take care of publicity free for the annual benefit of the Fraternal Order of Police so the boys in blue are naturally grateful.'

'What did you expect would happen?'

'Gloria was to be put in the clink temporarily, but you decided to be Lancel – '

'And made a fool of myself,' said Henry bitterly.

'You were real sweet, even if the whole thing did look like a scene from *Lancelot's Return* as filmed by Aldo Palmieri. We made front pages all over the country, to say nothing of *News Week* and *Time*. Did you read what Willy the Dilly said about you?'

'Yes. She might as well have put me in a paddock like any other stud. What has she got against me anyway?'

'Our Wilhelmina is a fierce partisan when it comes to women's rights, so any man who can make women swoon the way you do is a natural enemy.'

'I've never even spoken to the woman, except at the press conference,' Henry protested but Patty shook her head.

112

'For the world's greatest lover, you are incredibly naive sometimes, darling.'

'Somebody's always telling me that or comparing me to Walter Mitty. What does it mean this time?'

'Women like Willy Dillingham are naturally competitive, when it comes to men. To put it baldly, Henry, she's bucking for a piece of the action.'

'My God! They're coming out of the woodwork!'

'After yesterday afternoon, you're a marked man. If that raincoat you were trying to put around Gloria had been two inches shorter, we'd probably even had coverage by the *Wall Street Journal*. I hear London Fog's stock opened up two and a half on the Stock Exchange this morning.'

'Be serious, please.'

'How could I be anything but serious about the kind of gold mine you've latched onto? Barney Weiss told me this morning that bookstores all over the country are wiring in advance orders and the Publisher's Guild has upped the guarantee another ten grand. If that sort of success bugs you, Henry, it should happen every day.'

'It's just that I'm not quite used to seeing myself labelled a sex maniac.'

'But a nice sex maniac, Henry – one no woman can resist. I'm sorry I couldn't be in the courtroom yesterday to hear your gallant defence of Gloria but Calvin Peebles and I have worked together on several Fraternal Order of Police Benefits. He usually judges the beauty contests because he has a keen eye for feminine pulchritude, but if he'd seen me there, he might have smelled a rat. You handled it just fine, though; they tell me you were real dramatic when you opened that raincoat and showed Peebles why God created woman.'

'By the way,' Patty added. 'Because of what happened yesterday, Aldo has retained me to promote the film, too, so I'll have to work closely with him.'

'You've done so well with this gimmick about the press conference, I want you to take on a job for me,' Henry told her.

'Name it.'

'All of this really got started because I've been in love with Selena McGuire for years. After what's been happening lately, though, it will take your most powerful gimmick to even get me back on first base with her.'

'From what I've heard about Selena, if she lets you get to first base occasionally, you're going to win the ball game eventually. She's the serious – and marrying – kind.'

'But she's thrown me out of her life forever.'

'Why get back into it then, when you're doing so well outside the corral?'

'I told you I'm not cut out to be a sex symbol.'

'Maybe not, but right now you're giving the best imitation I ever saw of it. Wait until the book's published and the royalties start rolling in; some women can resist a handsome and sexy man – though I never could understand why – others – fools that they are – even resist millionaires. But practically nobody in skirts can hold out long against the combination.'

'Selena can – '

'That I doubt,' said Patty. 'With your track record, you're bound to win the next race, Henry. All you have to do is wait and go to the post at the proper time. Meanwhile, don't rest on your laurels. The old adage of gather ye rosebuds – '

'The very idea is beginning to make me nauseous.'

'Get your friend, Dr Schwartz, to prescribe belladonna, then. If your stomach starts churning, the rest of you might rebel, too. Then we'd all be in the soup.'

ix

Two weeks from finishing *Superstud*, Henry found himself faced with a plot block that brought the narrative to a sudden halt. When four days passed with no production from his usually facile pen, he telephoned Harry Westmore.

'I can't think of anything new to write,' he said when the agent answered.

'You don't need anything *new*, Henry, just new ways of describing the same thing.'

'I've run out of those, too.'

'Can't Gloria help?'

'She's already done everything she knows how to do.'

114

'You really are in trouble, then,' said the agent. 'Why don't you take a few days off?'

'I just finished telling you I've been off for four days.'

'These blocks are always psychological,' Westmore assured him. 'Do you have any idea where the trouble lies?'

'I know just exactly where it lies. I haven't been able to figure a way yet to get Bart and Leonora together at the end of the book.'

'I suppose you're not getting anywhere with Selena either.'

'She won't even speak to me.'

'I hate to bring this up, Henry, but Big John Fortuna won't like it if you don't finish the book on schedule.'

'That's only making it worse, Harry.'

'By the way, Barney thinks there's a good chance of making Gloria into another Marilyn Monroe. He's going to get Palmieri to give her a screen test.'

'I'm glad for Gloria.'

'That makes things even worse for you, though. If the book falls through, Palmieri will probably renege on Gloria's test and Fortuna's wife isn't going to like seeing little sister unhappy.'

'So what can I do?'

'Find something that's not related to writing. Wait! I may have the answer. Why don't you go to the Artists' and Models' Ball tomorrow night? The Bart in – on – you ought to find plenty of inspiration there.'

'I've got enough troubles as it is. If the women wear as little at this one as they did when I went to one years ago – '

'They're wearing less – if that's possible.'

'Then I'm liable to wind up in Justice Peebles's court again.'

'You could do worse, but we've already mined that vein pretty thoroughly, so we'd better leave it for the last resort.' Harry sounded more cheerful now. 'Tell you what; I'll get Patty to send you a couple of tickets by messenger. Meanwhile, you can call Selena and see if she doesn't want to go.'

'And get kicked in the teeth again?'

'I doubt that. Selena's female, which means she'd give anything she's got to go to that ball with a male sex symbol of our time, even though she claims to have given you up for Lent. I'll call Patty and have her send you the tickets. She always does the publicity for the ball so she'll have no trouble getting a pair. All you have to do is call Selena right away and set it up so she can have her hair done.'

Gloria had been out but came in shortly after Harry hung up the receiver.

'I'll be ready to work in a few minutes, Henry,' she said. 'Just give me time to take my clothes off.'

'Don't bother, Gloria. I can't figure out how to get Leonora and Bart together again.'

'I read a story once where you couldn't tell at the end whether the hero would marry the girl or be eaten up by a tiger.'

'That's a famous short story called "The Lady or the Tiger".'

'Couldn't you leave the ending up to the reader?'

'It wouldn't do for the movie.'

'I guess not, but you could always change the ending of the book right up until it's being printed, if you think of something, can't you?'

'Probably. The most important question right now is what will your brother-in-law do if it turns out that I can't finish this book.'

'Oh, my goodness!' Gloria's eyes widened. 'He'd have to be the tiger, wouldn't he?'

'What I'm asking is, would he be?'

'Sis is awful proud of my being on the book jacket and everything. She's been telling all her friends that she and John are going to be invited to the premiere of the movie.'

'Which means they wouldn't like it if things fell through.'

'I'm afraid not, Henry. Remember what happened before?'

'I'm remembering. I guess I'll just have to get myself out of this the best way I can.'

'Are you going to do any more work today?'

'No. Why?'

'Barney Weiss is taking me to the Artists' and Models' Ball tomorrow night. I was going as Eve but we couldn't find anything to hold the three fig leaves on I'd have to wear except that crazy glue that takes the skin off, too, when you try to remove what's stuck on with it.'

'What are you going to do, then?' Henry asked.

'Oh, I can get by with a net bra and pants like burlesque strippers use. The costume people will sew the leaves right on to the net and at a distance, you can't even tell anything's there

116

besides them. But I have to have the fitting so we can get the leaves exactly right.'

'I can understand that,' said Henry. 'Harry Westmore and Patty O'Flynn want me to take Selena but I don't think she'll go.'

'She's got to hate you a lot more than I think she does not to,' Gloria assured him.

The telephone rang shortly after Gloria left. It was Harry Westmore's secretary with the news that two tickets to the Artists' and Models' Ball were on the way to Henry's apartment from Patty O'Flynn's office by special messenger. He found a half dozen excuses not to call Selena, but when they were exhausted, he finally dialled the Bennett Press number.

'This is Henry,' he said when she answered.

'What's the other bad news?' she asked coldly – but didn't hang up.

'I've got a couple of tickets for the Artists' and Models' Ball tomorrow night.'

'So?' Somehow he felt that Selena wasn't surprised. 'Who stood you up at the last moment.'

'Nobody. Why?'

'Twenty-four hours is short notice to invite a girl to a costume ball.'

'I just learned that Patty O'Flynn could get me the tickets. Will you go?'

'Against my better judgement – and we'll come right home when it's over.'

'If you want to, we'll come home *before* it's over.'

'Get this straight at the beginning, when the ball is over, you'll take me to my apartment and then go straight to yours.'

'If that's the way you want it.'

'What gives you the idea I might want it any other way? After all, I can only be pushed so far.'

'I don't know what you're talking about, darling, but I'm so happy that you're going I won't worry about it. Incidentally, what kind of costume are you going to wear?'

'How would I know? You only asked me five minutes ago.'

'You'll be lovely, whatever it is. I'll come by for you about ten tomorrow night. Any suggestions for my costume?'

'I've got the perfect one.'

'What is it?'

'Paint a white stripe down your back and go as a skunk.'

X

Selena was ready when Henry arrived at her apartment in Gramercy Park. Over her costume she wore a long white evening coat buttoned high at the neck and down the front, so he had no hint of what she was actually wearing.

With the biggest *bal masque* of the year scheduled for that evening, practically every suitable male costume in New York had already been rented before Henry started looking. The best one he'd been able to find at a rental shop on Lexington Avenue was that of a satyr, with a pair of pipes hanging around his neck and small horns sprouting from the helmet that covered his head. The breeches, representing the hindquarters of a goat, were a bit tight, but he hoped they would survive the evening without splitting. His chest was bare.

'At least you've reverted to type,' Selena greeted him. 'But you're certainly the palest goat man I ever saw.'

'I was in the hospital over a month,' Henry protested, 'and I couldn't get a suntain in twenty-four hours.'

Selena looked him up and down again with a marked lack of enthusiasm. 'It's probably hopeless but maybe I can tone down that white skin above those crazy tight britches. How did you ever get in them anyway?'

'With a lot of body powder and a shoe horn. If I forget and bend over too quick, we'll have to leave in a prison lock-step.'

'What a revolting prospect,' she said as she disappeared into the bathroom.

Selena came out immediately with a bottle bearing the label of a familiar tanning lotion guaranteed to give the wearer the look of six weeks in Miami in an hour. Pulling on a pair of thin plastic gloves such as are sold with hair-dyeing kits, she started to spread the tanning lotion on his back.

'Be still,' she said when Henry shivered with pleasure at her touch. 'You'll have to stay away from me this evening on account of the lotion getting on me, so don't start getting ideas.'

118

'I always get ideas when I'm with you, ideas like love, marriage, children – '

'Wife-swapping, woman-chasing. You didn't just choose this costume; it's your unconscious mind taking over.'

'All I want is you,' he protested.

'And what have you done to deserve me? Double-crossed me by writing that book for Barney Weiss.'

'Selena, I had to.'

'Give me one reason why – after promising me you'd give it up.'

'I can't explain, but when the book is finished and you read it, you'll know why.'

Selena shrugged, an action that brought an odd sound like metal rattling from inside the long coat she wore. Impulsively, Henry reached out to part its folds and see what was underneath, but she slapped his hand away.

'No you don't, you satyr. I agreed to go with you under duress but that doesn't give you any licence to paw me.'

'What do you mean, "under duress"?'

She didn't answer but stood back and studied her handiwork. 'That will have to do, I suppose. At least you don't look like a fish stuffed into the lower half of a goatskin any longer.'

'I want to know what you mean by "under duress",' Henry insisted as she was putting away the tanning lotion and removing the plastic gloves.

Selena turned to face him. With flushed cheeks and eyes afire with indignation, she had never been more beautiful and desirable.

'Don't try to con me, Henry Walters. As if you didn't know Nick Darby read the riot act to me before you called and threatened to demote me to the position of reader, if I didn't co-operate with you in every way.'

Henry brightened. 'Every way?'

'Except the one you're thinking about.'

'And you thought I asked Nick to do that?'

'I know how devious you can be.' She studied him for a moment. 'Are you saying you didn't?'

'I haven't seen or talked to Nick in over a month. You know I've never lied to you, Selena.'

'You did once – when you told me a stinger was a mild drink.'

'Come on, now; you've been around long enough to know better than that. What really happened that time was you felt sorry for me because Bennett Press had just turned me down for *Superstud*.'

'Well – maybe. But you didn't have to go rutting around like you've been doing lately.'

'That isn't the real me, darling. It's the demon in Bart Bartlemy I inherited, along with the transplant.'

'Do you expect me to believe that?'

'*I* believe it and your friend, Dr Schwartz, half way agrees.'

'I may have been unfair to you,' she conceded reluctantly in the face of his obvious sincerity. 'But if *you* didn't ask Nick Darby to put the heat on me for tonight, who did?'

'Harry Westmore would be my first guess. I'm having some trouble with the book and he suggested I take you to the ball to get the story off my mind. He knew I was going to call you so he must have called Nick first to make sure you wouldn't hang up on me.'

'Are you telling the truth, Henry?'

'Cross my heart.' He drew his fingers across his chest, making white streaks in the tanning lotion, which had not yet dried.

'Now look what you've done!'

Picking up a tissue, she smoothed over the white streaks of skin that had been laid bare, but her touch was far more gentle than it had been when she was anointing his back. In fact, it was almost like a caress.

'Whatever you're wearing under that coat just clanked again,' said Henry. 'Mind telling me what it is?'

'A suit of armour where it could count – what else? Do you think I would go anywhere with you without protection?'

xi

The National Guard Armoury was crowded with people in various types of dress – or undress for the most part. Henry surrendered their tickets at the door and gave the light coat he'd worn over his costume to the hat-check girl in the cloakroom. Selena, however, didn't remove the long cloak she was wearing.

120

'I'm going to powder my nose,' she said. 'I'll check the wrap when I come back. 'Why don't you get us each a drink?'

It took Henry all of fifteen minutes to purchase two stingers for them at the crowded bar. All the while he was wondering what Selena's costume would really turn out to be. Masked, it was difficult to recognize anyone and he was looking in the crowd for her when a Turkish dancing girl in a rather startling brief girdle under diaphanous trousers and small metal breast-plates that only emphasized what they were designed to cover, reached over and took one of the two glasses from his hand.

'Hey!' he cried, reaching for the drink. 'That's not – '

He broke off suddenly, realizing that the dancing girl was Selena.

'You're practically naked,' he spluttered. 'I don't like my fiancée going around publicly in the nude.'

'I'm safe. The girdle is really a chastity belt.'

'I don't believe it. Those things went out during the Middle Ages.'

'Give me your watch.' He slipped the metal wristband over his fingers and, when she tapped it against the brief girdle she was wearing, heard an unmistakably metallic sound.

'How do you keep the darn thing on?' he asked.

'There are rubber suction cups around the waistband, but I do have to be a little careful.'

'I still don't like it. Too much of you is exposed.'

'I seem to remember you didn't mind having considerably more of me exposed on another occasion,' she said.

'That was different. We didn't have an audience.'

She drank her stinger without apparently remembering that three of them had set in motion the chain of events which had ended, some eighteen hours later, with her storming from Henry's apartment after Gloria appeared looking for her earrings.

'Gloria's around somewhere,' said Henry. 'She said she would be dressed as Eve.'

'So are half the women here – but I'm sure you'd recognize her.'

A Brunhilde swept by, then turned and came back. 'Why, it's old Supergoat himself,' said Wilhelmina Dillingham. 'And what

121

an appropriate costume! Bart wore one like it in the film of *Satyr's Quest*. I recognize the cod-piece.'

Beside him, Henry heard Selena snort but Willy the Dilly went on unperturbably: 'I'm sure you already know how lucky you are, Miss McGuire, to have such remarkable masculine capabilities at your disposal.'

'How is *she* in bed?' Selena asked in a tone of controlled fury as Brunhilde moved on.

'How would I know? I was never closer to her than we were just now.' Then he added. 'But I know one thing; she wouldn't be super – like you. You're everything a man could want in a woman.'

'A lady in the parlour, a graduate of the Cordon Bleu in the kitchen, and a slut in the bedroom?'

'Not a slut – a wanton,' he protested. 'There's a difference.'

'Don't bother me with semantics at a time like this. I've got to go to the powder room again and adjust this girdle, it's killing me.'

'Is that really a chastity belt Miss McGuire is wearing?' the hat-check girl asked while Henry was waiting.

'So she said.'

The girl smiled warmly. 'It's a little late to find a locksmith tonight, but from what I've been reading about you, Mr Walters, I'm sure you'll manage.'

In the powder room, Selena made the adjustments to the girdle so it would be somewhat more comfortable. As she was finishing, she saw in the mirror a somewhat familiar looking blonde come in but the mask hid the other woman's face – though her costume of three fig leaves hid little else. Selena went on with her adjustments until the blonde spoke.

'You're Leonora!' she exclaimed.

'I beg your pardon,' Selena said stiffly.

'I'd recognize you anywhere,' said Gloria.

'I'm sorry but my name is Selena McGuire.'

'I know that, Miss McGuire, but in Henry's book you're Leonora. I've typed that name so many times in the past month I don't know you by any other.'

Selena's mouth dropped open. 'You're – ?'

'Gloria, Henry's secretary; I didn't recognize you either with

122

your clothes on,' Gloria laughed. 'Not that either of us is wearing much, are we?'

Selena was not too dumbfounded to realize that Gloria was trying to be friendly.

'I'm afraid I've never seen you with yours off before,' she said.

'I guess that makes us even,' Gloria said, laughing. 'When I left the apartment after lunch yesterday, Henry didn't think you would come but I told him no girl would turn down a chance to attend the Artists' and Models' Ball.'

'You didn't work today, then?'

Gloria shook her head. 'Henry's run dry.'

'How unfortunate.'

Gloria frowned at the note of sarcasm in Selena's voice. 'Doesn't it bother you?'

'Should it?'

'It's just about the worst thing that could happen for both of you.'

'I assure you that what happens to Mr Walters is of no concern to me,' Selena said loftily.

'You mean you're not in love with him?'

Selena evaded the question. 'Are you?'

'Goodness, no; I could never hope for anybody as fine as Henry to fall in love with me. I'm not even in his league.'

'You do seem to be very fond of him.'

'Why shouldn't I be?' Gloria demanded indignantly. 'Didn't he allow me to pose for his research? And for the front jacket of the book? There's a good chance that I'll be going to Hollywood soon, too – and all because of Henry. But it's you he really loves; those other women – and me – don't mean a thing to him.'

'From what I hear he's been giving a pretty good imitation of meaning – '

'Oh, that's just research,' Gloria assured her. 'The important thing now is that if he doesn't get back to writing again, Leonora and Bart – I mean you and Henry – are going to be in serious trouble.'

'Why should what happens to a character in a book he's writing make any difference as far as I'm concerned?'

'Because you're the character. Everything that happens

123

between you and Henry goes into the book – only it's between Bart and Leonora, the heroine. And you should read his description of you, it's almost like he's painting a picture even down to the strawberry birthmark on your tush. When the book's published, every woman in the country is going to wish she was in your place.'

'Every woman except me!' Selena snapped, anger surging up within her at the realization that Henry had written about the intimate part of their relationship.

'Look now – ' Gloria protested but Selena had already left the room, slamming the door behind her.

Gloria started to follow, then stopped and shrugged. *Poor Henry*, she told herself, *whichever way the story ends now, it looks like he's going to wind up with a tiger.*

xii

People were still pouring into the armoury past where Henry waited for Selena. Among them was a tall Mephistopheles with a svelte Little Bo Beep in practically transparent dotted swiss cloth over a G-string and two over-large dots that kept shifting their place, revealing a rather interesting mammary development. She passed Henry as he stood waiting for Selena, then turned and came back to where he was standing near the main entrance.

'Is that you, Henry?' He recognized the voice of Elena Hartsfield.

'In the flesh,' said Henry. 'And a goatskin.'

'I want you to meet Arthur Coneyman.' Elena turned to her escort. 'Mr Henry Walters, the famous author.'

'Chawmed.' The tall Mephistopheles bowed rather unsteadily, obviously somewhat the worse already from early imbibing. 'Where's your, er, herd?'

'In the powder room,' said Henry. 'I'm surprised that Raschid let you off tonight, Elena.'

'He didn't like it and he'll be mad when I get home,' she said with a smile.

Selena came out of the powder room in time to hear and

Henry saw by the fire in her eyes that something had happened in there.

'Get my wrap, Henry,' she ordered. 'We're leaving.'

'But the fun is just about to begin,' Elena protested.

'It's already ended for my horned friend here,' said Selena grimly.

Elena Hartsfield laughed. 'From what I've been reading, that should be spelled with a "Y".'

'Come on, Henry, unless you're planning to stay.' Turning sharply, Selena was pushing her way through the stream of people still entering the armoury when Henry caught up with her, carrying her wrap and the topcoat he had worn over his costume.

'Which one of your paramours was that?' Selena demanded.

'Elena Hartsfield is a neighbour. Walks her cat every day in the park.'

'And you haven't invited her up to your apartment yet for catnip and stingers? You're losing your touch.'

They were outside now with Selena pretending Henry wasn't there.

'Will you call me a taxi, please?' she asked the doorman.

'You don't have to be nasty just because I saw a friend or two in the armoury,' Henry spluttered.

'This seems to be my day for meeting your cast-off paramours. Another one of them was in the powder room.'

'That would be Gloria; I saw her go in. What did she say that upset you?'

'Only that you're telling the whole world how I – ' Selena choked on her words.

'That isn't the way it is at all, darling – '

'Don't you darling me. I'll be happy if I never see you again.'

'That can probably be arranged.' Henry's patience had snapped at last, but he regretted the words immediately. 'What I really mean is – aw hell! What's the use!'

They rode in angry silence until the taxi drew to a stop in front of Selena's apartment house in Gramercy Park. She opened the door on her side before he could get out.

'Don't bother to go up with me,' she told him, 'or ever try to see me again.'

Knowing it would only make things worse, Henry didn't try

125

to follow her but his conscience wouldn't let him leave without making sure she was safely home.

'Wait for me,' he told the driver and crossed the street to where he could see the windows of Selena's apartment. When he saw the light go on in the bedroom and, moments later, the shade pulled down, he went back to the cab, got inside and closed the door.

'Fifth and Nine – ' he started to say, then changed his mind. 'The armoury,' he told the driver instead and leaned back against the cushions, acutely conscious that Selena's perfume still lingered in the cab and convinced that it was probably the last memory he would have of her.

BOOK IV

ELENA

i

'No locksmith, Mr Walters?' the girl in the cloakroom asked
when Henry once again gave her his coat.

'It's a bad night for satyrs.'

'And devils; the tall one who came with Little Bo Peep passed
out a few minutes ago. They've got him stretched out on the
couch of the manager's office snoring it off.'

Henry's interest began to rise with the knowledge that Elena
Hartsfield was now without an escort. Just because Selena had
gotten mad when she'd heard he was using her as the model
for the heroine in his book and gone home didn't mean he still
couldn't salvage something from the evening for himself. And it
would serve Selena right if the salvage turned out to be a
shepherdess who didn't mind associating with a goat herder.

'What happened to Bo Beep?' he asked the cloakroom girl.

'She's inside somewhere. You can't very well miss her
considering how much of Bo is peeping out of that costume.'

It took Henry half an hour and two wrong Bo Beeps before
he located Elena Hartsfield.

'So you came back,' she said, when he broke in on the cowboy
she was dancing with. 'I was hoping you would.'

'I hear your escort came a cropper. Too bad.'

'On the contrary; look who I'm dancing with now. And who's
going to take me home, I hope.'

127

'It must be ESP. I just had the same idea.'

'What are we waiting for, then. I've had all I want of this bash.'

'How about Satan?'

'Good old Arthur wouldn't feel at home at the end of an evening, if he didn't wake up on a strange sofa.'

'Looks like Little Bo Peep found herself a sheep,' said the cloakroom girl when Henry went to get his and Elena's wraps.

'I'm a goat.'

'With her for a shepherdess, you ought to be pawing the ground. From the way I hear it, you're really a tiger, though. I get off around four in case you strike out again and would like to try once more.'

'You're very kind,' said Henry, 'but don't wait up for me.'

'I guess I'd better not at that. Judging by the way Bo Peep was holding onto you when you were dancing just now,' said the girl a little sadly.

Half way home, with Elena Hartsfield cuddled against him in the taxi, Henry said: 'I'm hungry. Want to stop somewhere for ham and eggs?'

'How about my apartment?' said Elena.

'Best offer I've had all night,' said Henry gallantly.

At the apartment Elena handed him the key and he let them in. 'Use Carling's bathroom at the end of the hall,' she told him. 'Give me a few moments and I'll be ready for the kitchen.'

'Sure,' said Henry and moved down the hall to the bathroom, which had two doors. Curious to know where the second one led, as he was leaving he opened it to find himself in a bedroom, with a very large water bed. He was about to go back through the bathroom, when Elena Hartsfield came through a door on the other side of the room – minus the dotted swiss cloth but wearing an equally transparent négligée.

'I guess I used the wrong door,' said Henry.

'This was Carling's bedroom. Both our bathrooms have two doors.'

'That's the biggest water bed I ever saw.'

Elena laughed. 'It's great for playing games, too – like "Catch me if you can".' Dropping the négligée, she jumped on the bed.

Henry jumped, too, but the effort was more of a strain than the tight goatskin pants he was wearing could stand. He heard

128

the sound of tearing cloth as the goatskin split back to front exposing a considerable portion of bare flesh. The tearing cloth also released the demon Bart and, his control stretched beyond caring any more after the quarrel with Selena, he let it take charge.

When he rolled across the broad expanse of the bed to where Elena was lying, laughing, her arms went around him, holding him tight, as did limbs that were strong from tennis and golf. Naturally, then, the demon did his thing.

The resulting action soon reached a natural peak, but just as Elena squealed with esctasy, Henry heard a harsh spitting sound from the foot of the bed. The next moment he was howling with pain after a heavy weight landed on his bare backside and needle-sharp claws raked across it, tearing both flesh and goat-skin simultaneously as Rashid struck in defence of his mistress.

Scrambling frantically to get away from the spitting clawed menace that had attacked him, Henry reached back and lifted the angry Rashid, flinging him away. And, realizing now what had happened, Elena leaped from the bed to capture the cat before he could renew his attack upon Henry.

While she was busy secluding the angry feline in another room, Henry looked into the door-length mirror in the bathroom and shuddered at the sight of a startlingly white backside, in contrast to the chemically acquired tan of his torso, where drops of blood were already beginning to flow from ten, long furrow-like slashes made by Rashid's needle-sharp claws.

'You poor thing!' Elena cried when she came back in the room and saw the damage to Henry's anatomy. 'Does it hurt much?'

'When it happened, I was having too much fun to know,' said Henry gallantly. 'But now – '

'Those scratches look pretty awful. I took a first aid course once and the teacher said that after a bite or deep scratch, the victim always needed protection against lockjaw.'

'I had a toxoid injection when I was in the Army Reserve.'

'We'd better go to the Emergency Room at New York Hospital and let them give you a booster shot,' she said. 'It's only a short distance from here but I'll put some bandaids on those scratches first.'

ii

'Haven't I treated you before, Mr Walters?' The nameplate pinned to the jacket of the tall, young surgeon in the Emergency Room identified him as Dr James Crawford, Resident Emergency Surgeon.

'That was my fiancée after a subway accident.'

'I remember now. What can I do for you?'

'I need a shot of tetanus toxoid.'

'I can't just give you toxoid because you want it, Mr Walters. Have you had an accident?'

'You could call it that. A cat scratched me – or maybe I should say clawed me.'

'Might I ask where?'

'Well, it's sort of – '

'Mr Walters and I left the Artists' and Models' Ball early and were having breakfast in my apartment,' Elena Hartsfield volunteered. 'My Burmese cat is pretty jealous and attacked him.'

That did it, Henry realized. Even a tired Emergency Room surgeon couldn't help but jump to one conclusion, particularly when he saw where the claw marks were located.

'I'll still have to examine the wounds,' said Dr Crawford firmly. 'Scratches can become infected and there's always the possible danger of rabies.'

'But this is a pet cat.'

'I still must take every precaution,' the doctor insisted.

'Could we be a little more private, then?' Henry asked.

'Of course.' Dr Crawford nodded toward a curtained-off cubicle at one side of the Emergency Room. 'Go in there and lie down; I'll be with you in just a moment.'

Henry went into the cubicle and peeled down his torn goatskin before lying face down on the table. A few moments later, Dr Crawford came in and, with a quick, skilled movement, ripped off the adhesive Elena had applied, taking with it, Henry was certain, several outer layers of his epidermis.

'That certainly must have been a big cat!' The doctor's voice was filled with wonder. 'I'm surprised that he didn't knock you down.'

130

'Well – he did – sort of.'

Dr Crawford whistled softly. 'Your name didn't ring a bell, Mr Walters, until a woman reporter who hangs around here a lot at night told me who you are and who the lady is who brought you in. May I congratulate you on your taste in women? Also, on the fact that your famous transplant doesn't appear to have been injured either.'

Henry jumped suddenly as novacaine was injected into his tender flesh.

'I'm going to excise these puncture wounds to reduce the danger of infection and put in a few stitches,' Dr Crawford explained.

'You said something about a reporter.' Henry was hoping he hadn't heard right.

'Wilhelmina Dillingham often drops by after a big social function, looking for material she can use in her column. You'd be surprised to hear about some of the accidents we get in here after a bash like tonight's ball, but I've got to admit yours is the most unusual one so far.'

Henry groaned.

'Those claws went in deep,' said Dr Crawford, mistaking the cause of Henry's misery. 'How did you happen to let the cat get the drop on you?'

'I guess you could say I didn't know the cat was watching and by the time I found out, I was a casualty. Are you about through?'

'Just have to give you a shot of tetanus toxoid and an injection of penicillin. You're not allergic to it by any chance, are you?'

'The only things I'm allergic to right now are women and cats.'

'With the sort of reaction you seem to generate, we should all have that kind of allergy,' said Dr Crawford. 'That will be forty dollars. You pay as you go out.'

iii

It was almost noon when Gloria finished typing what Henry had dictated in the early morning hours.

'You seem to have had a lot more excitement after the ball than I did at it,' said Gloria, neatly stacking the sheets the word processor printer had just produced. 'I guess I'm spoiled, though, after spending so much time here with you.'

'The feeling's mutual,' Henry assured her. 'By the way, on your way home today would you drop what's left of that goatskin off at the costume rental shop on Lexington? It's in the closet on the floor.'

Gloria took one look at the costume and shook her head. 'I doubt that the costumer will take it back. I guess you could say this goat really had it last night – in more ways than one. Bart Bartlemy would have been proud of you, Henry.'

'That's not much of a compliment.'

'I think it is. I've been pulling for you and Selena to get together but right now I don't think you ought ever to marry.'

'Why not?'

'You should be preserved for the women of the world, Henry – like a national monument or something.'

Gloria left for the day when she finished printing what Henry had put into the word processor and, after taking two percodan tablets, Henry slept the rest of the afternoon – on his face. The telephone rang about eight o'clock – it was Patty O'Flynn.

'Congratulations,' she said. 'It doesn't look like you need old Patty's services any more, Henry.'

'What are you talking about?'

'Haven't you seen Willy the Dilly's column in the afternoon edition?'

'I've been asleep.'

'Did you ever try sleeping at night? And alone?'

'Cut the funny stuff, Patty. My tail's sore and it hurts to laugh. What did she say about me this time?'

'You've got to read it to get the full flavour. I'm coming to expect the unusual from you, Henry, but this has to be the caper to end all capers. I hope you're writing it down.'

'Gloria just finished taking it off the printer.'

'Good! That scene has to be preserved for posterity. Besides, it will add another fifty thousand sales.'

'Selena's thrown me out of her life for good and all you can

132

think about is sales,' Henry exploded. 'You and Barney Weiss – Harry Westmore, too – are a bunch of vultures.'

'I though you looked especially virile at the Artists' and Models' Ball last night in that goat suit. Selena was lovely, too. Was that really a chastity belt?'

'So she said.'

'Don't you know?'

'Gloria saw Selena in the powder room at the armoury and told her she's Leonora in the book and I'm writing down everything that's happened between us. Selena got mad as hell and I had to take her home before midnight.'

'If she's read Willy's column "Dallying with Dilly", you're probably in more hot water than you were last night,' Patty told him. 'But with Elena Hartsfield in your camp – '

'I still love Selena.'

'Mind telling me how you managed to make out so fast with Elena?'

'Well, a cat on a leash isn't something you see very often. She walks in the park with one every day so it was calculated to stir an author's imagination. Besides, she knew Bart rather well in Hollywood and has given me a lot of helpful information about what he was like then.'

'How is the lovely Elena in bed, by the way?'

'A gentleman wouldn't tell.'

'That's one trouble about getting old. Somebody's always inventing something you don't have the strength to try,' said Patty sadly. 'We've all been a little worried lately about the book, Henry. For a while you seemed to be losing your zest for what every red-blooded American male has the hots for, but it looks like you're okay after last night. Give me a ring when your tail isn't too sore to sit down and we'll blow some of Barney's money some place – unless you know a doctor who'd be willing to give me a giant hormone shot.'

When Patty hung up, Henry rummaged in the closet for the loosest pair of slacks he could find and put them on with a yellow polo shirt and sandals. At the drugstore he regularly patronized around the corner, he bought a copy of the *Post* before taking the seat at the lunch counter.

'What's your pleasure, Mr Walters?' the pert red-haired girl behind the counter asked when he took a seat gingerly. 'Or shouldn't I ask?'

'What's good in the ice-cream category?'

'Well, there's a banana split – if you're up to it, after that orgy Willy the Dilly said you took part in last night.'

'When you've seen one orgy, you've seen them all, Mabel,' Henry assured her. 'I'll take the split.'

'So I hear, Mr Walters. So I hear.'

While Mabel was concocting the confection, Henry unfolded the paper to 'Dallying with Dilly'. A photograph of him and Elena Hartsfield leaving the ball – he in his goatskin but without his mask, and she costumed as Little Bo Peep – was at the head of the column. He wondered where it had been taken, then remembered that a news photographer had been outside the armoury, snapping departing and arriving celebrants and recognizable celebrities.

Beneath the cut was a short headline such as columnists use to call attention to an item in the column:

WHAT THE CAT SAW?

Almost anything can happen after the annual Artists' and Models' Ball – and usually does. The Emergency Room of New York Hospital isn't an unlikely place to find out what did happen either – as this writer has noted more than once. But even these blasé eyes were somewhat startled early this morning to see Elena 'Bo Peep' Hartsfield, the ex-Mrs Carling, and Henry 'Billygoat Gruff' Walters, the Casanova of Upper Fifth Avenue, appear in the aforesaid Emergency Room with a new emergency – ten deep furrows across the bare backside of the virile author of *Superstud*

'*I didn't know the cat was watching*,' Henry explained. What the cat was watching if other than a Henry-in-the-buff, I leave to my readers' imagination. With only the final note that 'Billygoat Gruff', patched-up posterior and all, departed the ER – in the jargon of Doctor Novel Devotees – with 'Little Bo Peep.'

What did the cat see? There's the mystery of the day.

Or is it?'

134

Henry walked home from the drugstore in the warm early evening twilight. As he got off the elevator on his floor, he noticed a tall man standing before the door of an apartment at the end of the short hallway, ringing the doorbell. Only when he came nearer, did he realize that the bell being rung was his own.

'Can I help you?' he asked politely.

The tall man turned and looked him up and down. 'Not unless your name is Henry Walters,' he said belligerently.

'I am he,' said Henry, conscious of how awkward the correct grammatical form sounded. 'What can I do for you?'

'It's more a question of what I'm going to do *to* you,' said the stranger. 'My name is Carling Hartsfield.'

Henry's first impulse was the same as any lover would have felt when meeting an angry husband upon whom he'd recently put horns – flight. Hartsfield stood between him and both the elevator and the fire escape, however, besides being several inches taller and far broader of shoulder.

'Why don't you come inside?' he told the visitor politely. 'We can talk more privately there.'

When Hartsfield still appeared to be inclined toward forthright physical action, Henry added soothingly: 'Perhaps over a drink? I bought a fresh bottle of Wild Turkey bourbon yesterday – the hundred-and-one proof variety.'

The prospect of sour mash tipped the scales and Henry quickly unlocked the door and let the visitor in.

'Have a seat, please,' he said. 'I'll get the drinks.'

When he came back, bearing a double for the guest and a single for himself, Hartsfield was examining the word processor and the pile of manuscripts Gloria had stacked beside the printer.

'Is this where you write that stuff the newspapers have been full of?' he asked, taking the glass.

'I'm writing a book, yes.' Henry was relieved to see that Hartsfield hadn't turned the top page of the manuscript pile. His rather realistic account of the affair the night before with

Elena, somewhat elaborated upon to make the part of Bart a bit more heroic, was only a few pages deeper in the stack.

'Cheers,' he said, lifting the glass.

'Che – ' The visitor suddenly remembered why he had sought Henry out. 'What the hell were you doing with my wife last night?'

'It was all perfectly innocent, Mr Hartsfield.' Henry hoped he was achieving a sufficiently virtuous note to soothe a tipsy ex-husband.

'Then what's that Dilly woman writing about?'

'Nothing but circumstantial evidence, I assure you. Your wife was kind enough to take me to the Emergency Room after the cat scratched me – '

'Rashid sleeps in a bedroom,' said Hartsfield still on a note of suspicion. 'What the hell were you doing where Rashid could get to you?'

The point could well have been argued that neither the apartment nor its lovely occupant belonged to Carling Hartsfield any longer, even though he was probably paying a considerable sum for the upkeep of both in alimony. Henry, however, didn't even consider the point.

'I took my fiancée to the Artists' and Models' Ball but we had a lover's quarrel and she insisted upon going home alone,' he explained. 'I was about to leave when I saw Mrs Hartsfield leaving – also alone – after her escort passed out.'

'Arthur Coneyman?'

'Yes.'

'He always passes out.'

'So your wife told me. We had met casually before in the park where she sometimes takes the cat for a walk and, knowing we were neighbours, I offered to see her home. We had both been deserted, so to speak, and she was kind enough to invite me in for breakfast. Almost,' he added piously, 'you might say we were sharing our sorrow.'

'Are you sure you didn't share anything else?' Hartsfield's words were a little slurred, courtesy of the drinks he'd had earlier plus the double bourbon.

'Scouts honour,' said Henry, neglecting to mention that he'd grown up in a rural area where there was no Boy Scout Troop. 'I guess Rashid must have mistaken me for a goat. It was the

136

only costume I could rent at the last moment, after Patty O'Flynn managed to get me some tickets for the ball. Anyway, the cat attacked me.'

'The column implied that you were bare-assed at the time.'

'A natural conclusion on Miss Dillingham's part, I am sure, considering the location and nature of the wounds,' Henry was talking around the main issue, desperately seeking an explanation that would allay even an ex-husband's suspicions. Then the answer came to him – the goatskin pants the rental agency had refused to take back. 'I'll get the costume I was wearing and show you.'

Going to the closet, Henry found the damaged costume and showed it to Hartsfield. 'These trousers were pretty tight to start with,' he explained as he lifted the tattered garment for Carling Hartsfield's somewhat bleary-eyed examination. 'You can see the places where the cat's claws went through.'

Hartsfield studied the garment for a moment, then drained his glass and put it down.

'Anybody can see that you were wearing the pants when the damned cat attacked you,' he said. 'It looks like I pretty nearly made a fool of myself, Mr Walters. Obviously, you're a gentleman, sir – a gentleman and a scholar. I want to thank you for bringing m'wife home safe.'

'It was a pleasure,' said Henry. 'I hope you two are going to be reconciled.'

'I'm on m'way there now.' The guest rose and made his way toward the door while Henry sighed a deep sigh of relief. Halfway there, Hartsfield stopped and turned back, albeit rather carefully. 'They say you have a strange power over women, my fren',' he said. 'Just for information, mind you – if the cat hadn't tore yer pants would you have tried to take advantage of Elena?'

'Your wife is a very lovely woman, Mr Hartsfield, and you *are* divorced. Would you have blamed me if I had?'

'Can't say I would've. Can't say 'tall. Looks like I owe the damned cat a favour – mushn't forget to take 'm a fish.'

'Good night, Mr Hartsfield. You're a lucky man.'

When Henry had seen the visitor safely into the elevator and on the way to the ground level, he returned to his apartment and rang Elena.

'How are your wounds?' she asked.

137

'Sore but healing. I just had a visitor – your ex-husband.'

'Oh! Oh! What did Carling want?'

'He'd read Wilhelmina Dillingham's column and came here planning to slug me but I talked him out of it. He's on his way home, if you want him back.'

'I do,' she said. 'Until last night I'd almost forgotten how nice it can be to have a man around the house – even Carling. How did you manage it?'

'The way the tale went, we were both stood up at the ball and came home together, quite innocently, for breakfast. The cat resented it and attacked me.

'That's what really happened.'

'Considering what was in progress at the time, it was a natural mistake on Rashid's part,' Henry conceded. 'Anyway, when I showed your husband the goatskin pants, they convinced him.'

'He must have been pretty drunk not to have noticed that they were split down the middle. You could have done that easily getting out of them. Anyway, I'd better run and get ready for Carling. I could kiss you for what you've done, Henry.'

'I'll take a rain check. Maybe sometime when Rashid's at the vet's for his annual check-up.'

V

Henry was having a cup of coffee at the kitchen table when Gloria came in next morning.

'I hope you've got plenty of Java,' she called to him as she crossed the living room to the bedroom. 'I need it.'

Henry turned up the Silex and, by the time Gloria came back into the kitchen wearing the string bikini that was her working garment, the coffee was perking merrily.

'Don't get up,' she said, taking a cup and saucer for herself to the small table where Henry usually ate his meals. 'How are the wounds, by the way?'

'By wearing two cushions whenever I have to sit down, I only feel like I'm being stabbed in the tail with a Roman short sword. You don't usually drink coffee at this time of the morning. What happened?'

138

'I'm not usually out with Barney Weiss two nights in a row. Talk about your Casanovas; when you finish *Superstud* you ought to write a book about Barney. He could give Bart a run for his money any day.'

From the living room came the sound of the doorbell. 'I wonder who that could be?' Gloria put down her coffee cup. 'Don't get up, Henry. I'll go.'

When Gloria opened the door leading to the corridor outside, a uniformed messenger was standing there.

'Message for Mr Henry Walters,' he said holding out an envelope.

'I'll take it,' said Gloria. 'I'm his secretary.'

'I wish more secretaries dressed like you do, ma'am.' The messenger handed her the envelope and a clipboard for her to initial the address written there. 'You've made my day.'

'Thanks!' Gloria laughed as she initialled the sheet and handed it back. 'Sorry I don't have any place to carry my purse.'

'It's a special delivery message – from a woman,' said Gloria when she came back into the kitchen. 'That perfume costs more than the paper.'

'Open it,' said Henry. 'I don't have any secrets from you.'

Gloria took out the card inside, glanced at it, raised her eyebrows and handed it to Henry, who read the name stencilled upon the card and the message beneath it:

MS WILHELMINA DILLINGHAM
United Nations Apartments
At home June 25, 5pm.

'I've heard about those "at homes" Willy the Dilly stages,' said Gloria. 'There's only one guest and she serves tea and crumpets.'

'I'm not going,' Henry said firmly. 'That column she wrote about me made me look like a fool.'

'You've got to go,' Gloria told him. 'If you don't, she'll write in that column of hers that you were challenged and refused to fight.'

It was one minute to five when, after being swisked skyward in an elevator, Henry pressed a button beside the door of Wilhelmina Dillingham's suite. It was opened promptly by Willy

139

herself, looking gorgeous in a long hostess gown zipped up to her chin.

'How nice of you to come, Henry,' she said warmly, giving him her hand and, when he hesitated instinctively, pulling him over the threshold. 'And so prompt, too. I hope you don't hold it against me for suggesting in print once that you might not be the man to handle the legacy of my late good friend, Bart Bartlemy.'

Still holding Henry's hand, she led him to a chair before taking a seat on a sofa across a tea table from him. Nor was he surprised to see a tea service on the table with a plate of delicious looking crumpets.

'It's a heavy responsibility,' Henry mumbled.

'As I remember Bart – and I did know him pretty well – that's a very good description.' She was pouring. 'Cream or lemon?'

'Lemon. And two lumps.'

'Nothing like pure sugar to give one energy.' Wilhelmina raised her cup. 'To our closer friendship.'

'By the way,' she added studying him over the rim of her cup like a lioness, Henry thought, examining a prospective dinner. 'How's *Superstud* coming along?'

'I'm rewriting.' Which was true for, with all further story progress having once again come to a grinding halt, Henry had fallen back on every writer's remedy for plot block, revision.

'Nobody but another writer knows how much of that we have to do,' Wilhelmina conceded putting down her tea cup. 'Have another crumpet?'

Henry accepted, having decided that every crumpet he ate delayed that much longer the inevitable moment of truth, for which he couldn't summon up any real desire. His hostess, however, wasn't as hungry – for crumpets – as he was. He still had a fourth of a plate to go, when she stood up and looked down at him, smiling in a way that would ordinarily have set Henry's hackles rising all the way from his scalp to his sacral nerves. But oddly enough, the only emotion he felt at the moment was apprehension.

'Well, darling,' Wilhelmina said warmly reaching for the zipper at her throat. 'Shall we "Have at it?" as the English say.'

The zipper sped downward, revealing what Henry had

suspected from the first – that underneath was only vintage Wilhelmina. He took one look at unclothed loveliness that could have graced a Wagnerian opera, a view that normally would have brought Bart's part – as the columnist herself had named it – actively to life. But when nothing happened, he did the only thing he could do under the circumstances – and fled.

Back in the taxi in front of the towering apartment house, Henry scurried for home. There, his hands trembling, he poured a jolt of bourbon and drank it down. When the desired effect didn't settle his nerves, he poured another and remembering the green pills Dr Schwartz had prescribed, swallowed a couple of those, too, undressed and piled into bed.

vi

Henry was still asleep the next morning, when Gloria let herself in with her key and came to the doorway to the bedroom which he had left open.

'Are you all right, Henry?' she asked, awakening him.

'No,' he said. 'I had a couple of bourbons and two of those tranquillizers Dr Schwartz gave me about seven o'clock last night and I guess I overslept.'

'You could have killed yourself,' Gloria said. 'I'll go in the kitchen and get the percolator going before I change into working clothes.'

'I'll take a cold shower,' said Henry getting out of bed. 'Maybe it will wake me up.'

In the bathroom, he showered, shivering in the spray from the cold water faucet, and considered shaving but gave up the idea because his hands were shaking so he was afraid he might cut himself.

He was sitting in the kitchen at the small table, drinking a cup of coffee from the percolator, when Gloria came in wearing her usual string bikini.

'Feel better?' she asked pouring a cup of coffee for herself.

'Not much.'

'What happened at Willy the Dilly's apartment yesterday afternoon?'

'We had tea and crumpets.'

'Was that all?'

'Not for her, but for me. She started the game but I struck out.'

'What do you mean struck out?'

'Just that. I couldn't get it up.'

'You?' Gloria said on a note of unbelief.

'The transplant didn't work.'

'You didn't have any bourbon to fortify yourself on the way there, did you?' Gloria asked.

'Not a drop,' said Henry. 'Willy was willing but Bart's part reneged.'

'That's hard to believe.' Gloria came over to the table and reached over to put a couple of pieces of bread in the toaster.

Henry found himself looking down the deep cleft that had got him into trouble with his class ring on the subway. Usually just that was enough to give him a feeling as if he was about to have St Vitus dance – but nothing happened.

'What's wrong, Henry?' Gloria asked, a distant note of apprehension in her voice now.

'I don't feel a thing.'

'Not even in the transplant?'

Henry shook his head bleakly; at the moment he was beyond speech at the realization that the disaster of yesterday afternoon was continuous and not an isolated incident. 'I don't feel a thing.'

'My God!' Gloria cried. 'You've lost it!'

'We've all lost it,' Henry croaked in agreement.

vii

'With everything going so well for you, according to the press you've been getting lately, you'd be the last man I'd expect to see here,' Dr Schwartz greeted Henry when he tottered into his office shortly before lunchtime.

'I'm a nervous wreck! Look at these hands; I can't even hold a drink without spilling it.'

'Obviously, you're suffering from an acute anxiety state.' Dr

Schwartz went to the medicine cabinet and shook three green capsules out into his palm, then went to the adjoining wash room and drew a paper cup of water.

'Take these,' he said and Henry swallowed the capsules obediently before dropping into the chair beside the desk.

'Now tell me what your trouble is, Mr Walters,' said the psychiatrist soothingly.

'I've lost it,' Henry croaked.

'It?'

'The demon! It's left the transplant – and me.'

Dr Schwartz frowned. 'Not long ago you were anxious to get rid of the urge to use the parts Bart Bartlemy gave you. Now you say that has happened of its own accord, so it seems that you would be pleased to be simply yourself again.'

'I've even lost the urges I had *before* the accident.'

'Are you saying you no longer experience *any* sex impulse?'

'I told you I've lost it. *Kaput!*'

'Has Dr Sang examined you?'

'An hour ago; I came directly here from there. He says the transplant is completely normal anatomically.'

'Then things might not be as bad as you think. What you are experiencing could be a simple case of psychic impotence, Mr Walters. I see patients with that complaint at least once a week, particularly bridegrooms.'

'Then for God's sake, do something. My whole future is at stake.'

'Maybe we'd better start at the beginning,' said Schwartz, 'and let you tell me everything that's happened since your last appointment.'

'I must say you've packed a heap o' livin' into the past several months,' Schwartz said on a note of admiration – and envy – when Henry finished the tale of his amours. 'About as much romance in fact as most men are fortunate enough to get in during a lifetime.'

'If you can't put me back like I was before yesterday afternoon, there isn't going to be any lifetime,' said Henry. 'I won't be able to finish *Superstud* and the Syndicate will send me swimming – with cement waterwings.'

'Do you have any idea what happened – to your psyche, I mean?'

'It was all because of that damn cat.'

'I'm inclined to agree – at least partially.'

'But why? And how?'

'We'll analyse the *how* first; it may give us a clue as to the *why*. You are aware, of course, that emotions play an important role in the sex urge.'

'If I didn't know that by now, I must be dead from the neck up.'

'Aptly put,' said Schwartz, 'but from what you say, hasn't the direction been reversed?'

'Please, no conundrums. Right now my head and my tail both hurt too much.'

'Did you ever read Dr A.A. Brill's lectures on psychoanalytic psychiatry?'

'I don't believe so.'

'It would be very valuable to a novelist – particularly the section on Freudian slips.'

'What has that got to do with my not being able to do what used to come naturally?'

'Let us look at what you said just now. I'll repeat your exact words which were: "Right now my head and my tail both hurt" '

'You left me somewhere between the tail and the head.'

'We'll examine each phrase separately, then,' said Schwartz. 'The psychological side of the sexual function is in the head, the brain, where it is one of the strongest of human emotions.'

'You can't know just how strong – until you've lost it.'

'Well put,' said Dr Schwartz. 'On the other hand, the physical side is in the tail, since the sacral nerves emerge from the spinal cord in its terminal portion and control the function of the sexual apparatus itself.'

'I came here for help, not an anatomy lecture.'

'It's a simple psychological fact that, when the psychic portion of the sex urge is in a state of repression for various reasons, the physical side will not function at all.'

'Even with Bart Bartlemy's equipment?'

'I'll grant you that the psychic block would have to be extraordinarily strong in that case.'

'Stop quibbling,' said Henry. 'Can you fix it?'

144

'Even superficial observation suggests that yours is far from a simple case.'

'But why? I was doing fine until that damn cat – '

'Exactly,' said Schwartz. 'I strongly suspect that the wounds in your tail act to keep you from performing your normal capabilities as a lover.'

'But the soreness is leaving fast.'

'Nevertheless, your unconscious mind still remembers that the last time you exercised your by now well-publicized sexual proclivities, you sustained painful wounds. In other words, your unconscious mind seeks to protect you from possible pain by making certain that you cannot engage in the activity that resulted in the painful accident in the first place.'

'Is that the tail wagging the dog or the dog wagging the tail?'

'Some of both, I suspect.'

'It's certainly a shock to have a spitting cat sink its claws into your behind under the circumstances that this happened,' Henry admitted. 'But I don't understand why that would make me lose both the desire and the ability.'

'I can see at least two reasons for that,' said Dr Schwartz. 'For one thing, your amorous exploits with other women have interfered with the relationship between you and Miss McGuire. Knowing that further dalliance may cause you to lose her, your unconscious has simply made it impossible for you to function as a lover – except perhaps with her.'

'A fat chance I'll ever have to prove that. Anyway you look at it, I'm in one hell of a fix.'

'There's one other possibility,' said the psychiatrist. 'You might try the hair of the dog – '

'And be looking over my shoulder all the time wondering when I'll get clawed? Not even Casanova could make love under such circumstances.'

'The whole purpose of the procedure would be to convince your unconscious mind that the cat isn't going to attack you again. Once the unconscious is sure you'll not experience pain, your mind should be freed, along with your physical side.'

'I'll see what I can do,' Henry agreed. 'But you'd better put me down for another hour tomorrow.'

'I've got a few more aces up my sleeve, if this one doesn't

win the pot,' Dr Schwartz promised. 'Take heart, Mr Walters. A little fasting certainly won't hurt you.'

At the corner drugstore, Henry dropped a coin into the pay telephone and dialled the number of Elena Hartsfield's apartment. He was prepared to hang up if a man answered, since he didn't know Carling Hartsfield well enough to ask him for permission to sleep with his ex-wife, but Elena answered.

'This is Henry,' he said. 'Are you alone?'

'Yes – except for Rashid.'

'I need to see you for a few minutes.'

'I don't know . . .'

'Please, Elena. It's urgent and I can't talk to you about it on the telephone.'

'I *could* take Rashid for a walk in the park. Are you at home?'

'No. I'm at the entrance to the Park on Eighty-fifth.'

'I'll enter the Park at the Eighty-fifth Street entrance.' she said. 'There's a bench just inside the entrance and we can meet there.'

'I'll be there before you are,' Henry assured her.

He was sitting on the bench when she appeared, with Rashid tugging at the leash. Henry sat at one end of the bench and Elena at the other, with the cat between – no doubt convinced, Henry thought, that he was protecting his mistress.

'You look terrible,' said Elena.

'I feel worse.'

'From your wounds?'

'Not the ones you're talking about. Dr Schwartz says that, when Rashid stuck his claws into my hide, he put them into my brain as well.'

Elena frowned. 'I'm afraid I don't understand.'

Henry looked around and, seeing that no one was nearby, moved a little closer along the bench so he wouldn't have to speak very loud – until a baleful gleam in Rashid's eye warned him against getting any nearer. Quickly he told Elena what had happened, in spite of his embarrassment in having to admit his condition to a beautiful young woman, with whose love-making capabilities he was familiar and which he now needed badly to repeat.

'Couldn't this be merely a temporary condition?' Elena asked.

146

'You were being remarkably effective just before Rashid intervened.'

'Dr Schwartz thinks it goes deeper. And that only *you* can help me.'

'What could I do?'

Knowing he must be more eloquent than he'd ever been before, Henry took a deep breath. 'The doctor says I need to re-enact the crime – '

'What?'

'He says if we follow the exact procedure we did that night – without the cat attacking again, of course – my unconscious mind may accept that love-making won't always end up like it did.'

'I guess I should be flattered,' Elena said on a doubtful note.

'Just once more wouldn't hurt you – and it might *cure* me.'

'Being made love to by you under normal circumstances, Henry, is an experience no woman should be without at least once in her life, I admit – '

'Then, it's very sim – '

'Carling and I were married this morning, so what was fun after the ball would be adultery now. I know you're too fine a person to want me to do that.'

When she put it like that, Henry could hardly do less than admit to a certain amount of *noblesse oblige*, though he doubted that either Bart Bartlemy or the demon would have done the same.

'Believe me, Elena,' he said earnestly, 'I didn't know you were married again when I asked.'

'I'm sure you didn't,' she assured him. 'Actually, if I'd had any idea that you were going to ask me, I would have put off the wedding at least another day, just to re-enact the crime, as you put it. But now – ' She dropped the leash she'd been holding and reached over to put her hand upon his in a consoling gesture.

Touched by her concern, Henry started to lift her hand to his lips – when Rashid struck again.

Chronologuing later for his manuscript, via the word processor, the series of events that followed, Henry decided Rashid had interpreted the movement as another attack upon his mistress. This time Henry was able to move swiftly enough, however, to repel the attacker by seizing the cat behind his ears and tossing him unceremoniously into a bush behind the bench, but not before the needle-like claws had ripped the skin on the back of his hand.

'One thing is sure,' Henry said as he wrapped a handkerchief around his bleeding hand, 'Rashid doesn't have any intention of ever making up with me.'

'You naughty cat!' Elena scolded the feline who had once again resumed a sitting position on the bench between them. But in the slitted pupils, Henry was sure he saw a light of triumph.

viii

Harry Westmore called shortly after Gloria left the apartment at five o'clock.

'For God's sake, Henry!' said the agent. 'Didn't you know better than to tackle Willy Dillingham?'

'Tackle – hell! I had to run for my life!'

'Have you seen the early edition of the *Post?*'

'No.'

'Then get it as soon as I hang up. What the hell were you doing yesterday afternoon?'

'She invited me to tea at her apartment yesterday but nothing happened.'

'I'll say! I hate to be the one to tell you, Henry, but this afternoon's "Dallying with Dilly" is also your epitaph.'

'She invited me – the royal command.'

'Couldn't you have pleaded sick or something?'

'She would have just blown it all up in her column,' said Henry. 'I didn't want to go but Gloria convinced me that I couldn't afford not to.'

'I suppose she's right,' Harry Westmore admitted. 'But if Bart's Parts could only have made the grade with Willy and you'd put it in *Superstud*, we would have sold another hundred thousand copies – '

'Here I am dying and all you can think about is selling books,'

Henry spluttered indignantly. 'Besides, I don't know what the hell you're talking about.'

'You'll know when you read the paper. Dilly didn't dally this time.'

'How about getting off the phone then, so I can get one and see what this is all about.'

'I can tell you in a few succinct words; she's just made you the laughing stock of New York. Get a paper and read your obituary, but take a tranquillizer first.'

'I'm practically living on them already. Goodbye.'

Henry picked up the *Post* from the rack in front of the apartment, but didn't open it until he was back in his own quarters.

'Dallying with Dilly' was in a box on the front page of the second section. If it had featured anybody else except him, Henry would have been willing to give it a Pulitzer prize.

The columnist had chosen to paraphrase, in a piece of brilliant writing, one of the most beloved poems extolling a bucolic side of American life, 'Casey at the Bat'. Only her version was titled, 'Henry Hangs His Head' and it went:

'It looked like certain rapture for the feminine sex that night,
For Henry's Bart-born fervour had never burned so bright.
With hands outstretched and waiting, fully conscious of his
     power,
Our Henry at the ready was the lover of the hour.

'E'en the hardiest damsels, vets of many amorous passes,
Had met their fate and yielded to our hero – all the lasses.
What swain could know tomorrow that he would not surely
     lose
His loved one's warm affection if Henry her should choose.

'What home was safe? What marriage vow could hope to
     last a day?
When Henry, unresisted, began to make his play.
With moans of sudden passion, on every side they'd yield,
When Mighty Henry, SUPERSTUD, Bart's borrowed pow'r
     did wield.

'Like Lochinvar or Elvis, Frank, Peter, Dean or Sammy

149

Our hero conquered maidens with his famed transplanted
  whammy.
But e'en Goliath fell at last, and Samson's locks were shorn,
When fair Delilah's scissors left him weak as a newborn.

'Our Henry always rode roughshod, and flushed by much
  success
Sought to keep the favors won and shut out all the rest.
But days of man are numbered and nights still even more,
While he who dances yet must pay the piper as of yore.

'There came a day when Henry sought to couch again fair
  maid,
Forgetting that to Venus sacrifices must be paid.
Like mighty Casey at the bat, quite certain of his pow'r,
Our Henry strove to hold his fame, as 'lover of the hour'.

'But just as Casey learned at last that human strength can
  quail,
And vaunted powers of champions sometimes must also fail,
E'en mighty Henry lost his grip and with it lost the bout,
When on a boudoir playing field at last he, too, struck out.

'Now let the fate of him 'gainst whom no lass could dare
  resist,
Remind each knight who would upon the field of love enlist.
Don't spread yourself too thin, Sir Knight, lest when you'd
  start the bout
You find like Hanging Henry that you, too, have just struck
  out.'

A key grated in the lock just as Henry finished reading and
Gloria came in.
  'I saw Dilly's column in the *Post* as I was leaving just now,
and came back to see if I could help you, Henry. That
Dillingham woman should be shot.'
  'Thank you, Gloria. You're the first of the mourners – and
probably the last.'
  'Has anybody else called?'
  'Only Harry Westmore – to tell me I'm dead.'

'Can't you sue that woman – or the paper?'

'She didn't actually mention my last name, Gloria.'

'But everybody knows she was writing about you.'

'Granted, but I could never make such a suit stick.'

'Something's still bound to work out so you can finish the book, but I don't like to see anybody as nice as you are taking a beating, when you haven't done anything.'

'That seems to be the trouble.' Henry managed a faint chuckle, then added soberly, 'If working for me is going to be embarrassing for you, Gloria, I'll under – '

'Are you trying to fire me?' she asked indignantly.

'No. I'm just thinking about your welfare.'

'After all you've done for me, I'm certainly not going to let you down the way Miss McGuire and that Elena did.'

'I'll muddle through with your help then.' Henry spoke with a pretence of certainty he was far from feeling. 'How is your brother-in-law going to take this?'

'I haven't talked to Sis yet but I don't imagine John will be very happy. Can't Dr Schwartz do anything?'

'He says I've got to get my psyche straightened out.'

'For that, I'm afraid you're going to have to get away from here,' said Gloria.

'That's the best idea I've heard today,' said Henry. 'When I was at Dr Schwartz's office earlier today, he said he thought he had an ace or two up his sleeve. I'll call him and see what he had in mind.'

'You do that,' said Gloria. 'I'll see you in the morning and you can tell me what he said.'

Henry rang Dr Schwartz at his office and found the psychiatrist still there.

'Have you read "Dallying with Dilly" in the *Post?*' he asked.

'Just finished it,' said Schwartz. 'It's certainly a masterpiece of that sort of writing.'

'Masterpiece or not, what are you going to do to help me?'

'There's one more possibility.' Schwartz even sounded cheerful.

'Name it. I'll do anything.'

'A friend of mine runs a place in the Catskills. It's pretty sophisticated and caters to people who've lost the power to

151

communicate with others the way they want to and are helped by encounter therapy.'

'I've read about that sort of thing in California and I think I even saw a movie about it once. Is this one some sort of a nut house? I'm slowly going crazy but I don't think I'm quite there yet.'

'It's nothing like that. I often send people to Springhaven who've lost the ability to reach out to each other, or didn't have it in the first place.'

'I'll go anywhere; this is a life or death emergency.'

'I'll see if I can arrange for Horace Aiken to accommodate you,' said Dr Schwartz. 'I'll call you in the morning and tell you what the situation is.'

'Just give me time to pack. But one more thing. If this Horace Aiken you mention can do any good for me, I can probably start to work on *Superstud* while I'm up there. Do you think he'll allow Gloria to go with me?'

'I'm sure he will when I explain what's involved,' Schwartz told him. 'I'll call you tomorrow, Henry.'

When Dr Schwartz hung up, Henry called Bennett Press and asked for Selena.

'I believe she's out of town, Mr Walters,' said the switchboard operator. 'I'll put you through to Mr Darby.'

The Chief Editor came on the line almost immediately. 'What's up, Henry? Or maybe I shouldn't ask.'

'The operator says Selena is out of town –'

'She's been pretty upset since you two had that fight at the Artists' and Models' Ball,' said Nick. 'Yesterday she told me her doctor had recommended that she get away for a while, so I imagine she's had another mild nervous breakdown. She had something like it a few years ago and took some sort of a rest cure for several weeks. When she came back she was a different person, so if she's going to have the same sort of treatment again, things between you may be better when she gets back.'

'Don't you know where she is?'

'I haven't the foggiest notion.' There was a moment's hesitation, then Darby added: 'Are you in real trouble with your book, Henry? I don't mean to pry, but there are rumours all over the place.'

'I'm sunk and now I've got Selena to worry about, too. If you hear from her will you let me know?'

'Certainly. And good luck, Henry.'

'Thanks, Nick. When they fish me out of the Hudson a few days from now, contributions should be made to the 'Authors' League Fund.''

Henry's telephone rang as soon as he hung up from talking with Nick Darby; it was Dr Schwartz.

'You're all set for Springhaven, Henry, as soon as you can go there,' he said. 'Hold on and my secretary will tell you how to get there.'

After copying down the secretary's instructions, Henry telephoned Gloria. 'How soon can you pack?' he asked.

'In ten minutes. Where are we going?'

'To a place called Springhaven. Suppose I pick you up around noon tomorrow; we'll have a bite somewhere along the way.'

'I'll be ready.'

'We'll take the portable typewriter and the tape recorder, just in case Bart's Parts rise again.'

BOOK V

LEONORA

i

The narrow road they'd been following since leaving Interstate 87 wound through the lower reaches of the Catskills toward the Poconos. Henry found himself feeling better and better as his sleek new sports car – with the top down – put more and more distance between them and New York City. He'd called Harry Westmore before leaving that morning, telling the agent only that he was going away for a while, seeking to regain control of the narrative flow that had produced everything but a satisfactory ending sequence for *Superstud*.

Gloria was driving expertly, as she did practically everything. The day was warm, the air fragrant with the aroma of the forest through which they were passing, broken only now and then by a bridge over a bustling little stream that appeared to descend from the higher ground to the north-west. Henry relaxed against the cushions with the sun on his face dozing every now and then. By mid afternoon, they were only a few miles from their destination, according to the directions Henry had been given the previous afternoon by Dr Schwartz's secretary.

'If this Springhaven is as nice as the country we've been driving through, it's bound to do wonders for you, Henry,' said Gloria.

'I almost feel like I can start writing again.'

'That's the best news I've heard in days.'

As Gloria expertly guided the car around a sharp curve in the narrow road, Henry turned to look at her. She was wearing a white summer dress, with a light-coloured bandeau about her blonde hair. She had slimmed down considerably, too, he noticed, since the day they had first met in the subway. Now that he looked at her closely – for the first time in weeks – he could see that she had changed in other ways, too.

From the beginning, Gloria had possessed a high degree of self-assurance, but much of what had appeared to be brassiness at first was gone now. No little, he understood, because he had come to know her so much better in the month or so of their close relationship. Even her voice had changed as well as her choice of words and in every way she was far more sophisticated – though still possessing the innate warmth that had attracted him to her from the beginning – than when she had come to his apartment the day after their encounter in the subway with the photographs.

'Anything wrong?' Gloria's voice broke into his thoughts.

'No. Why?'

'You were looking at me like I was somebody you'd never seen before.' She chuckled. 'In spite of the fact that you've seen about as much of me as is possible to see – except maybe on the table in a doctor's office.'

'I was thinking how much you've changed since the day I first met you.'

'For the better, I hope.'

'Decidedly for the better – though you were a very real person to start with.'

'You know why I've changed, don't you?'

'Not entirely.'

'Having somebody like you trust and depend on them would make anybody a better person, Henry. Besides, the Gloria in the book is so much nicer than the old me was that I guess I had to change to be like her. You see, nobody ever treated me like a lady before. Even while we made love, you've always been tender and careful that it should mean something to me, too. A woman can recognize that in a man, even if he doesn't say a word.'

'I think that's the nicest thing anybody ever said to me, Gloria.'

155

'It's true. That's why I get so mad when I see people making fun of you like that Dillingham slut. And when I think of the women like Elena and Leonora that you've been good to not being willing to help you, when you need help so badly, I could kick 'em where it might do some real good.'

'What are you going to do if I don't finish the book and you don't get the screen test?' Henry asked.

'Go on working for you – if you'll have me.'

'I'm not sure I can even write historical novels any more. And even at best, I wouldn't be able to pay you very well – nothing like you were making as a model.'

'I'm not going back to that – ever. When I didn't know any better, I was happy enough doing what I was doing. But now – ' She chuckled again. 'I guess you're Professor Higgins where I'm concerned and I'm your Eliza – like it was in *My Fair Lady* – always ready to bring your slippers. Anyway, I'm what you made me and I like it so well, I'm just going to stay the way I am now.'

'I don't think I can ever really love anybody except Selena,' Henry warned.

'That's all right,' said Gloria. 'I suppose I could fall in love with you, if I let myself go, but I know my place. That's in your bed when you need me and in your office, but not really in that part of your life where your wife should be.'

'Is that fair to you?'

'I'm content with it.'

Henry didn't say more but he couldn't escape the conviction that he didn't really have any choice now, except to become his old self again, not only to save his own skin but to repay Gloria for the trust she'd given him.

ii

'Looks like we're almost there.' Henry had been lying back in the bucket seat with his eyes closed enjoying the peace merely getting away from the city had brought, when Gloria's words called his attention to the road.

They were crossing a narrow bridge over a bubbling stream,

and ahead of them at the road's end was what appeared to be a rustic lodge. On each side of the main building, like the wings of a stage set, tall fences of weatherbeaten timbers, standing upright like palisades, extended into the woods and disappeared among the trees. Pulling the car to a stop before the steps leading to the entrance, Gloria cut the motor.

'Whatever they do here, they don't want the rest of the world to know it,' she observed.

'We won't find out by staying in the car. Let's go inside.'

Beside the door of the main lodge was a small sign that said: 'Ring bell, door will open.'

Henry pushed the bell and the sound of a sliding bolt could be heard before the door opened silently. They had seen no other human beings yet and, when Henry looked at Gloria, she raised her eyebrows and shrugged as he stood aside for her to pass through the door ahead of him.

They found themselves in a fairly large room furnished comfortably like the lounge of a country hotel. Across the back was a countertop with rows of pigeon holes behind it against the wall. Mail and other papers had been stuffed into most of them and, from what seemed to be an office adjoining the counter, came the sound of rapid typing, which stopped as they crossed the lobby to the counter.

The door to the office opened and a smiling young woman came out. She was tall, statuesque in fact, raven-haired, very beautiful – and completely nude.

'Well, what do you know,' said Gloria. 'A nudist camp.'

The girl smiled. 'Welcome to Springhaven; you must be Mr Walters and Miss Manning. We're expecting you.'

'Is this really a nudist camp?' Henry managed to stammer.

'In a sense. My name is Jacqueline Broders – most people call me Jacque. Horace Aiken is my uncle.'

'Don't you feel' – Henry stumbled for a word – 'self-conscious?'

Jaque Broders laughed. 'I did at first but only for a day or two. You get over it rather quickly. Here's Horace now.'

A tall man, wearing only sandals and a pipe, came through a door at the back of the lobby. He was grey-haired, looked to be about fifty, and was craggily handsome.

157

'This is Mr Walters and Miss Manning, Horace,' said Miss Broders. 'They just arrived.'

'Miss Manning,' Horace Aiken bowed in a courtly, old-world sort of way. 'You're even lovelier than your photograph in the newspapers.'

'Thank you,' said Gloria.

'And Mr Walters.' Aiken's handshake was firm and friendly. 'I've been an admirer of your writing for a long time. You don't often find an author who combines literary skill with the highest traditions of scholarship.'

'Then runs out of things to write,' said Henry.

'Let us hope that will prove to be only a temporary condition,' said Horace Aiken cheerfully. 'I was more than pleased when Dr Isadore Schwartz called me about a reservation for both of you.'

'Mr Walters was just asking me whether this isn't a nudist camp?' the statuesque Miss Broders told Aiken.

'A natural assumption and correct – to a degree,' said Aiken. 'We believe that by freeing the body of restrictive clothing, you take the first step toward breaking the fetters of convention and repression that can bind the soul and keep it from reaching out to others.'

'Is – nudity a requirement for admission?' Henry asked somewhat doubtfully.

'Yes. But we arrange it so those who come to us for help can attain that state gradually. Jacque will show you how.'

From behind the counter, Miss Broders produced two small packets, one of which she gave to each of them. When Henry opened his, he saw that it contained a fairly large domino mask, such as one might wear to a masquerade ball, hiding the upper part of the face from just above the mouth to the top of the forehead, along with a pair of dark glasses.

'The embarrassment that goes with nakedness is really a reflection of what one thinks he sees in the eye of the beholder,' Aiken explained. 'By taking off one's clothing and at the same time putting on a mask and dark glasses that hide one's features, so he will not be recognized, much of the shock of being naked in public is removed. We suggest that most of our lodgers wear the mask for twenty-four hours – or as long as they feel at all

158

uncomfortable without clothing.' He held up the mask to show that a numeral had been painted on it.

'During the period that you wear the mask and the dark glasses, you are known only by the number of your cottage unit, which you can see here. We also use only first names here, too, so anonymity is preserved.'

'Does this gimmick of hiding your nakedness by hiding only your face really work?' Henry managed to take his eyes off the decorative Miss Broders long enough to ask.

'Beautifully,' said Horace Aiken. 'You'll see.'

'Dr Schwartz didn't tell me exactly what sort of treatment you give here, Mr Aiken.'

'We don't have any set routine, although we are part of the Human Potential movement,' Aiken explained. 'I became interested after spending some time at Esalen.'

'Is that where you got the idea for the nudity bit?'

'Most of that is my own idea. I'm sure you and Miss Manning will find Springhaven a very comfortable place to be, Mr Walters. When you wish to participate in our programme, you merely join a group; nobody will force you until you're ready.'

'Sounds fair enough,' said Henry.

'One of the main reasons why I chose this spot,' Aiken explained, 'is the warm sulphur spring that bursts from the rocks here. The temperature of the water remains practically constant the year round at about eighty-five degrees.'

'A natural hot tub,' said Henry.

'Exactly. Some guests like to soak for days in what we call the "Womb Pool" after the one at Esalen. Others take an active part in our programmes from the very start.'

'Want to stay?' Henry asked Gloria.

'If you do.'

'We'll give it a try, then,' he told Aiken. 'From now on, though, I'd rather be referred to as Bart.'

'Of course,' said the Springhaven director. 'Jacque has already reserved units eleven and twelve adjoining. Meal hours are posted in your rooms and no one will disturb you, unless you fail to show up for two meals in succession. Dinner is from six to eight.'

'Did Dr Schwartz tell you my trouble?' Henry asked.

'Yes, but our files are secret, if that's what's troubling you.

159

Considering your – fame, shall we say? – I would advise you to wear the mask, else you might find yourself challenged.'

'Heaven forbid,' said Henry fervently.

'Tomorrow you and I will have a long talk, Mr Walters, and afterward I will assign you to a therapist; Jacque is one of them. If you will give me the keys to your car, I'll have your luggage put in units eleven and twelve while Jacque takes down the information we need for our records. You'll probably want to rest a while before dinner.'

'Do we undress here?' Henry asked Jacque Broders when Horace Aiken had left with the keys to the car.

Miss Broders laughed. 'You see how easy it is, Mr Walters? You've been here less than ten minutes and already you don't find the idea of nudity objectionable.'

'On you certainly not,' said Henry gallantly.

'The moment I saw this place I knew it would be good for you, Henry,' said Gloria. 'You're more relaxed already – like Bart in the book.'

iii

The cottages housing the guests at Springhaven were scattered among the trees surrounding the great spring, which had been enlarged to form a rectangular pool in the midst of which the 'boil' of the spring erupted. Although open to the sun, the pool was protected by a wall of sliding glass doors that could be opened to allow the breeze to flow through in hot weather or closed to shut out the wind on a cool night. The cottages themselves were served by a road that wound just inside the fence. When Henry and Gloria were taken to theirs by Jacque Broders they saw that their luggage was already inside.

'Your car will be quite safe parked in our lot outside the fence; nothing is ever locked at Springhaven,' she told Henry. 'You'll find a terrycloth robe hanging in each closet,' she continued. 'Some of our guests like to soak in the warm pool at night but the air can be a little cool after sundown, so we recommend wearing the robe when you come out to avoid a chill.'

The rooms were standard motel type of construction, the beds king-sized and the furnishings comfortable, though somewhat rustic. Each room had its own colour television set.

'They think of everything,' said Gloria when Jacque left. 'Well, what's the programme, Henry – I mean, Bart?'

'I'm going to take a nap,' said Henry. 'How about you?'

'Think I'll go skinny-dipping in that hot spring. I'll wake you up in time for dinner.'

There wasn't much point in unpacking his bags so Henry settled for taking out his shaving kit and a pair of tennis shoes to wear. Removing his clothes, he hung them in the closet and put on the mask Horace Aiken had given him. Surveying himself in the full-length mirror on the closet door, he studied the picture he presented critically.

The events of the past few days didn't appear to have made him look any different physically, which surprised him for he certainly felt different. He was twisting his neck with his back to the mirror, trying to see whether the scars from Rashid's claws were still visible, when Gloria opened the connecting door.

'How do I look?' Gloria was wearing her own dark glasses over the mask, a pair of ballet slippers – and nothing else.

'Like a million bucks.'

'Care to spend a little of that million?'

'Let's not push our luck yet.' He gave her an affectionate slap on her rear. 'Go take your swim but be sure to wake me when you come back. We'll have a drink or two – so I can get up enough courage to go to dinner.'

Henry didn't think he'd be able to sleep but, to his surprise, dropped off immediately and didn't waken until Gloria came in about a quarter to six and shut off the TV.

'You should have gone skinny-dipping.' She was surveying herself in the mirror. 'That pool is very relaxing but it sure made me look like a parboiled lobster. How about fixing the drinks you promised while I take a cold shower?'

'Sure. Did you meet anybody interesting?'

'A couple from Weehawken – Lois and Bob. I read something in one of your books about a pocket Venus and Lois certainly fits the picture.'

'What about Bob?'

'He's a clod but he's built like a Greek god. I gather that

161

Lois caught him making out with some other woman and they're up here trying to save their marriage. For my money, he isn't worth saving, except maybe as a stud.'

Henry made them double bourbons and took the drinks into Gloria's room. She was still in the shower but came out and started towelling herself with one hand while holding the drink he gave her in another.

'You didn't tell your friends from Weehawken who we are, perchance?' he asked.

'Not a word. I didn't see many people but they certainly obey Horace Aiken's rule about using only first names.'

'Don't forget to call me Bart,' he reminded her.

'I won't. After all, it's really Bart we're up here trying to cure.'

'Did you feel a little awkward – without your clothes?'

Gloria laughed. 'You do feel like everybody's looking at you, but only for a few minutes. Then you remember you're looking at them, too, and right away it doesn't matter.'

By the time they'd finished the drinks and Gloria had dried her hair and brushed it into shape, it was six thirty. Henry was feeling warm inside from the bourbon – also hungry.

'Shall we go to dinner?' he asked.

'I was wondering if you were going to pass it up.'

'Horace Aiken said they come looking for you if you don't show up for the meals.'

'If he sent Jacque Broders, you might be better off. Ready for your début?'

'Ready as I'll ever be. Let's go.'

A winding path led from the cottages to the main dining room, located in a wing of the lodge through which they had entered Springhaven. They saw several people on the path, all nude like themselves, but didn't come face to face with anyone, until they stepped up on the porch of the dining room and met another couple coming out. They were middle-aged, wore no clothes and no masks and smiled a friendly welcome.

'Good evening.' The woman was grey-haired, pleasant and rather plump. 'The lobster is delicious tonight.'

'Thanks.' Henry was careful to keep his eyes up.

'New, aren't you?' the man asked.

'Just got here this afternoon.'

162

'You're probably still a little self-conscious but you'll get over it rather quickly. By the way, I'm George and my wife is Tettle – I call her Tet.'

'Bart and Gloria. We're from New York.'

'Did you notice George giving me the once-over?' Gloria asked, as Henry opened the door for her. 'He may have grey hair but he sure didn't miss anything.'

From the path the other two had taken toward one of the cottages, their voices floated back through the evening twilight.

'I know I've seen those two somewhere,' said Tet.

'That girl certainly looks familiar,' said George. 'Wouldn't it be something if they turned out to be celebrities?'

The dining room was bright, cheery and crowded. When the door started to close behind them, a loud squeak came from the automatic closer and, as if this were a signal, the sound of voices that had filled the room was suddenly stilled. Henry was quite certain every head in the room was turned towards them in one common movement and had to fight against a strong urge to flee. Gloria, however, seemed unaffected by the sudden scrutiny of perhaps fifty people, so Henry rigidly controlled both impulses and tried to look as nonchalant as if he were waiting for the maitre d'hôtel at the Four Seasons.

'Hey, Gloria!' A tall young man at one of the tables beckoned to them. 'We've saved places for you.'

'That's Bob and Lois,' said Gloria. 'Want to join them?'

'Why not?'

The chatter that had filled the room when they entered was resumed, as they made their way to the table where a tall, blonde young man – looking as Gloria had said like a Greek god – was sitting with a small brunette. Henry was quite certain the gaze of at least half of the people in the room were directed exactly at him, but his own eyes were drawn by some force he didn't understand toward a gorgeous red-head, who rose suddenly from a table where she'd been sitting with a half dozen other Springhaven patients, and moved toward the door leading outside.

She was masked and wore dark glasses, but something about her carriage and the exciting loveliness of her body and hair reminded him of Selena. The reminder was only momentary, however, for, as the red-head moved toward the door, he saw

163

that she lacked the strawberry birthmark Selena had said was an inherited family trait.

'Lois, Bob, this is Bart,' said Gloria, bringing Henry's attention back to those at the table.

Bob shook hands enthusiastically and Lois nodded pleasantly. As Gloria had said, Henry noted, Lois was indeed a pocket edition of Venus. Hardly five feet tall, her hair was raven black and everything Henry could see about her reminded him of some exquisite figurine modelled by a master sculptor.

'I don't drink but Lois was having a cocktail,' said Bob when they were seated. 'Can I get something for you, too?'

'We had a couple of drinks in my room.' Henry managed to smile. 'To shore up my courage so I could come over here.'

'You don't have any reason to be ashamed,' said Lois.

'Likewise, I'm sure,' said Henry and was rewarded with a smile.

'And Gloria certainly doesn't need to take a back seat to anybody either,' said Bob enthusiastically.

Henry could see why Gloria had said their marriage was probably beyond repair for Bob was obviously a big friendly animal with a natural prejudice against monogamy.

A waitress, identifiable from others in the room by the fact that she carried a tray and wore a perky little cap on her hair and a small apron, appeared and took their order for the lobster, which Lois and Bob were also having.

'Have you two been here long?' Henry asked, while they were eating their salads.

'A week,' said Bob.

'Do you like it?'

'When we first got here we were sort of self-conscious like you are tonight,' said Bob. 'But as soon as you learn the ropes, you'll discover this place can really swing.'

'*If* you want it to,' said Lois. 'Bob's managed to make out with a different girl every night since we came.'

'Is that part of the therapy programme?' Henry asked and the Greek god guffawed.

'What you do here in the day-time is called therapy, but at night it's called fun,' he explained. 'This is really a swinging place, Bart my boy.'

Henry looked at Gloria who shrugged, an action that made

Bob's eyes bug. He knew she was thinking the same thing he was – that this was the wrong place for anybody with his symptoms.

'I'm in public relations with Lois's father's plastic firm in Weehawken,' Bob confided. 'Mind telling me what you do, Bart?'

Henry hesitated only momentarily. 'You might say I'm an historian.'

'You mean you make history.'

Henry found himself laughing for the first time since he'd come to Springhaven.

'Bart's one of the history-makingest fellows you ever saw,' said Gloria.

'I only write about it,' Henry explained.

'History books?'

'You might say that.'

'I guess somebody has to write 'em,' said Bob. 'I was on a football scholarship at Rutgers, so I didn't get to study much history.'

'Or anything else,' said Lois. 'Bob's strong suit is making people happy, especially women, and he's very good at it.' Oddly enough, there seemed to be no anger in her voice and she even put her hand on her husband's shoulder in an affectionate gesture.

The lobster came then and was excellent, as was the baked potato, tender tips of asparagus wrapped in thin blankets of ham and baked with sauce Mornay, plus an excellent Chablis. Henry found that he had more appetite than he'd had in days, while Gloria attacked her dinner with obvious relish. Lois only toyed with her food but Bob ate with gusto.

'This sure beats the training table,' he said when he finally pushed his empty plate away. 'Take much interest in athletics, Bart?'

'Only as a spectator. I run in Central Park in good weather and try to work out at the Y twice a week.'

'Great place, the Y. Only one thing wrong with it – no women.'

'Looks like you've been going to the wrong Y,' said Gloria.

Bob shouted with laughter, then sobered. 'Mind if I ask what's with you two?'

'I don't quite understand,' said Henry.

'I mean are you married – or going to be?'

'Gloria's my secretary,' Henry explained. 'We're quite fond of each other but not the way you mean.'

'How do you manage to keep it that way?' Lois asked. 'I mean without things getting all fouled up.'

'Bart and I work together and, when we feel like it, we have sex together,' Gloria explained. 'But we each live our own lives separately.'

'Sounds like a good arrangement,' said Bob.

'Then you don't intend to get married?' Lois persisted.

'No,' said Gloria. 'Bart's in love with someone else.'

'What about you?' Bob asked Gloria.

'I'm very happy the way things are,' she said with a shrug. 'Being married might spoil what Bart and I already have.'

'Mind telling me why?' Lois asked and Henry could see that the question wasn't simply a casual one.

'If we were married, I guess either one of us might get to feel he or she owed something to the other,' Gloria explained. 'Then we wouldn't be free to be individuals any more.'

'That doesn't sound like a very permanent relationship,' Lois observed doubtfully.

'If Bart gets tired of having me as his secretary, he can just fire me,' Gloria explained. 'And if I'm not happy with him, I can quit.'

'Like having your cake and eating it, too,' said Bob. 'Sounds wonderful.'

'It certainly is an unusual relationship,' Lois conceded. 'But then you must be unusual people.'

Bob poured the rest of the wine evenly between the four glasses and lifted his own. 'To Bart and Gloria and Bob and Lois,' he said. 'Like in that movie, may we always be friends.'

They clinked glasses and drank.

'Feel up to a game of ping-pong, Gloria?' Bob asked as they were leaving the table after dinner.

'Sure. Don't you want to play, Lois?'

Lois smiled. 'Athletics are for athletes. What do you say we go for a walk, Bart? The moon should be out by now.'

iv

'Gloria described you as a "pocket Venus" when she came back from the pool,' Henry told Lois as they crossed the porch and descended the steps to a path leading down through the woods. 'I must say I agree. What do you weigh?'

'One hundred and ten without my sandals. I'm more solid than you might expect.'

'If I were Bob I wouldn't be hunting a different girl every night.'

'You're sweet, Bart,' she said and moved closer to him. 'It's chilly out here; put your arm around me.'

Henry obeyed and found the contact pleasant, if not stimulating. The top of Lois's head came just level with his chin and, when she looked up at him, he found it easy to kiss her. But though her lips were soft and warm and the pressure of her body against his own far from unpleasant, he felt no urge to go farther – and was sorry for he was pretty sure he would have met little, if any, resistance.

'Would you care for a drink?' he asked. 'I've got some excellent bourbon in my room.'

'That sounds like a good idea,' she said. 'Bob doesn't drink; he thinks it stunts his power. And I don't like to drink alone.'

It was warm in Henry's room and he flicked on the TV before pouring a drink.

'It took me a while at dinner to figure out who you are,' Lois told him, when he handed her the glass.

Henry almost dropped his own. 'What did I do wrong?'

'Nothing. It was when you told Bob you were an historian. I read several of your novels when I was in college and one of them had your picture on the jacket.'

'In that case I might as well take off the mask.'

He did and Lois nodded. 'I like you better without it,' she said. 'Bob took his off the afternoon we came here when we stripped for the first time. He's pretty proud of his body.'

'With good reason. Gloria described him to me when she came from the pool this afternoon as a Greek god.'

'He has Zeus' penchant for making love to beautiful women, too,' said Lois.

167

'Don't you mind?'

'I did – and still do, a little; that's really why we came here. With Bob, making love is something like kleptomania – he can't keep from doing it every time he gets the opportunity.'

'I had the same experience until recently,' Henry confessed. 'But I still don't see how he could neglect *you*.'

'He doesn't. Our troubles don't come from that.'

'What then?'

'I guess I'm old-fashioned – '

Henry laughed. 'Nobody could say that to see us now.'

'The trouble was I felt like I ought to have a monopoly,' Lois explained. 'But Bob feels like he's God's gift to women – '

'I know how that is,' said Henry, then added, 'Or, rather, *was*.'

'Was?'

Henry debated how to make the admission that seemed indicated and finally confessed: 'Wilhelmina Dillingham compared me to "Casey at the Bat". You remember the poem, don't you?'

'I think so.'

'Casey struck out at the crucial moment – and so did I.'

'And you're at Springhaven seeking a cure?' Her eyes were warm and sympathetic as was her voice. To Henry she seemed to have developed an aura, setting off her small but extremely symmetrical perfection as if she were a lovely painting in a frame. Nevertheless, he felt no other impulse than simply to enjoy talking and looking at her.

'Maybe we'd better have another drink,' said Lois. 'Have you tried the pool?'

'No. But I'd like to.'

'We'd better take the drinks with us while we can still walk. Take your robe, though; it can be really cool when you come out of the water, and you'd better put your wallet into the pocket. Horace says there have been some thefts here, he thinks by some of the employees.'

It was almost midnight and Henry was lying on the bed watching the late TV news, when Gloria came in from her room looking a little the worse for wear.

'How was the ping-pong?' he asked.

'It was all right but got a little monotonous after a while.'

168

'You seemed interested enough when Bob suggested the game.'

'I was curious to see how he operated. Besides, I could see that you were attracted to Lois, so I tried to keep Bob out of the picture for a while and let you have room to play a few games yourself. Any luck?'

'Casey didn't even lift the bat.'

'Too bad,' said Gloria. 'The main reason I went with Bob was because I could see that Lois was beginning to get the hots for you – as who wouldn't.'

'Thanks for the sacrifice,' Henry told her. 'I'm sorry it was to no avail.'

'Oh, it wasn't that rough. Bob was fullback at Rutgers, but I used to play tag football with the boys in our block when I was a girl. Got to be a pretty good pass receiver, too, if I do say so myself.'

V

Horace Aiken leaned back in the chair behind his desk and tapped his knuckles gently with a ballpoint pen. Henry had just finished giving his life history, including the non-adventure of last evening.

'Lois is a very lovely young woman,' said Aiken. 'You say there was no desire at all on your part?'

'Plenty of desire but nothing happened.'

'Too bad; a healthy bout of love-making would have been good for both of you. When Bob and Lois came here a week ago, she was about ready to divorce him. You see, Lois grew up in a very narrow family and she's never really learned to shed her inhibitions the way we made her shed her clothes. As a result, she hasn't learned yet to communicate easily with others.'

'Including Bob?'

Aiken nodded. 'As you gathered, he's an intellectual light-weight – went through Rutgers on a football scholarship. He's an expert at the purely physical side of love-making but Lois expected more when she married him. The truth is that it simply

169

isn't there and, when Bob kept playing the field, she tried to hem him in with a lot of rules.'

'I imagine that would be like trying to turn Old Faithful into a drinking fountain.'

'Just about,' Aiken conceded. 'Lois's defences were so fragile at first that we had to handle her very gently, but she's beginning to see that she's actually better off than most women.'

'How did you manage that?'

'By showing her that Bob should be regarded simply as a love-making machine to be put to work for her needs whenever the oestrous cycle demands his services. The other part of her nature, requiring communication with others upon a much higher plane, can now be developed independently of Bob. Once she got to see that, she began to realize that she could actually have the best of two worlds and not feel guilty about either one – something perhaps one woman in a thousand ever achieves in marriage.'

'Do you think you've taught her that?'

'Frankly, I'm not as sure this morning as I was yesterday.'

'Why?'

'You came yesterday afternoon, remember?'

'Why would my being here make any difference to Lois?'

'Because you're exactly what she – and millions of other women – dream of, a man who can satisfy both the physical and the intellectual sides of their nature. In fact, I'd be willing to wager that therein lies much of your really fabulous success as the Lochinvar of Megalopolis.'

'You're giving me too much credit, Horace.'

'I don't think so, particularly after the talk I had with Gloria last night.'

'Where was that?'

'At the pool. She was on her way back to the cottage from an evening with Bob and stopped to soak a while. I often lie in the pool late at night to think and we had a nice chat.'

'Gloria's a little prejudiced in my favour,' Henry warned.

'Of course she is. But for you, she'd still be no more than a model – as she called herself then.'

'And I'd probably never have become a sex symbol without her, so I guess we do owe each other a lot.'

'Anyway, I'd appreciate it if you would avoid Lois as much

as you can,' Aiken told him. 'I don't want her comparing you to her husband too much at this stage of the game, or we might lose everything we've gained with her.'

'Where does that leave me?'

'Where you were – or maybe not. Have you stopped to think what an important part you've played in several women's lives lately?'

'Only a little,' Henry admitted.

'You're far too modest where your own accomplishments are concerned then. After all, you are Pygmalion to Gloria's Galatea and she's more proud of it than anything else in her life. Besides that, from what you say, you brought Carling Hartsfield and his wife back together again.'

'And got attacked for my pains, to say nothing of losing my manhood – to use the vernacular.'

'I don't think the two are really connected,' said Aiken.

'What!' Henry looked at the psychologist in astonishment.

'Just what I said. The loss of your manhood, is probably not connected with the attack by the cat.'

'But Dr Schwartz – '

'Isadore is a very smart psychiatrist and an old friend. He sent me a summary of your case; it arrived the day before you did. You see, Henry, psychiatrists don't often have emergencies like yours, where something has to be done in a hurry. They like to move rather slowly, while guiding the patient into discovering for himself the mechanism that produces the symptoms. In your case, Schwartz had to improvise and the cat theory seemed to be one you'd accept – '

'Especially with my tail hurting like crazy.'

'Exactly. Schwartz's spur-of-the-moment diagnosis was enough to convince you that you need to be treated. After all, nothing comes as a greater shock to a young man than to find out he can't perform in the sack. My guess would be that the unconscious part of your psyche – '

'The Id?'

'Some call it that, though I like to think of it as the primitive man inside us all. Cave men had no instinct for monogamy and courtship was practically unknown. Some of those same instincts survive in the masculine ego, so the Id – as some call it – can

171

see no reason to settle for one woman when the world is full of them.'

'By those standards, Bart Bartlemy was certainly a primitive.'

'Exactly, which accounts somewhat for his tremendous appeal to women – plus, of course, his remarkable physique.'

'In more ways than one as I can testify.'

Horace Aiken smiled. 'So can practically everybody at Springhaven by now; your physical accoutrements are the talk of the hour. Nevertheless, civilization has decreed that a man shall cling to but one woman – at least until they're divorced, which isn't very long in nearly half of the marriages today. In the early stages of courtship, the female flatters the male by making him believe he has selected her from all the rest, while leaving him with the conviction that, if he really wanted to, he could have a lot of others.'

'Which happens to be true.'

'In your case certainly,' the psychologist agreed. 'The trouble comes when a female has convinced the particular male *she* has selected that he wants her alone. Then the primitive man in the courting male sometimes realizes he has been sold down the river and decides to do something to ward off disaster. Your fabulous success as a lover, since the transplant, proves that in spite of the fact that you're a scholar and also undeniably a gentleman – qualities that appear to have been largely absent in the case of your unfortunate twin – your primitive unconscious is also exceptionally strong.'

'Either that, or more likely the parts I received from Bart have taken over and are running my life, like they seem to have run his.'

'I don't accept that,' said Aiken.

'Then how do you explain what's been happening?'

'Off the cuff, I'll say that before the accident, you were a man of strong impulses where women are concerned, who sublimated them into your writing – and very successfully, too.'

'Authors of romantic fiction are largely describing their own fantasies,' Henry agreed.

'Other writers have told me the same thing. In your case, through sublimation, you managed to convince yourself you wanted only Miss McGuire but then the accident happened. Your primitive self suddenly found itself capable of feats of sexual conquest it probably never even dreamed of accomplishing, with the result that your conscience – Freud called it the Super Ego – was almost overwhelmed.'

'But not quite.'

'Exactly. The Super Ego led you to try various methods of control with tranquillizers, isolating yourself or whatever. All of them failed, though, according to the story you just told me, so it finally used the ultimate weapon, a block between your emotions and the transplant.'

'You may be right,' Henry conceded. 'How long do you think it can hold out?'

'I can't tell,' Aiken admitted. 'For the past month or so your reaction to every woman you've seen has been to make her a conquest. And since you had temporarily convinced your Super Ego that it couldn't prevent the primitive man in you from having his own way, you've been on what might be called a rampage. Now, though, with your Super Ego riding herd, I'd say the simplest way to regain the correct balance between the two is to develop non-sexual relationships.'

'Is that possible – with women, I mean?'

'Here at Springhaven we think it can often be accomplished through Encounter Therapy, by discovering things in other people you never realized were there. Through that discovery, you're able to find out more about yourself.'

'I hope you're right,' said Henry doubtfully. 'But don't underestimate the strength of Bart Bartlemy's spirit.'

'Bartlemy's spirit is wherever it went the minute his brainwaves ceased,' said Aiken. 'It's Henry Walters' spirit – or rather his conflicting spirit – we have to deal with. Give us a chance and I'm sure we'll have you finishing your book, with Bart winning Leonora – '

'Wait a minute,' said Henry. 'Was that name in Dr Schwartz's summary?'

'Yes, but Gloria told me about Leonora last night.'

'And the fact that Selena and Leonora are the same?'

'Yes.'

'I don't quite understand,' said Henry. 'How would Dr Schwartz have known more about Selena McGuire that what I had told him?'

Horace Aiken looked at Henry in surprise. 'Didn't you know she had been a patient of Dr Schwartz's?'

'Selena did send me to him in the first place, so I suppose I should have made the connection. But I really didn't think about it.'

'Didn't she ever tell you about Springhaven?'

'You mean she's already been here, walking around naked – '

'You're naked, aren't you Henry?'

'Yes, but – '

'And Gloria?'

'Well – yes.'

'Did you see anything wrong about Lois's being nude?'

'No, but I still can't believe it of Selena.'

'I hope I'm not violating a confidence when I tell you that Miss McGuire was here several years ago. Until then, she had been something of a shrinking violet, I gather, working as a senior reader for Bennett Press and not getting anywhere. When Schwartz referred her to us, she was so inhibited at first that she wore a mask for three days before she would take it off.'

'You've always got unattached men around here, haven't you?' said Henry.

'Yes.'

'Did she – I mean – '

'I'm pretty sure the answer is no, though I don't ride herd on our guests after dark. Anyway, once we got Miss McGuire to shed her clothing and the mask, she made rapid progress.'

'I remember now that she went on a vacation about that time and came back a different person. I used to see her around the Bennett office before but she would hardly even speak to me. When she came back she was assured, even aggressive and the next thing I knew, she was my editor.'

'The way I look at it,' said Horace Aiken, 'when you discovered that you were near the end of the book and, in all probability, that you would stop being Bart in your fantasies and become yourself again and marry Selena, the primitive Henry Walters – '

'That's Bart. He's like Bob – takes his women where he finds them.'

'All right, if you insist. Bart took control and shut down the flow of nervous energy to the psycho-sexual apparatus.'

'Wasn't that like cutting off his nose to spite his face?'

'The Bart inside us all isn't very logical,' Horace Aiken conceded. 'What we try to do here is to help our visitors strip the covering off their primitive selves the way they do their clothing. Then once they see themselves for what they are, they can learn to communicate with others at both the primitive and the conventional levels.'

'Which one wins?'

'The ideal is a mixture of both, but I like to see people get back to a fair proportion of the primitive while they're here. That way they have a lot less trouble later.'

'So what'll I do?' Henry asked.

'You've already taken a giant step by removing your clothing. The only worry I have now is what will happen when somebody recognizes you and my female guests in particular learn your identity.'

'One has already – Lois.'

'Then the cat's probably out of the bag and you're liable to be eaten alive – like the Bacchae used to eat the males sacrificed during the festival of Dionysus in ancient Greece,' Horace Aiken said with a smile.

'That prospect might be pleasant with a red-head I saw briefly in the dining room last night. She was wearing a mask and dark glasses but still looked familiar. Actually, for a moment I thought she might be Selena but then I discovered that she didn't have a telltale birthmark in a very strategic place like Selena has. Mind telling me who – '

'Sorry,' said Horace firmly. 'I must preserve the identity of all my guests, just as I will protect yours.'

'I'll have to scout around a bit then,' said Henry. 'I'd certainly like to see more of her – or at least what's behind the mask.'

'You're improving already,' Horace assured him.

The door of the office opened and Jacque Broders came in. 'I'm about to hold a session in the Tank,' she said. 'You have Bart down for a tentative this morning, Horace.'

'We just finished this discussion,' said the director. 'Are you ready to start your therapy programme, Bart?'

'Do I have to?'

175

'No. Everybody's a free agent here, but I strongly advise you to take part in all our programmes.'

'Okay,' said Henry and followed Jacque from the office.

vi

'What's this "Tank" we're going to?' Henry asked as he and Jacque left the lodge and followed a winding path toward a rather utilitarian looking building visible through the trees.

'It's one of the two main activities here at Springhaven,' Jacque said as he held a branch aside for her to pass.

'I take it that the other building over there – the one without a roof – is the "Womb Pool"?'

'Yes. Some of our guests – '

'I notice you never refer to us as patients.'

'Because you really aren't, at least not in the sense that the word is usually used.'

'Come again?'

'Horace has a PhD in Psychology and I have a Masters but we don't claim to treat the mentally ill, only to help people help themselves. Some of our guests refer to the Tank as the "black hole", but it's not really that bad.'

'You said you had a Masters; did you come to work here right after you graduated?'

'Not for several years. Like a lot of students at Berkley, I didn't have much purpose except what I thought was my own pleasure. I lived in Haight-Ashbury for a while and was tripping regularly when I wasn't smoking pot. Even shot horse occasionally until I almost died from an OD. They straightened me out at Synanon, and when Horace learned I was there, he came out and brought me back here with him.'

'How did they go about curing you at Synanon?'

'I didn't say cure. If I ever got into an emotional situation serious enough to threaten my defences, I might go back on drugs. What they did at Synanon was teach me to act as if I didn't need the drug. Once I learned to do that, I got to where I really didn't need it, as long as I was able to cope. Horace has helped me a great deal there.'

176

'Is that what he plans to do for me?' Henry asked. 'Teach me I don't need sex?'

Jacque Broders smiled. 'Is that what you want?'

'My God! No!'

'Then we'll just let nature take its course. It's really able to take care of itself to a surprising degree, you know.'

They had reached the dark building Henry had noticed through the trees and he saw now that it was windowless. Jacque opened the door and they went inside. The entire building was painted black inside, as was the tank itself, a circular walled excavation that appeared to be about ten feet deep.

A dozen people were standing around inside the building in the light of four bulbs set into the wall. Half of them were wearing masks, as Henry had been since yesterday afternoon. Among the latter was the red-haired young woman he'd noticed in the dining room last night. Looking at her again, Henry was again impressed with the remarkable likeness of her body to Selena's but when he moved a little so he could see her better, he was able to determine that she did not possess the identifying birthmark Selena had once said she had inherited as a family trait.

'Good morning,' said Jacque to the group. 'For the next two hours you will all remain in the tank, unless an emergency arises. If it should, you have only to call out to me and I will have the ladder brought down and will help you out. The darkness will be absolute and we request that you remain silent, communicating only with other senses. At first you might find it quite oppressing, even frightening, but stay with it and I think you'll learn something about yourself.'

'Once over with feeling?' said Bob but not many laughed.

'When the lights go out, I want each of you to lie on the floor of the tank,' Jacque continued. 'At first, pretend that you want to be alone, until you can't stand it any longer. Then start to move until you touch another person but be sure to keep silent at all times unless there's an emergency.'

Jacque descended the steps and at the foot waited for the others to climb down one by one. Henry was among the first to descend, acutely conscious of what his naked lower half must look like to those already on the bottom. The red-head was among the last and while waiting for the other guests to reach the floor of the tank, he tried to work his way toward her unobtrusively. When all were on the floor of the Tank, Jacque Broders pressed a button on a small control panel and the ladder rose smoothly, like an airplane landing stairway, and was folded up on the rim of the Tank above them quite out of reach.

'Each of you pick out your own spot,' Jacque instructed them. 'Get as close to the floor and the wall as you can and crouch in the foetal position, staying there until you feel you must move.'

They all looked pretty silly, Henry thought as he crouched against the side and bottom of the Tank, curling himself up into a ball so as to fit into as small an area as possible. When Jacque pressed another button the Tank was suddenly pitch black. One woman screamed and a man cursed under his breath, but there was no other sound except breathing and the soft shuffle of bodies against the plastic material lining the Tank.

As he had been instructed, Henry tried to shut everything out of his mind except the blackness and after a few moments, felt a pleasant sort of languor begin to envelope him. Although he could feel the pressure of the Tank wall and floor against his body, he seemed to be growing steadily more weightless, as if suspended in space. It was an infinitely pleasurable sensation and, pleased by the lessening of the anxiety that had been with him for so long, he found his spirits rising until he felt like shouting aloud that he was free. At the same time, he experienced a sensation almost as if he were floating upward, out of the tank and through the roof into an endless dark void, where no stimuli could reach him, no sense of contact with anything save his own body. Gently he touched himself here and there, almost surprised to find that he was still a corporeal entity.

When the primordial fear began to assert itself after a while, Henry couldn't understand at first what was happening, beyond the first anxiety of claustrophobia anyone felt at being closed in. The sense of separation from people and the world had been infinitely pleasurable at first; now it was replaced by something else, an actual fear of being alone and without contact with another person. As the fear rose, he fought against the need to touch another to reassure himself that somehow all of them, save himself, had not been spirited away leaving him to face eternity alone. Finally, he could stand the rising anxiety no

178

longer and had to reassure himself he wasn't the only person in the tank.

Moving slowly, crawling on the floor and pushing always against the wall, so he would have some contact with reality, he began to follow the curving wall of the tank. He had gone perhaps six feet, though it seemed many miles, when his fingers touched human flesh and he heard a quick gasp – feminine – in the darkness. Not sure just what he should do, he waited until a hand tentatively touched his shoulder and went on to explore his face. At the same time the body of the woman, drawn, he sensed by the same anxiety he was experiencing, moved closer to his own.

Now his exploring fingers outlined the unmistakable contours of her breasts, the nipples turgid beneath his fingers, the skin of the aureole around them becoming pebble-grained and erect to his touch. Slowly, too, the warm body he was touching, faintly fragrant with perfume, accustomed itself to his own until all the skin surface that could be brought together was touching, as they lay there in the warm darkness.

He had no idea who his companion might be, nor wanted to know. It was enough to be certain he was not alone in the universe, that this other person had experienced the same desperate loneliness which had gripped him and that the same loneliness was now assuaged for her through contact with another person, just as it was for him.

Strangely, there was no element of sexual desire in the great affection he felt for this unnamed other person who shared his world and the mutual freedom from fear they had obtained through each other's presence. Nor did the lack of any impulse to sexual union trouble him, for an integral part of this mutual communion of the mind seemed to be the certainty that an equally mutual communion of their bodies, far exceeding in pleasure any casual sexual encounter, was possible whenever both should come to desire it.

He was content to lie there, while a flood of sensations flowed from her body into his through the contact points where their surfaces met, and an equal though opposite current flowed from his body to hers. Nor was the unnamed – though no longer strange – woman in his embrace really an individual to his newly inspired touch. Rather she was a symbol of all mankind,

179

animate and inanimate, with their exploring embrace only a physical expression of the wish, normal he was sure to all mankind, to share the small world in which they both found themselves.

The happy communion was broken by the sudden intense glare of a photographer's flash bulb. Blinded momentarily like the rest, Henry wasn't even able to identify the partner with whom he had shared what he knew was an almost divine communion before guilt and the fear of what others would think tore them apart.

'Horace and I beg your forgiveness for startling you like that.' Jacque's voice sounded disembodied coming from the darkness. 'We need the photographs for our records and for the seminar after lunch. The lights will go on gradually in the next few minutes, so I would suggest that, if any of you find yourself in what might be a compromising position, you effect a change before I turn on the lights.'

'Damn!' A masculine voice Henry recognized as Bob's spoke from the darkness. 'Somebody's always messin' up my playhouse.'

The laughter that followed was overloud, a natural reaction, Henry sensed, to the experience they had all shared. People were moving about in the darkness now, too, laughing when they bumped into each other. When the lights went up Henry could gain no idea of who, among the dozen or more women in the Tank, had shared his terror and his outpouring of completely asexual love at finding themselves sharing a private world of their own. But he did know that it was one of the most moving experiences he'd ever shared, whether or not he'd ever know the identity of his companion. Or was actually helped by the experience in solving his particular problem.

vii

When Henry came into the dining room for lunch, he saw Gloria at a table for two in the corner. She was with a tall, athletic appearing man with the clean-cut features of an aristocrat. He wore his mask but Gloria had discarded hers almost from the first, and Henry judged from the greying hair of his secretary's companion that he was in his sixties – probably a man of prominence.

Henry looked for the red-haired girl, convinced that it had been she who had lain in his arms in the darkness, but she was nowhere to be seen. Moving to a small table he sat by himself, until Jacque Broders came into the dining room and crossed over to where he was sitting.

'Mind if I join you?' she asked.

'Please do.'

'How did it go in the Tank?'

'It was a real experience.'

'More than you expected?'

'Much deeper, at least. I'm not normally claustrophobic, but when you cut off those lights, I felt – '

'As if the whole world had deserted you?'

'Why, yes,' he said. 'Did it affect you that way the first time?'

She nodded. 'Except that I know where my difficulty came from. When I was a little girl, we used to go to Red Bank on the Jersey coast in the summer.'

'I've been there; worked as a waiter in an ocean-front boarding house one summer after my freshman year in college.'

'We had an old house on the shore; the kind they built at beach resorts seventy or seventy-five or so years ago. It was three storeys high and the outside was covered with cypress shingles. There was one spot under the stairway between the second and third floor – '

'I never could understand why that play was titled "*The Dark at the Top of the Stairs*",' said Henry. 'Everybody knows the dark place is always behind the bottom part of the steps.'

'I had to pass that dark spot every night when I went to bed and I always felt as if a hand was reaching up to grab me,' Jacque continued. 'Once an older cousin of mine stood there and really did grab me. I fainted and, when I came to, he had my clothes off. I didn't let a boy touch me for two years after that.'

'Did you relive that experience when you first went into the Tank?'

'In every detail and it taught me a lot about what was troubling me then. What did you feel?'

181

'Just an overpowering need to touch someone else and reassure myself that I wasn't really alone in the world.' Henry laughed a little self-consciously. 'That was a woman; I haven't the least idea who but I guess she wanted to be touched. Anyway, we were in close communion.'

'Did you – '

Henry shook his head. 'Frankly, the idea never occured to me. I guess that proves I've struck out for good.'

'My guess would be that it proves you're capable of a very intense feeling for another person – something that goes beyond sex,' said Jacque. 'The reason you aren't the same man you've been writing about any longer is that you've become yourself again, the one who wants to share the whole loving process, not just gain pleasure from the body of another.'

'Horace said much of the same thing. But how will I know? Unless I find the girl I was with in the Tank.'

'I'm sure you'll find her – or someone else. Once you've learned to touch, not just the body but the very soul of another person, you'll find that every encounter starts the current flowing again between you.'

viii

Henry decided not to participate in the after-lunch conference, when those who had been in the Tank that morning told what it meant to them. His own experience, as he had told Jacque Broders, had been on such a lofty plane that, even though words were his tools, he didn't feel like trying to translate what had happened for anyone else. Instead, he went for a long walk, following a path that wound through the woods.

Springhaven, Henry discovered, was in one sense a prison, or at least a large enclosure. The palisade barricade they'd seen stretching on both sides of the lodge, when they arrived the day before, soon gave way to a tall chain link fence that enclosed the whole area, comprising he estimated, perhaps several hundred acres. A stream traversed the property and flowed under the fence at the south boundary to continue its way. When he knelt to drink from it Henry discovered that the water

182

was still quite warm, with a mineral taste that identified it as the overflow from the spring Horace Aiken had mentioned as serving the Womb Pool.

It was pleasantly quiet in the woods and Henry felt more at peace than at any time in weeks – except perhaps during the period of communion with another in the Tank. Whatever the reason, the woods and the stream exerted a markedly soothing effect upon him and it was with some reluctance that he took a path marked by a rustic sign, 'To Lodge' several hours after he entered the woods.

When Henry left the cottage after lunch, he'd called Gloria to tell her he was going for a walk, so he knew she wouldn't be looking for him, In fact, it was pleasant to think that, at least for the moment, he had the woods of Springhaven to himself. As he approached the Lodge again, however, he saw baggage being carried to a small cottage almost hidden in the woods and surmised that an additional guest must have arrived.

Both rooms of their cottage were empty, so Henry deduced that Gloria was participating in some of the manifold activities that were a part of the Springhaven programme. Warm from the walk, Henry took a shower and lay down on the bed to watch a soap opera that was working out the tortured lives of its characters on the television screen.

Somehow, he knew, he had to make contact with the woman who had lain in his arms in the darkness of the Tank that morning, sharing with him a communion of spirit more intimate than any he'd ever known in the sexual embrace. And though it troubled him somewhat that, if he found her again, he'd be unfaithful to Selena, what he felt toward the girl of mystery was a greater sharing than even his love for Selena had ever enabled him to experience. Somehow he knew he must achieve once again at least that sense of communion, for in it, he was sure, lay the answer to the problem that had brought him to Springhaven.

ix

Gloria woke Henry before dinner, when she came into his room with the usual double bourbons and handed him one.

183

'Where were you this afternoon?' she asked, sitting on the side of the bed.

'I went for a walk in the woods.'

'Alone?'

'Yes. I had to think some things out.'

'Like how you could be getting the hots for that red-head and still be in love with Leonora – I mean Selena?'

Henry was so startled, he almost dropped his glass. 'Whatever gave you that idea?'

'At the end of those sessions in the Tank, Jacque takes a flash picture.'

'I remember. It damn near scared me out of my skin.'

'Did you know she shows the pictures with a projector when they hold what the calls a *post mortem* in the afternoon?'

'She told me that at lunch. Maybe that's why I skipped the sessions. Were you there?'

'It's just for the people who took part, but Bob was there and told me all about it. From what he said, you and the red-head were so close, you could have been mistaken for Siamese twins.'

'That's the whole idea here – touching,' Henry reminded her.

'You don't have to tell me *that*,' said Gloria. 'Have you been in the Womb Pool yet?'

'No.'

'You ought to try it. Why don't we go there after it gets dark, say around eight thirty.'

The bourbon was beginning to lift Henry's spirits once more. 'Sounds like a good idea,' he agreed.

X

Henry didn't see the red-head in the dining room at dinner either and briefly considered going to the office to ask whether she might have left Springhaven but gave up the idea. The afternoon walk and his talk with Jacque at lunch hadn't really solved anything, however, and he was sitting in his bedroom after dinner and after darkness had fallen outside, looking at a rerun on TV when Gloria came in. She was carrying a towel

184

and the terrycloth robe that hung in each closet for use, if desired, when the evening was cool.

'It's almost nine,' she said. 'Let's go to the Womb Pool.'

'I don't know – '

'Come on, boss.' Taking his own robe from the closet, she went into the bath and came out with a towel. 'You'll never have any fun sitting here moping. Want another drink before we go?'

'I don't think so.'

'Okay, we'll save it for later. That warm water certainly does make you thirsty.'

As they were leaving the cottage Henry suddenly remembered the admonition not to leave valuables there and turned back. 'I'd better take my wallet,' he said. 'Somebody said there's been a little occasional pilfering going on around here.'

He came out a moment later with the wallet in the pocket of the robe and they left the cottage and took the curving path leading to the hot spring. The pool was in a little clearing surrounded by pines. And since the night was warm, the glass doors in the wall surrounding it were open. A full moon shone down into the enclosure but the only sounds to be heard, except voices and music in the distance, were the faint rustle of a breeze in the pines and the soft rush of water from the boil that went into the pool, where a subterranean stream burst from the rock. No one else was in the water, however, and except for the boil, the surface was like dark molten glass.

'What do you know? I forgot to bring a bathing cap,' said Gloria when they paused at the edge of the pool. 'Back in a minute.' She was off before Henry could remind her that she'd never worn a cap in the pool before to his knowledge.

Dropping the robe and towel at the edge of the pool and slipping his feet out of his sandals, Henry descended the ladder and entered the water. It was warm, yet set his skin tingling, a product, he surmised of its high mineral content. The ladder was at the shallow end near where the overflow formed the brook he had followed for a while that afternoon until it went under the fence around Springhaven and disappeared in the woods.

There was a springboard at the deep end and Henry swam slowly to it, the strokes requiring little effort since the mineral content of the water added a buoyancy to his body strangely like what he had heard described as weightlessness. At the deep end, he turned on his back, floating lazily and moving his hands gently, causing ripples in the dark surface. When he closed his eyes, shutting out the light of the moon, he could imagine he was floating in a dark and formless void, without weight and almost without substance, the centre of a private universe all his own.

The pleasure was so great that he was loath to open his eyes and re-establish contact with reality. Then, as he floated there, he seemed to hear a voice, like a whisper intended for his ears alone, a woman's voice that was familiar, yet could not be.

'Bart,' she said. 'Bart, darling, it's Leonora.'

Certain that his own senses were betraying him and almost afraid to open his eyes, Henry floated there until the voice came again, this time above him. Opening his eyes then, he saw the lovely body of a woman silhouetted upon the springboard in the moonlight that was so bright it almost seemed like a spotlight in itself. His gaze travelled upward along limbs he was sure the goddess Diana herself would have envied, past loins and a torso that could have inspired the poet in King Solomon himself and on to the features of his beloved.

Only a moment did she remain poised there, then her body arched above him in a graceful dive. Turning quickly, he dived to meet her beneath the surface and their bodies strained together in a communion even more ardent than it had been that morning in the Tank. Her lips, when he found them, were bitter with the minerals of the water but, when they parted beneath his own, the warm cavity of her mouth was like the 'best wine' in the 'Song of Solomon'.

'I knew you looked familiar when I saw you in the dining room tonight,' said Henry – for it was indeed Selena. 'But you didn't have that birthmark on your – '

'The damn thing was irritated by that chastity belt I wore at the ball, so I had my gynaecologist remove it,' she explained.

When Henry sought to kiss her again, Selena pushed him away gently. 'I've got a confession to make,' she said. 'After this morning when you held me in the Tank, I realized that I'd been wrong about a lot of things so I went to see Gloria this afternoon. She set me straight about the subway accident and everything that's happened since – and promised to bring you to the pool tonight. Can you ever forgive me?'

His answer was to draw her close and the sudden flame of desire engulfing his own body told him the answer to the question that had brought him to Springhaven. Gripped by the fierce urgency of his now thoroughly aroused body he drew Selena toward the side of the pool, unwilling to break contact even for a minute. Reaching up he touched the ladder at the deep end and gently disengaged himself from Selena's embrace as he started to lift himself from the pool preparatory to swinging her up, too. His fingertips touched human flesh, however, and thinking Gloria had returned with the bathing cap she'd gone to get, he said quickly, 'Go back, Gloria, I've found Leonora.'

It was Selena who first realized that the other person wasn't Gloria and the stillness of the air was torn when she cried: 'Henry! It's the man who tried to kill me in the subway!'

Henry, too, looked up then, and in the bright moonlight recognized Al, the hood with the scarred face who had muscled him into Gregory Annunzio's car that morning so long ago, it seemed now, before the apartment house. How Big John Fortuna's muscleman had managed to find them Henry couldn't know but there was no doubting the purpose for which Al had been sent – or what Bart would do under the circumstances, now that he had re-discovered both Leonora and his own life force.

xi

For an instant Henry had been shocked into immobility by the knowledge of the hit man's presence at Springhaven and the Womb Pool, but not for long. Lifting himself half out of the water with his left hand gripping the tile edge of the pool, he reached up with the right and seized the other man by the ankle, jerking Al's feet from under him and toppling him into the water.

'Run, Selena!' he cried kicking himself away from the side of the pool toward where Al had disappeared beneath the dark surface of the water.

'Get Horace and whoever else you can.'

Al's head broke water just then and Henry seized him by the hair, shoving him down as he thrashed frantically with both hands. Occupied with trying to keep his struggling assailant submerged, Henry was too busy to see whether Selena had obeyed his command, until his hand touched her body and he realized she was fighting at his side against the invader.

'Save yourself!' he told her but she shook her head, and, when Al broke the surface this time, pulling air into his lungs in a great shuddering gasp, it was Selena who seized his head and thrust him beneath the surface of the water again.

'Come on!' Pulling himself up out of the pool, Henry seized Selena's hand to lift her up, hoping they might gain the safety of the woods surrounding Springhaven before Al could recover from the water he'd swallowed during the forcible dunking. Al passed them both, however, thrashing as fast as both arms and legs could propel him. Reaching the ladder at the shallow end of the pool, he pulled himself from the water and raced along the path toward the cottages as if pursued by the devil himself.

'We've got to get away before he comes back,' Henry told Selena.

'But where? He's between us and the Lodge.'

'Henry! Leonora!' It was Gloria running toward the pool. 'Al's here. I went back to call Big John and tell him he'd better not do anything to you or I'd spill the whole story to Senator Loring.'

'Is that the grey-haired man you were having lunch with today?' said Henry. 'I thought something about him looked familiar.' Loring was chairman of a Senate committee investigating rackets and racketeers and one of the most powerful men in Congress.

'He's a real nice gentleman,' said Gloria. 'We spent part of the afternoon together.'

'What did Big John say?' Henry asked.

'He swears they don't plan to do a thing to you; says it would be like killing the goose that might still lay some golden eggs. But when he told me Al was on the way here, I knew it must be for a hit on you and Selena, so I hung up and came to warn you.'

'Al was just here at the pool,' Henry told her. 'We almost drowned him but he got out and ran toward the cottages.'

The breeze striking Selena's wet body made her shiver and picking up the terry cloth robe she'd dropped before diving into the pool, Henry held it out for her to slip her arms into the sleeves. Gloria was wearing her robe and he quickly pulled on his own as his teeth started to chatter.

'Al must have gone back to get a gun,' said Gloria. 'We've got to get out of here.'

'He'd see us in the lighted area if we go toward the cottages,' said Henry. 'Selena and I will hide in the woods while you warn Horace and Jacque, Gloria. Al's not after you anyway.'

'I got you into this and I'm not going to leave you now,' said Gloria firmly. 'If we leave here, we leave together.'

'Don't be foolish,' Henry told her. 'Al's after Selena and me.'

'What would Bart do in this situation?' Selena startled Henry with the question.

'He'd follow the stream to where it goes under the fence around Springhaven,' Henry answered. 'Then he'd double back outside the fence – I noticed a path there this afternoon when I was walking in the woods.'

'What then?' Gloria asked.

'Bart would try to find a car that had been left unlocked or he'd jump a switch with a piece of wire from the fence and get the hell out of here.'

'What are we waiting for?' said Selena. 'Let's go.'

xii

Tooling along Interstate 87 south of the Tappan Zee Bridge, Gloria was driving the sedan from whose switch they had been fortunate enough to find a set of keys hanging when they finally reached the parking lot at Springhaven. It had taken a couple of hours to follow the warm stream flowing from the Womb Pool to where it emerged from the fenced-in area, crawl beneath the bottom strand of the fence by submerging in the stream itself, and make their way to the woods around the parking lot.

Certain that Al was stalking them somewhere in the darkness, they had waited until the lights went out in the Lodge before making another move and possibly revealing their presence. To avoid thus betraying their plan by starting the engine of the car they'd decided to take, they'd pushed it a hundred yards down the road leading from Springhaven to the highway before starting the engine.

At Gloria's insistence, Henry and Selena had taken the back seat while she drove. The distant towers of Manhattan's skyscrapers were just beginning to take form out of the morning blanket of pollutants, when Gloria spoke over her shoulder without, however, looking back.

'I hate to spoil whatever you two lovebirds have been doing,' she said. 'But could you disentangle yourselves long enough to tell me where to go?'

'My apartment,' said Henry. 'Angus sleeps in and has a passkey so he could let us in. We can get some clothes there and I'll phone Springhaven and tell Horace Aiken what happened so he can fix it with whoever owns this car and have mine brought to the city. I've got some writing to do, if I'm to meet the publication deadline on *Superstud*.'

'Upper Fifth Avenue it is,' said Gloria. 'Go on back to whatever you two were doing – as if I didn't already know.'

The streets were almost deserted at this early morning hour. Only a few trucks were abroad besides the garbage collectors, busy crashing cans against the sidewalk. When Gloria pulled the car to a stop before Henry's apartment, she stretched and yawned.

'Here we are,' she said. 'Let's all go upstairs and get some shut-eye.'

'Why don't we all go to the police station first?' an authoritative voice asked and Henry was startled to see a burly policeman standing on the pavement beside the car.

'What's going on here, officer?' he demanded.

'I don't know what's *been* going on, mister, though from the way you're all dressed I could make a pretty good guess. We've been waiting a couple of hours for you all to show up here driving a stolen car, Mr Walters.'

'But you don't understand – '

'I'm not paid to, that's Justice Peebles's job. You can see him in court at nine o'clock.'

'How about letting us get some clothes from Mr Walters's apartment?' Gloria asked.

'The judge is known to have quite an eye for beauty, miss,' said the policeman. 'I think he'd like to see at least two of you just the way you are.'

'By the way,' the officer added as he was ushering the three of them into the back seat of the prowl car, 'just what are those costumes you're wearing anyway – a new kind of mini-skirt or something? No offence meant, of course, Mr Walters.'

Henry was too tired and too dispirited by this unlooked-for turn of events to speak. To his surprise, Selena answered:

'You might call them togas, officer.'

'Like the Romans used to wear?'

'Yes. And, incidentally, Mr Walters is, without question, the noblest Roman of them all.'

xiii

Condemned men are allowed one telephone call and Henry insisted upon his rights, even though he had to borrow a coin from the arresting officer to make the call. On the third ring, a woman's voice answered: 'Mr Annunzio's office.'

'I'd like to speak to Mr Annunzio,' said Henry.

'This is the answering service, sir. I'll be glad to leave a message for him when he comes in.'

'This is Henry Walters. You'd better put me in touch with Mr Annunzio now.'

'But – '

'No buts,' said Henry. 'I'm calling from the jail and I'm only allowed one call. Tell Mr Annunzio I'll give him two minutes to call me back at this number or I'll blow the whole story sky high.'

After giving the answering service operator the number of the telephone booth in the police station, Henry pushed down the receiver rest and leaned against the telephone so anybody watching outside wouldn't know he wasn't still talking. The telephone rang in less than two minutes and he released the rest.

'Is that you, Annunzio?' he demanded.

'Yes, but – '

'But nothing! Gloria, Selena and I are in jail on a charge of stealing the car we used to escape from that hood Big John Fortuna sent to get us in Springhaven. I want you to get on the phone to Horace Aiken and tell him to square things with whoever owns the car we took – '

'Al called me around midnight; it's his car,' said Annunzio. 'He has a bad habit of leaving the keys in the ignition so he can get away in a hurry if he needs to.'

'Why did he – '

'Al wasn't there to get anybody, Mr Walters. He's very serious about his work and is convinced he failed in his duty where you're concerned, so he was naturally upset. Then he had a fight with his girl and coming on top of everything else, it gave him a nervous breakdown. We have used Mr Aiken's establishment at one time or another as a refuge for people who needed to be quiet for a while. I'm sure that, as a writer, you can see how going naked with only a mask to hide your features would be a very effective way of staying incognito – so to speak.'

'You mean all the trouble I went to wasn't – '

'Necessary?'

'Why – yes.'

'That would depend on how much enjoyment you got out of the company of two lovely women – and I think I know the answer to that. You can include all this in *Superstud*.'

'That's an idea,' said Henry.

'By the way, Al doesn't swim and you almost drowned him.' Annunzio chuckled. 'I think you made a Christian out of him, too. He swears he walked on water getting out of that pool.'

'So what happens now?'

'I've already called the authorities of the county Springhaven is in and told them the report of the stolen car was a mistake.'

'Then why did the New York Police arrest me?'

'The original order for your apprehension was probably put into a police computer bank by the sheriff's office in the Springhaven area before I called them.'

'My God! That means I'm liable to be on the wanted list for stealing a car the rest of my life.'

192

Gregory Annunzio laughed. 'The computers aren't quite that bad, Mr Walters. I'm sure it will be straightened out soon.'

'Meanwhile, I'm in jail!' Henry squawked. 'And so are Selena and Gloria.'

'Only for a little while; I'll have a bondsman there when court opens,' Annunzio promised. 'One thing more. How is *Superstud* going?'

'All I have to do now is to dictate what's been happening the past few days – since I struck out with Wilhelmina Dillingham.'

'Then Casey's back in the batter's box again?'

'And batting a thousand. Miss McGuire and I have plighted our troth, to use a phrase from the days of chivalry.'

Annunzio laughed again. 'Coupling in the Catskills; no wonder Rip Van Winkle stayed in those mountains so long. Can I ask one more question?'

'It's your telephone call.'

'How are you going to have Bart and Leonora live happily ever after when everybody knows he was killed in the accident?'

'I figured that out coming down from Springhaven,' said Henry. 'Bart and Leonora get together but as he's on the way to the altar, he stops at a bar for a few drinks. In the final scene, Bart's riding off into the sunset in the Rolls, loaded to the gills. Get it?'

'That's genius but don't let it happen in real life.'

'No chance. As soon as Judge Peebles finishes with us in court, we're going to ask him to marry us. We got our licence before your boys pushed Selena off that subway platform and damn near ruined everything; I've been carrying it in my wallet ever since it came in the mail.'

'I told you your fiancée was in no danger,' said Annunzio.

'Maybe – but I didn't know it at the time and neither did she.'

'Well, *Superstud* is going to be a smash hit so everything has turned out all right.'

'Only after I got a case of psychic impotence and Selena got so upset Dr Schwartz sent us both to Springhaven – separately, of course. She had been there before.'

'Anything I can do?'

'Not if you've already squared the car theft charge. Goodbye.'

xiv

Justice Calvin Peebles was not in a happy mood. For the first time in some thirty years he had been denied his usual three eggs and link sausages for breakfast, limiting himself instead to a grapefruit and dry toast – all caused by too high a figure for both his weight and his blood cholesterol at his annual physical examination two days before. The sight of Henry Walters on the front seat of his courtroom, even though flanked by two stunning beauties in rather scanty attire, could not entirely overcome hunger pains from a gastric void still demanding to be filled.

'Well, Mr Walters,' said the magistrate dourly, 'what brings you here this time?'

'It's a long story, your honour – '

'Yours usually are, Mr Walters. Perhaps the clerk has a shorter one.'

'Grand theft – auto, sir,' said the clerk. 'The defendants were arrested about five o'clock this morning in front of Mr Walters's apartment house on Fifth Avenue – in the stolen car.'

'In the car at five a.m.?'

'Yes, your honour.'

'When was the vehicle in question stolen?'

'Last night, your honour. The complaint is from the sheriff of a county in the Catskills.'

Judge Peebles turned back to Henry. 'Guilty or not guilty, Mr Walters?'

'Guilty, your honour, but there are extenuating circumstances – '

'There always are where you're concerned, Mr Walters. Let's hear the latest.'

Before Henry could speak, Selena said, 'We were on our way to City Hall, your honour – to be married.'

Judge Peebles eyebrows lifted. 'At five in the morning – from the Catskills?'

'By way of the Tappan Zee Bridge,' Gloria added.

'I understand that some hotels in the Catskills cater to honeymooners, Mr Walters.' The magistrate looked considerably more interested than when he'd seated himself on the bench, 'But aren't you engaging in what might be called vice versa?'

'I assure you that no *vice* is involved, sir,' said Henry, warned by the sudden fire in Selena's eyes that she, too, had gotten the point. 'Miss McGuire and I are to be married. Miss Manning is my secretary.'

'And you naturally took her with you to the Catskills on your honeymoon – before the wedding?'

'Like I said at the beginning, it's a long story – '

'And no doubt a very intriguing one. I only wish I had time to listen, but I feel it my duty to halt your career of crime at mid-flight, so to speak, by binding you over – '

The magistrate stopped, when the clerk beside him plucked at his sleeve and handed him a paper that looked to Henry like a computer readout. Judge Peebles studied it for a moment, then engaged in a whispered conversation with the clerk, before reaching for the gavel.

'Some are saved by the bell, Mr Walters,' he said. 'You, it seems, have been saved by a computer. Which, considering the way city records have been fouled up by that electronic devil's disciple, would seem to be the greater miracle. The owner of the car you are alleged to have stolen remembers now that he loaned it to you. Case dismissed.' The gavel crashed to the desk. 'I would strongly advise you and your lovely companions to flee before the computer changes its mind again.'

'One more favour, your honour,' said Henry. 'Would you be kind enough to marry Miss McGuire and me? I've been carrying a licence in my wallet for about a month.'

Judge Peebles took the folded and somewhat rumpled licence Henry handed him and studied it for a moment.

'Everything seems to be in order, Mr Walters,' he conceded. 'And, after all, perhaps marrying you and Miss McGuire is the least I can do, considering how much beauty you have brought into my courtroom in such a delightful state of unadornment.'

And he did.